The Company She Keeps

Books by Mary McCarthy

The Company She Keeps

The Oasis

Cast a Cold Eye

The Groves of Academe

A Charmed Life

Sights and Spectacles

Venice Observed

Memories of a Catholic Girlhood

The Stones of Florence

On the Contrary

The Group

Mary McCarthy's Theatre Chronicles

Vietnam

Hanoi

The Writing on the Wall and Other Literary Essays

Birds of America

Medina

The Seventeenth Degree

The Mask of State: Watergate Portraits

Cannibals and Missionaries

Ideas and the Novel

The Hounds of Summer and Other Stories

Occasional Prose

How I Grew

Intellectual Memoirs: New York 1936–1938

MARY McCARTHY The
Company She Keeps

A HARVEST BOOK
HARCOURT BRACE & COMPANY
San Diego *New York* *London*

Requests for permission to make copies
of any part of the work should be mailed to:
Permissions Department, Harcourt Brace & Company,
6277 Sea Harbor Drive, Orlando, Florida 32887-6777.

ISBN 0-15-620085-6   (Harvest: pbk.)

Printed in the United States of America

J K L

Acknowledgments are due *The Southern Review, Partisan Review,* and *Harper's Bazaar,* in which certain of these episodes first appeared.

Contents

ONE   *Cruel and Barbarous Treatment*

S H E could not bear to hurt her husband. She impressed this on the Young Man, on her confidantes, and finally on her husband himself. The thought of Telling Him actually made her heart turn over in a sudden and sickening way, she said. This was true, and yet she knew that being a potential divorcee was deeply pleasurable in somewhat the same way that being an engaged girl had been. In both cases, there was at first a subterranean courtship, whose significance it was necessary to conceal from outside observers. The concealment of the original, premarital courtship had, however, been a mere superstitious gesture, briefly sustained. It had also been, on the whole, a private secretiveness, not a partnership of silence. One put one's family and one's friends off the track because one was still afraid that the affair might not come out right, might not lead in a clean, direct line to the altar. To confess one's aspirations might be, in the end, to publicize one's failure. Once a solid understanding had been reached, there followed a short in-

termission of ritual bashfulness, in which both parties awkwardly participated, and then came the Announcement.

But with the extramarital courtship, the deception was
prolonged where it had been ephemeral, necessary where
it had been frivolous, conspiratorial where it had been
lonely. It was, in short, serious where it had been dilet-
tantish. That it was accompanied by feelings of guilt, by
sharp and genuine revulsions, only complicated and deepened its delights, by abrading the sensibilities, and by im-
posing a sense of outlawry and consequent mutual depend-
ence upon the lovers. But what this interlude of deception
gave her, above all, she recognized, was an opportunity,
unparalleled in her experience, for exercising feelings of
superiority over others. For her husband she had, she believed, only sympathy and compunction. She got no fun,
she told the Young Man, out of putting horns on her dar-
ling's head, and never for a moment, she said, did he appear to her as the comic figure of the cuckolded husband
that one saw on the stage. (The Young Man assured her
that his own sentiments were equally delicate, that for the
wronged man he felt the most profound respect, tinged
with consideration.) It was as if by the mere act of betray-
ing her husband, she had adequately bested him; it was
supererogatory for her to gloat, and, if she gloated at all, it
was over her fine restraint in not-gloating, over the integrity of her moral sense, which allowed her to preserve even
while engaged in sinfulness the acute realization of sin and
shame. Her overt superiority feelings she reserved for her
friends. Lunches and teas, which had been time-killers,

matters of routine, now became perilous and dramatic adventures. The Young Man's name was a bright, highly explosive ball which she bounced casually back and forth in these feminine *tête-à-têtes*. She would discuss him in his status of friend of the family, speculate on what girls he might have, attack him or defend him, anatomize him, keeping her eyes clear and impersonal, her voice empty of special emphasis, her manner humorously detached. *While all the time . . . !*

Three times a week or oftener, at lunch or tea, she would let herself tremble thus on the exquisite edge of self-betrayal, involving her companions in a momentous game whose rules and whose risks only she herself knew. The Public Appearances were even more satisfactory. To meet at a friend's house by design and to register surprise, to strike just the right note of young-matronly affection at cocktail parties, to treat him formally as "my escort" at the theater during intermissions—these were triumphs of stage management, more difficult of execution, more nerve-racking than the lunches and teas, because *two* actors were involved. His over-ardent glance must be hastily deflected; his too-self-conscious reading of his lines must be entered in the debit side of her ledger of love, in anticipation of an indulgent accounting in private.

The imperfections of his performance were, indeed, pleasing to her. Not, she thought, because his impetuosities, his gaucheries, demonstrated the sincerity of his passion for her, nor because they proved him a new hand at this game of intrigue, but rather because the high finish of her own acting showed off well in comparison. "I should have gone on the stage," she could tell him gaily, "or been a diplomat's wife or an international spy," while he would admiringly agree. Actually, she doubted whether she could ever have been an actress, acknowledging that she found it more amusing and more gratifying to play herself than to interpret any character conceived by a dramatist. In these private theatricals it was her own many-faceted nature that she put on exhibit, and the audience, in this case unfortunately limited to two, could applaud both her skill of projection and her intrinsic variety. Furthermore, this was a play in which the *donnée* was real, and the penalty for a missed cue or an inopportune entrance was, at first anyway, unthinkable.

She loved him, she knew, for being a bad actor, for his docility in accepting her tender, mock-impatient instruction., Those superiority feelings were fattening not only on the gullibility of her friends, but also on the comic flaws of her lover's character, and on the vulnerability of her lover's position. In this particular hive she was undoubtedly queen bee.

The Public Appearances were not exclusively duets. They sometimes took the form of a trio. On these occasions the studied and benevolent carefulness which she always showed for her husband's feelings served a double purpose. She would affect a conspicuous domesticity, an affectionate conjugal demonstrativeness, would sprinkle her conversation with "Darlings," and punctuate it with pats and squeezes till her husband would visibly expand and her lover plainly and painfully shrink. For the Young Man **no** retaliation was possible. These endearments of hers were sanctioned by law, usage, and habit; they belonged to her role of wife and could not be condemned or paralleled by a young man who was himself unmarried. They were clear provocations, but they could not be called so, and the Young Man preferred not to speak of them. *But she knew.* . . . Though she was aware of the sadistic intention of these displays, she was not ashamed of them, as she was sometimes twistingly ashamed of the hurt she was preparing to inflict on her husband. Partly she felt that they were punishments which the Young Man richly deserved for the wrong he was doing her husband, and that she herself in contriving them was acting, quite fittingly, both as judge and accused. Partly, too, she believed herself justified in playing the fond wife, whatever the damage to her lover's ego, because, in a sense, she actually was a fond wife. She *did* have these feelings, she insisted, whether she was exploiting them or not.

Eventually, however, her reluctance to wound her husband and her solicitude for his pride were overcome by an inner conviction that her love affair must move on to its next preordained stage. The possibilities of the subterranean courtship had been exhausted; it was time for the Announcement. She and the Young Man began to tell each other in a rather breathless and literary style that The Situation Was Impossible, and Things Couldn't Go On This Way Any Longer. The ostensible meaning of these flurried laments was that, under present conditions, they

were not seeing enough of each other, that their hours together were too short and their periods of separation too
dismal, that the whole business of deception had become
morally distasteful to them. Perhaps the Young Man really
believed these things; she did not. For the first time, she
saw that the virtue of marriage as an institution lay in its.
public character. Private cohabitation, long continued, was,
she concluded, a bore. Whatever the coziness of isolation,
the warm delights of having a secret, a love affair finally
reached the point where it needed the glare of publicity to
revive the interest of its protagonists. Hence, she thought,
the engagement parties, the showers, the big church wed-
dings, the presents, the receptions. These were simply socially approved devices by which the lovers got themselves
talked about. The gossip value of a divorce and remarriage
was obviously far greater than the gossip value of a mere
engagement, and she was now ready, indeed hungry, to
hear What People Would Say.

The lunches, the teas, the Public Appearances were getting a little flat. It was not, in the end, enough to be a
Woman With A Secret, if to one's friends one appeared to
be a woman without a secret. The bliss of having a secret
required, in short, the consummation of telling it, and
she looked forward to the My-dear-I-had-no-idea's, the
I-thought-you-and-Tom-were-so-happy-together's, the How-
did-you-keep-it-so-dark's with which her intimates would
greet her announcement. The audience of two no longer
sufficed her; she required a larger stage. She tried it first, a
little nervously, on two or three of her closest friends,

swearing them to secrecy. "Tom must hear it first from me," she declared. "It would be too terrible for his pride if he found out afterwards that the whole town knew it before he did. So you mustn't tell, even later on, that I told you about this today. I felt I had to talk to someone." After these lunches she would hurry to a phone booth to give the Young Man the gist of the conversation. "She certainly was surprised," she could always say with a little gush of triumph. "But she thinks it's fine." *But did they actually?* She could not be sure. Was it possible that she sensed in these luncheon companions, her dearest friends, a certain reserve, a certain unexpressed judgment?

It was a pity, she reflected, that she was so sensitive to public opinion. "I couldn't really love a man," she murmured to herself once, "if everybody didn't think he was wonderful." Everyone seemed to like the Young Man, of course. *But still . . .* She was getting panicky, she thought. Surely it was only common sense that nobody is admired by everybody. And even if a man were universally despised, would there not be a kind of defiant nobility in loving him in the teeth of the whole world? There would, certainly, but it was a type of heroism that she would scarcely be called upon to practice, for the Young Man was popular, he was invited everywhere, he danced well, his manners were ingratiating, he kept up intellectually. But was he not perhaps *too* amiable, *too* accommodating? Was it for this that her friends seemed silently to criticize him?

At this time a touch of acridity entered into her relations with the Young Man. Her indulgent scoldings had an edge to them now, and it grew increasingly difficult for her to keep her make-believe impatience from becoming real. She would look for dark spots in his character and drill away at them as relentlessly as a dentist at a cavity. A compulsive didacticism possessed her: no truism of his, no cliché, no ineffectual joke could pass the rigidity of her censorship. And, hard as she tried to maintain the character of charming schoolmistress, the Young Man, she saw, was taking alarm. She suspected that, frightened and puzzled, he contemplated flight. She found herself watching him with impersonal interest, speculating as to what course he would take, and she was relieved but faintly disappointed when it became clear that he ascribed her sharpness to the tension of the situation and had decided to stick it out.

The moment had come for her to tell her husband. By this single, cathartic act, she would, she believed, rid herself of the doubts and anxieties that beset her. If her husband were to impugn the Young Man's character, she could answer his accusations and at the same time discount them as arising from jealousy. From her husband, at least, she might expect the favor of an open attack, to which she could respond with the prepared defense that she carried, unspoken, about with her. Further, she had an intense, childlike curiosity as to How Her Husband Would Take It, a curiosity which she disguised for decency's sake as justifiable apprehension. The confidences already imparted to her friends seemed like pale dress rehearsals of the supreme confidence she was about to make. Perhaps it was toward this moment that the whole affair had been tend-

ing, for this moment that the whole affair had been designed. This would be the ultimate testing of her husband's love, its final, rounded, quintessential expression.
Never, she thought, when you live with a man do you feel
the full force of his love. It is gradually rationed out to you
in an impure state, compounded with all the other elements of daily existence, so that you are hardly sensible of
receiving it. There is no single point at which it is concentrated; it spreads out into the past and the future until
it appears as a nearly imperceptible film over the surface
of your life. Only face to face with its own annihilation
could it show itself wholly, and, once shown, drop into the
category of completed experiences.

She was not disappointed. She told him at breakfast in a
fashionable restaurant, because, she said, he would be
better able to control his feelings in public. When he
called at once for the check, she had a spasm of alarm lest
in an access of brutality or grief he leave her there alone,
conspicuous, and, as it were, unfulfilled. But they walked
out of the restaurant together and through the streets,
hand in hand, tears streaming "unchecked," she whispered
to herself, down their faces. Later they were in the Park,
by an artificial lake, watching the ducks swim. The sun
was very bright, and she felt a kind of superb pathos in the
careful and irrelevant attention they gave to the pastoral
scene. This was, she knew, the most profound, the most
subtle, the most idyllic experience of her life. All the
strings of her nature were, at last, vibrant. She was both
doer and sufferer: she inflicted pain and participated in it.

And she was, at the same time, physician, for, as she was the weapon that dealt the wound, she was also the balm that could assuage it. Only she could know the hurt that engrossed him, and it was to her that he turned for the sympathy she had ready for him. Finally, though she offered him his discharge slip with one hand, with the other she beckoned him to approach. She was wooing him all over again, but wooing him to a deeper attachment than he had previously experienced, to an unconditional surrender. She was demanding his total understanding of her, his compassion, and his forgiveness. When at last he answered her repeated and agonized I-love-you's by grasping her hand more tightly and saying gently, "I know," she saw that she had won him over. She had drawn him into a truly mystical union. Their marriage was complete.

Afterwards everything was more prosaic. The Young Man had to be telephoned and summoned to a conference *à trois*, a conference, she said, of civilized, intelligent people. The Young Man was a little awkward, even dropped a tear or two, which embarrassed everyone else, but what, after all, she thought, could you expect? He was in a difficult position; his was a thankless part. With her husband behaving so well, indeed, so gallantly, the Young Man could not fail to look a trifle inadequate. The Young Man would have preferred it, of course, if her husband had made a scene, had bullied or threatened her, so that he himself might have acted the chivalrous protector. She, however, did not hold her husband's heroic courtesy against him: in some way, it reflected credit on herself.

The Young Man, apparently, was expecting to Carry Her
Off, but this she would not allow. "It would be too heart-
less," she whispered when they were alone for a moment.
"We must all go somewhere together."

So the three went out for a drink, and she watched with
a sort of desperation her husband's growing abstraction,
the more and more perfunctory attention he accorded the
conversation she was so bravely sustaining. "He is bored,"
she thought. "He is going to leave." The prospect of being
left alone with the Young Man seemed suddenly unendur-
able. If her husband were to go now, he would take with
him the third dimension that had given the affair depth,
and abandon her to a flat and vulgar love scene. Terrified,
she wondered whether she had not already prolonged the
drama beyond its natural limits, whether the confession in
the restaurant and the absolution in the Park had not
rounded off the artistic whole, whether the sequel of divorce and remarriage would not, in fact, constitute an anti-
climax. Already she sensed that behind her husband's good
manners an ironical attitude toward herself had sprung up.
Was it possible that he had believed that they would return
from the Park and all would continue as before? It was
conceivable that her protestations of love had been misleading, and that his enormous tenderness toward her had
been based, not on the idea that he was giving her up, but
rather on the idea that he was taking her back—with no
questions asked. If that were the case, the telephone call,
the conference, and the excursion had in his eyes been a
monstrous *gaffe*, a breach of sensibility and good taste, for

which he would never forgive her. She blushed violently. Looking at him again, she thought he was watching her with an expression which declared: I have found you out: now I know what you are like. For the first time, she felt him utterly alienated.

When he left them she experienced the let-down she had feared but also a kind of relief. She told herself that it was as well that he had cut himself off from her: it made her decision simpler. There was now nothing for her to do but to push the love affair to its conclusion, whatever that might be, and this was probably what she most deeply desired. Had the poignant intimacy of the Park persisted, she might have been tempted to drop the adventure she had begun and return to her routine. But that was, looked at coldly, unthinkable. For if the adventure would seem a little flat after the scene in the Park, the resumption of her marriage would seem even flatter. If the drama of the triangle had been amputated by her confession, the curtain had been brought down with a smack on the drama of wedlock.

And, as it turned out, the drama of the triangle was not quite ended by the superficial rupture of her marriage. Though she had left her husband's apartment and been offered shelter by a confidante, it was still necessary for her to see him every day. There were clothes to be packed, and possessions to be divided, love letters to be reread and mementoes to be wept over in common. There were occasional passionate, unconsummated embraces; there were endearments and promises. And though her husband's irony remained, it was frequently vulnerable. It was not, as she had at first thought, an armor against her, but merely a sword, out of *Tristan and Isolde,* which lay permanently between them and enforced discretion.

They met often, also, at the houses of friends, for, as she said, "What can I do? I know it's not tactful, but we all know the same people. You can't expect me to give up my friends." These Public Appearances were heightened in interest by the fact that these audiences, unlike the earlier ones, had, as it were, purchased librettos, and were in full possession of the intricacies of the plot. She preferred, she decided, the evening parties to the cocktail parties, for there she could dance alternately with her lover and her husband to the accompaniment of subdued gasps on the part of the bystanders.

This interlude was at the same time festive and heart-rending: her only dull moments were the evenings she spent alone with the Young Man. Unfortunately, the Post-Announcement period was only too plainly an interlude and its very nature demanded that it be followed by something else. She could not preserve her anomalous status indefinitely. It was not decent, and, besides, people would be bored. From the point of view of one's friends, it was all very well to entertain a Triangle as a novelty; to cope with it as a permanent problem was a different matter. Once they had all three got drunk, and there was a scene, and, though everyone talked about it afterwards, her friends were, she thought, a little colder, a little more critical. People began to ask her when she was going to Reno. Furthermore, she noticed that her husband was getting a slight edge in popularity over the Young Man. It was natural, of course, that everyone should feel sorry for him, and be especially nice. *But yet ...*

When she learned from her husband that he was receiving attentions from members of her own circle, invitations in which she and the Young Man were unaccountably not included, she went at once to the station and bought her ticket. Her good-bye to her husband, which she had privately allocated to her last hours in town, took place prematurely, two days before she was to leave. He was rushing off to what she inwardly feared was a Gay Week End in the country; he had only a few minutes; he wished her a pleasant trip; and he would write, of course. His highball was drained while her glass still stood half full; he sat forward nervously on his chair; and she knew herself to be acting the Ancient Mariner, but her dignity would not allow her to hurry. She hoped that he would miss his train for her, but he did not. He left her sitting in the bar, and that night the Young Man could not, as he put it, do a thing with her. There was nowhere, absolutely nowhere, she said passionately, that she wanted to go, nobody she wanted to see, nothing she wanted to do. "You need a drink," he said with the air of a diagnostician. "A drink," she answered bitterly. "I'm sick of the drinks we've been having. Gin, whisky, rum, what else is there?" He took her into a bar, and she cried, but he bought her a fancy mixed drink, something called a Ramos gin fizz, and she was a little appeased because she had never had one before.

Then some friends came in, and they all had another drink together, and she felt better. "There," said the Young Man, on the way home, "don't I know what's good for you? Don't I know how to handle you?" "Yes," she answered in her most humble and feminine tones, but she knew that they had suddenly dropped into a new pattern, that they were no longer the cynosure of a social group, but merely another young couple with an evening to pass, another young couple looking desperately for entertainment, wondering whether to call on a married couple or to drop in somewhere for a drink. This time the Young Man's prescription had worked, but it was pure luck that they had chanced to meet someone they knew. A second or a third time they would scan the faces of the other drinkers in vain, would order a second drink and surreptitiously watch the door, and finally go out alone, with a quite detectable air of being unwanted.

When, a day and a half later, the Young Man came late to take her to the train, and they had to run down the platform to catch it, she found him all at once detestable. He would ride to 125th Street with her, he declared in a burst of gallantry, but she was angry all the way because she was afraid there would be trouble with the conductor. At 125th Street, he stood on the platform blowing kisses to her and shouting something that she could not hear through the glass. She made a gesture of repugnance, but, seeing him flinch, seeing him weak and charming and incompetent, she brought her hand reluctantly to her lips and blew a kiss back. The other passengers were watching, she was aware, and though their looks were doting and not derisive, she felt herself to be humiliated and somehow vulgarized. When the train began to move, and the Young Man began to run down the platform after it, still blowing kisses and shouting alternately, she got up, turned sharply away from the window and walked back to the club car. There she sat down and ordered a whisky and soda.

There were a number of men in the car, who looked up in unison as she gave her order, but, observing that they were all the middle-aged, small-businessmen who "belonged" as inevitably to the club car as the white-coated porter and the leather-bound *Saturday Evening Post,* she paid them no heed. She was now suddenly overcome by a sense of depression and loss that was unprecedented for being in no way dramatic or pleasurable. In the last half-hour she had seen clearly that she would never marry the Young Man, and she found herself looking into an insubstantial future with no signpost to guide her. Almost all women, she thought, when they are girls never believe that they will get married. The terror of spinsterhood hangs over them from adolescence on. Even if they are popular they think that no one really interesting will want them enough to marry them. Even if they get engaged they are afraid that something will go wrong, something will intervene. When they do get married it seems to them a sort of miracle, and, after they have been married for a time, though in retrospect the whole process looks perfectly natural and inevitable, they retain a certain unarticulated pride in the wonder they have performed. Finally, however, the terror of spinsterhood has been so thoroughly exorcised that they forget ever having been haunted by it, and it is at this stage that they contemplate divorce. "How could I have forgotten?" she said to herself and began to wonder what she would do.

She could take an apartment by herself in the Village. She would meet new people. She would entertain. But, she thought, if I have people in for cocktails, there will always come the moment when they have to leave, and I shall be alone and have to pretend to have another engagement in order to save embarrassment. If I have them to dinner, it will be the same thing, but at least I shan't have to pretend to have an engagement. I will give dinners. Then, she thought, there will be the cocktail parties, and, if I go alone, I shall always stay a little too late, hoping that a young man or even a party of people will ask me to dinner. And if I fail, if no one asks me, I shall have the ignominy of walking out alone, trying to look as if I had somewhere to go. Then there will be the evenings at home with a good book when there will be no reason at all for going to bed, and I shall perhaps sit up all night. And the mornings when there will be no point in getting up, and I shall perhaps stay in bed till dinnertime. There will be the dinners in tearooms with other unmarried women, tearooms because women alone look conspicuous and forlorn in good restaurants. And then, she thought, I shall get older.

She would never, she reflected angrily, have taken this step, had she felt that she was burning her bridges behind her. She would never have left one man unless she had had another to take his place. But the Young Man, she now saw, was merely a sort of mirage which she had allowed herself to mistake for an oasis. "If the Man," she muttered, "did not exist, the Moment would create him." This was what had happened to her. She had made herself the victim of an imposture. But, she argued, with an access of cheerfulness, if this were true, if out of the need of a second, a new, husband she had conjured up the figure of one, she had possibly been impelled by unconscious forces to behave more intelligently than appearances would indicate. She was perhaps acting out in a sort of hypnotic trance a ritual whose meaning had not yet been revealed to her, a ritual which required that, first of all, the Husband be eliminated from the cast of characters. Conceivably, she was designed for the role of *femme fatale,* and for such a personage considerations of safety, provisions against loneliness and old age, were not only philistine but irrelevant. She might marry a second, a third, a fourth time, or she might never marry again. But, in any case, for the thrifty bourgeois love insurance, with its daily payments of patience, forbearance, and resignation, she was no longer eligible. She would be, she told herself delightedly, a bad risk.

She was, or soon would be, a Young Divorcee, and the term still carried glamour. Her divorce decree would be a passport conferring on her the status of citizeness of the world. She felt gratitude toward the Young Man for having unwittingly effected her transit into a new life. She looked about her at the other passengers. Later she would talk to them. They would ask, of course, where she was bound; that was the regulation opening move of train conversations. But it was a delicate question what her reply should be. To say "Reno" straight out would be vulgar; it would smack of confidences too cheaply given. Yet to lie, to say "San Francisco," for instance, would be to cheat herself, to minimize her importance, to mislead her interlocutor into believing her an ordinary traveler with a commonplace destination. There must be some middle course which would give information without appearing to do so, which would hint at a *vie galante* yet indicate a barrier of impeccable reserve. It would probably be best, she decided, to say "West" at first, with an air of vagueness and hesitation. Then, when pressed, she might go as far as to say "Nevada." But no farther.

TWO *Rogue's Gallery**

M r. Sheer fired his stenographer in order to give me the job. It puzzled me at the time that he should so readily dismiss a professional whom he paid ten dollars a week to take on an amateur at eleven. I now see that he must have owed her money. Several times during that summer she would come into the gallery, a badly made-up blond girl in a dark dress that the hot days and the continual sitting had wrinkled at the waist. He would hold whispered conversations with her in the outer room, and at length she would go away. Later on, after I had quit, I, too, would make regular calls to collect my back pay, and there would be another girl sitting at my desk, while I, as a mark of special courtesy, would be led into the inner exhibition room reserved for customers. There he would whisper to me, and, on a few occasions, press into my hand, as if it were something indecent, a tightly folded five-dollar bill. After a great many visits I succeeded in getting, in such small driblets, all that was owed me, but my case was ex-

* *An extract from memoirs begun by the heroine.*

ceptional. Mr. Sheer's usual method of dealing with a creditor was simply to dispense with his services. This worked quite well with everyone but the telephone company, for, while there are many stationers, many photographers, many landlords, there is only one American Tel. & Tel.

Mr. Sheer was extremely resourceful in financial matters. It was he who taught me how to get a free lemonade on a stifling day. You go into the Automat (there was one conveniently located across the street from our building), and you pick up several of the slices of lemon that are put out for the benefit of tea drinkers near the tea tap. Then you pour yourself a glass of ice water, squeeze the lemon into it, add sugar from one of the tables, and stir.

Mr. Sheer was a dealer in objects of art, a tall, pale-eyed man with two suits and many worries. Downstairs in the building directory he was listed as The Savile Galleries, and the plural conveyed a sense of endless vistas of rooms gleaming with collector's items. Like Mr. Sheer himself, that plural was imaginative, winged with ambition, but untrustworthy. Actually, the Savile Galleries consisted of two small, dark, stuffy rooms whose natural gloom was enhanced by heavy velvet drapes in wine-red and blackish green which were hung from ceiling to floor with the object of concealing the neutral office-building walls. There was also another and still smaller room which had no drapes and was therefore more cheerful, but this was merely the inner office where the stenographer and the Negro boy assistant were herded, together with the office supplies, the *Social Register,* and *Poor's Business Directory,* and where the sitter for a miniature in progress was occasionally tied.

For Mr. Sheer's gallery was unique in one respect. On my first day there I had stared hopefully about at the shabby collection of priests' robes, china figurines, clocks, bronzes, carved ivories, old silver, porcelains, and seen only the scrapings of the Fifty-ninth Street auction rooms. In a glass case off in one corner, there were a few garnet chokers, some earrings in wrought Italian silver, and an improbable-looking sapphire ring in an out-of-date claw setting. On the walls hung a couple of faded paintings of the Hudson River School and some gaudy scenes of Venice, which, as I learned later, had been signed by Mr. Sheer with any Italian name that happened to come into his head. (As he said, there was nothing really wrong with this practice of his: it made the customer feel better to see *some* name on a picture, and it was not, after all, as if he were attributing them to Raphael.) But that morning, knowing nothing of Mr. Sheer, I had looked about at all those tarnished objects (I had been led to expect something grander, more artistic, more "interesting") and tears had come to my eyes as I wondered how I should describe this dreary job to my family and friends. It was then that I noticed the smell.

"Dogs," Mr. Sheer said. "Wear your dog on your sleeve." I stared at him. He went into the inner office and came back with a jeweler's box in which lay a pair of crystal cuff links. Buried in the crystals, one could see a tiny pair of scotties. "They're real portraits," he said. "We do them

right here in the gallery. Something newer than mono-
grams." He held them up for me to look at. "Isn't that a
beautiful bit of workmanship?" he asked. His face lit up
as he pronounced this sentence. "Look at that coat. You
can see every hair." The artist, he explained, was an elderly Frenchman who, before the War, had done *all* the
Kaiser's dogs in miniature, an achievement Mr. Sheer
never failed to linger over in the sales letters he dictated.
How much this meant to Mr. Sheer I did not understand
until I suggested one day that we should omit the part
about the Kaiser from a follow-up I was writing. It was the
only time he was ever angry with me. I saw then that it
was not solely Monsieur Ravasse's talents that made Mr.
Sheer treat him, alone of his associates, with a subservient
respect, made him pay him, take his scoldings, ask his ad-
vice. Unquestionably, Monsieur Ravasse's work did excite
Mr. Sheer's admiration—every pair of cuff links, every
brooch was for him a new miracle—but the greater miracle
had, I am afraid, taken place inside Mr. Sheer's head: he
had succumbed to the spell of his own salesmanship, and
Monsieur Ravasse had become interchangeable with the
Kaiser in his mind.

At any rate, commercially speaking, Monsieur Ravasse
was, virtually, our only asset, and it was these custom-made
dog crystals that Mr. Sheer was pushing all that hot summer
I worked for him. There was not a great margin of profit
to be made on them, and many inconveniences attended
their execution, but they were the only things we had that
tempted the rich people, who, on Long Island, in New Jer-

sey, in the Adirondacks, in Canada, were feeling themselves poor. In the letters I took from his dictation all our pieces were described as Extraordinary Bargains, Sacrifices, Exceptional Opportunities, Fine Investments Especially In These Times. But the rich people seldom believed. Mr. Sheer might insist that "an opportunity like this may never present itself again," but only when a man's own dog was concerned did the argument carry much weight. A seventeenth-century tapestry would still exist when times got better (if they ever did); one could afford to wait and pay a little more, if necessary. But one's own dog might die, or the aging artist, who after all dated from Louis Napoleon, might die himself. So one might perhaps hurry, as Mr. Sheer urged, to-take-advantage-of-this-remarkable-offer.

During that summer we turned out several Bedlingtons, a cairn, two Kerry blues, some German sheep dogs, and even a chihuahua, which, being itself a miniature, proved, in Mr. Sheer's opinion, the least interesting of all our subjects. There were also extensive negotiations with a lady who had thirty-one toy spaniels, but she and Mr. Sheer could never get together on the price (for she felt that the number of dogs entitled her to a cut rate), and the project was finally abandoned.

The dogs who came up from Long Island or New Jersey presented no particular problems. They arrived with their handlers, posed for a few hours, and then went home until the next day. Naturally, the miniature would have to be repainted at least once, for the owners never felt that their pets had been done justice, but this was a relatively simple matter. It was the dogs who were not within commuting distance that gave us trouble. Such a dog would arrive by Railway Express, boxed up in a cage and wild with hunger. Arrangements would have been made, of course, for it to be fed by the trainmen on the way, but, as far as we could tell, this was never done. We would take the cage into the inner office, open it, and the animal would shoot out and bite me on the leg. There was one cairn who came out like a black cannonball and was crazy ever after. The dogs were usually in such bad condition that extensive treatment by a veterinary was necessary before we could allow them to pose. The cairn was never able to pose at all. We kept him in the office for a long time, trying to soothe him back to sanity, but it was no use, and when he finally bit Mr. Sheer's red-haired mistress, we sent him home to his owner, who threatened to sue us for what had happened.

Yet in spite of the havoc created by this business, the nervous strain and the expense, the smell and the smallness of the profit, there was nearly always a dog boarding in my office, eating the choicest dog meat while Mr. Sheer went without his lunch. As the summer wore on, the smell of the dogs mingled with the damp, sour odor of the old velvet drapes, with the colored boy's personal smell, with the smell of Mr. Sheer's two suits, which were stiff with dried sweat, until our very skins were soaked with the gallery, and even outside, on the streets, we walked about with a special, occupational scent.

We were not making money. In spite of the commissioned crystals we were not so much as breaking even. The second morning I came to work I was met by a square man with a badge who was putting a sign on the door. The sign read, PUBLIC AUCTION TODAY.

I took out my key and said politely, "I didn't know there was to be an auction."

"Really?" said the man. "Maybe you want to pay this forty-three eighty-five then?" And he shoved a document at me.

"You mean," I said, "it's a debt?"

"Don't kid me, sister," said the man, "I'm the city marshal."

I began to talk very rapidly, to say that I was sure Mr. Sheer didn't know about this, that it must be an oversight, that he would be here any minute, that the marshal must wait till he came. But another man came up the hall and began to help him with the sign, and the city marshal's only replies were derisive and they were addressed, not to me, but to his assistant, who found them very amusing. I went into my office, put my head on the typewriter, and started to cry.

At once the city marshal was bending over me, his hand on my shoulder.

"For God's sake, sister, don't cry," he said. "What's the trouble? This guy your sweetheart?"

"No," I sobbed.

"He a relation of yours?"

"No."

"Then for God's sake what are you crying about?"

"Because I'm not accustomed to being spoken to in such a manner."

He dropped his hand in amazement. Then he went out and took the sign down.

"You think this guy will pay up?"

"Yes."

"All right. See that he has the money at my office at four o'clock sharp."

The two of them went away, carrying the sign.

Mr. Sheer slipped in at noon with an apprehensive air. I expected him to share my indignation at the law's high-handedness, but he seemed, rather, to take the city marshal's attitude. He listened to my story with some astonishment, and then laughed in a relieved way, and shook my hand several times and said I was going to make a wonderful secretary.

"But you must pay the money right away," I said.

"Yes," he answered vaguely.

However, I nagged him about it until he made some phone calls, in the inner office, with the door closed. He then went out, and the city marshal never came again, so, presumably, the debt was paid.

In conversation Mr. Sheer frequently reverted to the city marshal's visit. In his eyes, one could see, it marked a turning-point in his career. Obviously, as I recognized later, he had been expecting the city marshal and his sign, had tried in all quarters to raise the money and failed. That was why he had not come in until noon, for in the face of danger Mr. Sheer always disappeared. He had re-signed himself to the loss of his business and the concomi-tant loss of prestige. He had seen himself condemned, cast back into the outer darkness from which he had risen, back into that nether world where a public auction or a bankruptcy or a jail term carried no stigma. He had al-ready accepted his sentence when he discovered that he had been reprieved, as if by a miracle, at the eleventh hour. He had been given, as it were, a second chance, and with it came a second wind that enabled him to effect, easily, by a few telephone calls, what for weeks had been the impos-sible—the settlement of a debt of forty-three dollars and some odd cents. After this, Mr. Sheer's hold on respecta-bility was much more tenacious, for after this Mr. Sheer no longer believed that his clutching fingers *could* be shaken off.

However unappetizing, however eccentric his gallery might appear to the sophisticated world, to Mr. Sheer these rooms with their dark velvet, their porcelain urns, their statuary, their dirty chasubles hung from the ceil-ing, their little rococo chairs, and their deep, velvet-covered sofa incarnated a double dream. From his Western boy-hood, he said, he had loved dogs and culture. There was a rich man back in San Francisco whose dogs he had valeted and whose lawn he had watered; now and then he had been allowed to look at this man's fine library, which contained, he declared with reminiscent awe, "all these wonderful works on Shakespeare and vice versa." Today, as at that time, the dog was the natural highway to culture, and Mr. Sheer perceived no incongruity between the tarnished luxury of his setting and the homeliness of his liveliest line of goods.

He had begun as a bootlegger shortly after Prohibition had come in. He had perhaps been jailed (his accounts of his past were always vague and contradictory), but at any rate he had left the liquor business to become a veterinary's assistant. After a short period as a prize fighter's handler, he had bought himself a small kennels, and he had but recently progressed from selling dogs to selling their miniatures. He had met Monsieur Ravasse at his kennels one day, and had been inspired by him to open a novelty jewelry business in which the crystals played a leading part. His imagination, however, had been kindled less by the stones he dealt in than by the clocks, the carved ivories, the church vessels, the china mantel ornaments—all the rich and bizarre oddities that clutter the fringe of the jewelry trade; and it had not been long before *I. F. Sheer, Jeweler* had melted into *The Savile Galleries*. His gallery was the least rewarding of all his ventures, but it was dearer to him than any. Having pursued the luxury trades with considerable single-mindedness, he had now arrived at a point where the Right People, who had almost all his life been his customers, were now to become his clients—if he could only persuade them to buy.

For if Mr. Sheer loved culture, he loved Money too, and he could not always keep them apart in his mind (it was *a rich man* that had owned that library). Indeed it was sometimes difficult to tell whether he loved culture simply as an appurtenance of wealth or whether he loved it genuinely, for its own sake. He was fond of the fine arts, fond of long words, and fond of me, but was this simply because he felt that between us we could make a prosperous gentleman out of him? I am not sure. He could never use the long words correctly and he could hardly tell a Cellini from a Remington; yet surely there was a kind of integrity in that very lack of taste.

He was really proud of his stock; he admired everything indiscriminately. If he had nothing else to do, he would walk about the gallery, studying the pieces. When he could no longer contain himself he would summon me from my desk and point to a canal or to a bit of foliage in a picture and exclaim, "Isn't that a wonderful piece of painting?" Or of a vase, "Come here, Miss Sargent, and look at that glaze." It was all wonderful to him.

He worshipped any kind of ingenuity: boxes with false bottoms, cuckoo clocks, oval miniatures of the school of Boucher that opened if you pressed a button and disclosed a pornographic scene. He liked little statues that became fountains, Victorian banks made to resemble birds' nests, where the bird grasped the coin in its beak and dropped it when the lever was pulled. And for him the supreme ingenuity was the great *trompe l'oeil* of art itself, which made a painted canal look exactly like a real one and a bronze statue simulate a man. He had no use for modern art or modern design (although he knew them to be fashionable); it puzzled and annoyed him that anyone should, for example, make a set of book-ends that looked, simply, like themselves. The whole conception of functionalism was odious to him, for since art was in his eyes a splendid confidence game, the craftsman who did not, in some fashion, deceive his public seemed to him a sort of stool-pigeon, a high-class rat.

The colored boy who worked for us had far more taste, and he and I, in the little inner office, formed a Connoisseurs' League to pass on the new objects as they came in. But such distinctions, whether they came from me, from the colored boy, from another dealer, or from a customer, only angered Mr. Sheer. They smacked of disloyalty, not only to Mr. Sheer's business, but to art itself. And they seemed to him unnatural: he always suspected a hidden motive. Another dealer was plainly trying to run down Mr. Sheer's business for competitive reasons; the colored boy was making himself disagreeable because his salary had not been paid; the customer had a prejudice against the genre in question; and I was a college girl whose head had been stuffed with faddish preferences for modern design.

It is possible that it was merely the pride of ownership that was coloring Mr. Sheer's vision: his objects, being all extensions of his own personality, were all therefore equal in his heart. Certainly, I have often, walking down Fifty-seventh Street with him, seen a tapestry that was, to me, indistinguishable from one in Mr. Sheer's possession, and heard him, pausing, compare it unfavorably to his own. But there was always a certain fretfulness in his voice which came from the fact that he really felt the other tapestry to be quite as wonderful as his.

In any case, if the pride of ownership was working in Mr. Sheer, that pride was, characteristically, unreal, since the ownership was factitious. Mr. Sheer did not, I discovered, own a single one of the objects he displayed; indeed, so far as the ornamental arts were concerned, he had never owned anything more than a tie-pin in his life.

His gallery was stocked with loans from other dealers, merchandise that he held "on consignment." Some of it had been freely offered: another dealer who happened to have an unfashionable marble on his hands, a trade-in, say, that he despaired of selling to his own clients, would promise Mr. Sheer a commission to dispose of it. Others had been more artfully extracted. Mr. Sheer, hearing of a fine jade that was owned by someone else, would pretend to have a client who was interested in just such a piece. The other dealer would yield up the jade, and Mr. Sheer would promptly display it in his gallery. He would then have to stall off the owner with a variety of excuses until a real client could be found to take the place of the imaginary one. If no real client materialized, the jade would eventually have to be returned, but a long time usually elapsed before Mr. Sheer would admit defeat. In these ways, Mr. Sheer kept his gallery well populated with objects. That excessive secrecy and cunning, so characteristic of the trade, played directly into his hands. Each dealer assumed that he was the only one using the Savile Galleries as an outlet. There would have been considerable astonishment in Fifty-ninth Street circles had the dealers learned that they had unwit-

tingly formed a combination to provide Mr. Sheer with
what was really the capital for a rival gallery.

As for Mr. Sheer himself, he was careful to wrap all his
affairs in such a cocoon of falsehoods that, of all the people
associated with him, only the colored boy, whose job it was
to call for and deliver merchandise, had any suspicion of the
truth. Like all my own discoveries about Mr. Sheer, this
one was made painfully and by accident. He was not given
to confession, and any unsolicited information he advanced
about himself was likely to be either unimportant or false.
In general, his aversion to truth-telling was fanatical—to
tell the truth, at any time, on any matter, to any hearer,
was, he believed, profoundly dangerous: any fact, however
small, however harmless, provided it *was* a fact, was better
concealed: facts were high explosives. Never, for example,
during the time I worked for him, did I learn where he
lived. He would disappear at night and return in the
morning. If he were late, customers and creditors would
have to wait for him; there was no way, I was continually
explaining, of reaching him by phone. Since those days, I
have often badgered him about this question, and he has
told me a number of different stories. He has said that he
was living with a woman, which I suspected, that he was
passing back and forth between dollar-a-night hotels and
flophouses, and was ashamed to tell me, which is possible,
that he was sleeping on the divan in the gallery, which I
know to be true, for one morning when he had overslept
I found him there, in a rumpled pair of shorts, his close-
curling hair damp with summer-morning sweat. Yet these

explanations, taken separately or together, do not satisfy
me. They may one or all be true, but there must have been
something more.

All during what I now think of as the dime-novel period
of my employment with Mr. Sheer, I had no idea of the
facts about the gallery. I did not find out until the very
end. Had I been able to shake off the idea that Mr. Sheer
was an ordinary businessman who was a little bit hard up,
I might have been in a better position to understand what
was going on.

The thing began with a series of telephone calls from a
man named Bierman, to whom Mr. Sheer was always out,
but for whom a message was regularly left, a message so full
of consideration and empty of meaning that it was clear that
Bierman was a special case, a creditor perhaps, but no run-
of-the-mill creditor.

"Tell him I'll call him back in an hour," Mr. Sheer in-
variably whispered, or if he were stepping out, as he called
it, for a few minutes, he would not fail to remind me, "If
Bierman calls, tell him I'll call him back in an hour." Since
Mr. Sheer never did call Bierman back, and since, as the days
passed, the frequency of Bierman's calls increased until they
were coming at fifteen-minute intervals, I protested against
having to repeat this farcical sentence, and begged Mr.
Sheer to change the message, to suppress it altogether, or
to speak to Bierman, who was getting very angry. But Mr.
Sheer refused. The sentence, in his eyes, was a mark of
civility to Bierman. To leave no message would be the equiv-

alent of cutting him on the street. The sentence, moreover, had, for him, a kind of magic that I did not understand until I had had a longer experience of Mr. Sheer and his promises. Mr. Sheer's promises were a kind of fiat money issued at will and with no regard to fulfillment, or, indeed, to plausibility. He differed from the ordinary debtor who, under pressure, offers a promise as a substitute for cash, in that the ordinary debtor is not deceived by the substitute, but expects the creditor to be, while Mr. Sheer was himself deceived and concerned himself hardly at all with what the creditor might think. And it was not only to creditors that Mr. Sheer extended his gilded pledges. He showered them about him like an obstinate philanthropist. He knew where he could get me an ermine wrap for practically nothing (I had nowhere to wear it). He knew a man that would place Elmer, the colored boy, in the Cotton Club floor show (Elmer was a serious-minded youth who did not dance). Objectively, none of the promises had any validity. Their usefulness was of a different sort. They acted as a kind of transmission belt to the real world from the world of Mr. Sheer's fancy, the powerhouse of dreams that kept his life's wheels turning. So this sentence which I kept passing on reassured Mr. Sheer in the same measure that it infuriated Bierman.

When the man commenced to shout at me on the phone and, what was worse from Mr. Sheer's point of view, to mention a lawyer, Mr. Sheer reluctantly abandoned that particular magic. Instead, he drew me into the dark inner room, seated me on the velvet couch, and announced with an appealingly gloomy air that he was going to take me into his confidence. Bierman was a jeweler, he said, and it was a question of diamonds. The story branched out and became more elaborate, and on subsequent days he gave me different versions of it, but this was all I was ever certain of: Bierman was a jeweler and it was a question of diamonds.

I know this because very early in the game I talked to Bierman himself in his office.

Even here perhaps I am too cocksure, for I remember, uncomfortably, a scheme by which Mr. Sheer at a later date staved off a creditor. He had borrowed a hunting bronze featuring some falcons from a lady art dealer, and had got Abernethie and Rich to display it in a window full of hunting equipment. Through them, he had sold it to one of the Long Island sporting people. When Mrs. Martino, the dealer, wanted her money, it had already been parceled out to the landlord, the stationer, the photographer, and the telephone company. It was true, Mr. Sheer informed her, that he had sold the picture, but he had not yet been paid. This held Mrs. Martino at bay for some months, but at the end of that time, she began to make herself unpleasant, and Mr. Sheer saw that it was time to act. He went around to Abernethie's and asked for the loan of one of their offices "to talk to a client in." They gave him an office marked VICE-PRESIDENT. He arranged to have Mrs. Martino meet him there, and arrived himself a little ahead of time, accompanied by an old vaudeville actor he knew. The vaudevillian hid his hat and sat down behind the desk. When Mrs. Martino was shown in, the man was introduced by Mr. Sheer as Mr. Brown of Abernethie's. The vaudevillian then explained to her in a Keith-time version of a fox-hunting dialect that the bronze had indeed been sold "to an old and valued client," who "settled his accounts" only once a year, "the English system, you know; we can't hurry a man like that. Mrs. Martino, who was Spanish, was powerfully impressed, and it was six months before she went back to Abernethie's to question Mr. Brown again. Then Mr. Sheer was obliged to pay up instantly, but the next day he borrowed back half the money from Mrs. Martino's husband.

Bierman must have been real, however, for in the interview Mr. Sheer projected it was I who was to pretend to be someone else.

He had borrowed some diamonds from Bierman, he said, to show to a friend, a playboy named Carew. But Carew, who was considering buying them for a chorus girl he was keeping, had disappeared with the diamonds before coming to any decision. It was a criminal offense to let jewelry that you had taken on consignment go out of your possession, so Bierman would have to be kept from legal action until Carew could be found. Now supposing I were to go to Bierman and say that I was a rich widow who had bought the diamonds from Mr. Sheer but would be unable to pay until my next dividend fell due. . . .

"But what if he should ask to see them?" I said.

"Tell him you sent them home to Pittsburgh to have them reset."

"But I don't *look* like a rich widow—"

"You married young," said Mr. Sheer. "Do you want me to go to Sing Sing?"

In the end I persuaded him that my impersonation of this character would only evoke catcalls from Bierman. But I would go to him in my own person, I said, tell him the truth, and beg him to wait a little. I could go, Mr. Sheer finally conceded, if I promised not to mention Carew. I should merely say that the stones had been sent out for resetting and there had been an unavoidable delay.

Just as I was leaving, Mr. Sheer had an afterthought. I was to tell Bierman, he said, that if anything *should* go wrong, Mr. Sheer would make good because his mother had a diamond that was worth more than all of Bierman's stones put together, and he would be glad to wire his mother in California to send this diamond for Bierman to hold as security.

"But does your mother really have a diamond?" I asked, and indeed I was surprised to hear that Mr. Sheer really had a mother.

"Of course," he replied impatiently. But he never spoke of it again. Whether it was out of respect for Mr. Sheer's mother or out of respect for Mr. Sheer's imagination, I do not know, but neither Bierman nor I, whatever the provocation, was ever so tactless as to remind him of this promise.

In a little office back of a jewelry store I told Bierman, a small, all-gray man, the story Mr. Sheer had prepared for me, including, at the end, the vision of the fabulous diamond in California. I did not expect him to believe me. But when I finished he seemed convinced. It was not so much that he believed in a literal sense what I was saying (he could hardly have been so naïve), but he appeared to trust what was behind what I was saying, the intention to make things right. It occurred to me after this episode that Mr. Sheer was fond of me and sometimes paid my salary, not, as I sometimes thought, out of snobbism because he believed me to be a lady, nor out of cultural aspiration because he believed me to be educated, but simply because I was the only one of his retinue who had an honest face.

Already I had fobbed off the city marshal, now I had pacified Bierman, and it was not long before I was being sent on errands of the most dubious nature, leaving Mr. Sheer behind in the Savile Galleries, secure in his confidence that my good faith would not be questioned. After this, it was I who was sent to get credit from tradesmen, I who cashed checks, I who would walk down Madison Avenue with a clock under my arm, going from door to door of the jewelers in the attempt to sell it for cash. It was even I who in a dark room taken by the hour in a questionable hotel showed a tiny, eight-by-ten Rembrandt, which I now think must certainly have been stolen, to various rat-faced men who came by appointment to examine it, while Mr. Sheer in the closet waited for results.

Of course, if I were to remain valuable to Mr. Sheer, I would have to believe that the checks were good, that the Rembrandt was genuine and legally acquired, that if the story I was telling Bierman were false, nevertheless the story that lay hidden behind it was true and not discreditable. And here lay Mr. Sheer's dilemma: if he kept me in a state of innocence (which was difficult since I handled all his business), I might blunder on one of my errands and get him into trouble; but if he allowed me to be corrupted by knowledge of his affairs, I would lose that earnest sincerity that could never be properly simulated. The dilemma was insoluble, as he discovered later. Meanwhile, his brain was kept working overtime, for each of his deceptions had to be double-barreled, one set of lies for his creditors and one for me.

Looking back, I see that, in the Bierman case, the Carew story was the lie intended for domestic consumption. Surely Carew must have been fictional, for when the finale of the diamond business took place, there was no Carew in it at all, and, in the years I have known Mr. Sheer since, I have never seen or heard of that playboy, as Mr. Sheer always called him, who figured so largely in my life that summer. Neither have I ever seen the name in Winchell's column.

I returned to the gallery from Bierman's store, ready for action. The thing to do, I said, was to find Carew at once. Mr. Sheer, it seemed to me, had been strangely apathetic about looking for him. He had heard a rumor, he finally murmured, that the girl Carew was keeping had been seen in Atlantic City.

"We must look for him in Atlantic City then," I announced energetically. "What hotel do you think he would be staying at?"

Mr. Sheer named a hotel and I called it by long distance. There was no Thomas Carew registered there. I called a second and a third, but there was still no Carew.

Mr. Sheer began to find the search enlivening, and together we called all the hotels in Atlantic City, but it was quite fruitless. Then I remembered having read in detective stories that people who went to seaside resorts with girls would often register under false names but use their own initials so that the name on the register would match the luggage. I suggested that we try asking for anybody whose initials were "T. C." Mr. Sheer was enthusiastic about the idea, and we called all the hotels over again, but either the clerks would not co-operate with us or the people we got on the wire were indignant when Mr. Sheer would open the conversation by asking if they were Tom Carew. Mr. Sheer was positive, however, that none of the men he talked to had Carew's voice. We passed a whole afternoon this way, an afternoon we both enjoyed, I because I felt myself hot on the trail of the fugitive, like a particularly bright and wily bloodhound, and Mr. Sheer, no doubt, because he had a taste for practical jokes, and found this search for an imaginary Carew a pleasant diversion from his troubles.

But his mood changed when I remarked that though we had not been able to find Carew, our idea was still good, and we might now try looking for the girl. What was her name, I asked. Mr. Sheer did not reply directly.

"You know, Miss Sargent," he said, getting up, "I've just been thinking that we're wasting our time this way. The best thing to do is to get a detective on it. I think I'll just run around and talk to O'Bannon. If Bierman calls tell him I'll call him back in an hour."

He took up his hat, paused at the door as he always did to look up and down the corridor, and went on out.

O'Bannon was a friend of Mr. Sheer's, a private detective who was known in the trade for having a particularly choice collection of strikebreakers on call, but who had lately achieved a wider notoriety when he had been jailed for an attempt to burgle the district attorney's safe during a political investigation. I had seen him once or twice waiting for Mr. Sheer, a short, thick-set man with flat feet who smoked a black cigar and wore his hat on the back of his head. With these salient occupational characteristics, he had intensified the sinister air of our outer room as he sat in a red velvet chair and stared pugnaciously at the glittering priests' robes on the wall. (Mr. Sheer generally had a friend waiting for· him in the outer room—there were a silver forger, a racetrack tout, a typewriter salesman, a men's tailor, a professional gambler, and there was also, of course, Billie, Mr. Sheer's red-haired mistress who drank. He would keep them there for hours while he talked to me in the office or made phone calls or "stepped out" on mysterious errands. When he was finally ready to see them he would come out and beckon them into the inner room with that hushed, ingratiating, yet faintly sadistic air that a dentist uses to summon his patients from the anteroom. At this time, however, O'Bannon, though fully qualified by his unprepossessing appearance, was not an habitué.)

After this day, there was a lull during which O'Bannon was supposed to be looking for Carew. At length, Bierman began to call again, and soon Bierman was replaced by his lawyer, whose telephone manners were more suave but also more ominous. Still O'Bannon reported no success. I was growing frightened, and Mr. Sheer took on a hunted look; his nose stood out more sharply in his sunken face and his pale-green eyes burned with a desperate light. We stopped writing letters altogether and made no attempt to solicit business. I took to bringing a volume of Proust to the office with me, and Mr. Sheer passed the days listlessly reading the *Social Register*. But finally one morning Mr. Sheer brought the news that O'Bannon had got on the track of Carew's girl. Carew himself, he said, had completely disappeared. The girl had the diamonds all right, but she demanded five hundred dollars before she would give them up. She and Carew had had a fight, Mr. Sheer said, and she maintained that Carew owed her money, and she was holding the diamonds as security.

"But the diamonds don't belong to her," I exclaimed. "She will have to give them up."

Mr. Sheer shook his head sadly. "It's just a hold-up," he explained, with a certain worldly resignation.

"I wouldn't do it, Mr. Sheer," I protested. "And where are you going to get the five hundred dollars?"

For it seemed obvious to me that if Mr. Sheer had had anything salable he would already have sold it.

"Well," he said thoughtfully, "there's that bronze."

"What bronze?"

"Oh, you know, *Custer's Last Stand*," he answered impatiently.

I had never heard anything of this bronze before, and it

was a surprise to find Mr. Sheer dealing in Americana. His tastes in general were sumptuous and European, and while every other dealer of Mr. Sheer's category would feature a portrait of Lincoln or a Revolutionary bedspread showing the Continental Congress, Mr. Sheer, for some reason, eschewed anything with a patriotic theme, and would even speak contemptuously of Paul Revere silver. But what I did not yet realize was that he would sell anything he could get his hands on. Now and then he would sell a live dog, and on the day I was displaying the Rembrandt in the hotel room, I was also empowered to offer an Isotta-Fraschini for a thousand dollars. And, of course, if he were telling the truth, he had been trying to sell Bierman's diamonds.

When the colored boy had gone out and returned with a huge bronze, showing one tall American with a gun and a cowboy hat standing on a hill, surrounded by some dervish-like Indians, I could see that the work had a certain sporting character that must have attracted Mr. Sheer. But I could not imagine that it would be readily marketable. I was mistaken.

Mr. Sheer telephoned Caporello, the little white-faced Italian silver forger who spent his spare time in the outer room of our gallery.

"What are you going to do?" I said. "It would take him quite a long time to forge a copy of this thing, and besides how do you know that he can work in bronze?"

Mr. Sheer was displeased by this levity toward the bronze, which he was in the very act of admiring.

"He told me once he thought he could sell it," he replied shortly.

When Caporello arrived, Mr. Sheer took him into the inner room, and after a time Caporello went away and then came back again, and the colored boy wrapped the bronze in brown paper and took it down in the elevator and put it in a taxi with Caporello, who drove off and was not seen again for three days.

"He's lit out for Italy, it's a sure thing," Mr. Sheer would say, pacing gloomily up and down the gallery. And each time he said this we would both laugh. For Mr. Sheer had a kind of calamitous humor, which when his mishaps seemed to take on an artistic shape or unity, he would turn wryly on himself. Death was always comic for him, and even while he was telling you that so-and-so's end was "a terrible thing," you could see the tension with which his face was held grave and almost hear the laughter bubbling underneath. He told me once of the death of his closest friend. "He was drunk," he said, "and dived in a swimming pool [pause, and then the explosion of laughter], but there was no water in it." Next, with a quick recovery of sobriety, "Oh, Miss Sargent, it was a terrible thing. He broke his neck." Another time, several years later, I came to see him in his office and found him convulsed with merriment. "You know what happened?" he said. "My best customer just dropped dead." One of his most hilarious anecdotes concerned the death of an old man, a wealthy soap manufacturer ("Miss Sargent, he was like an uncle to me"), who met his end in a Broadway hotel, signing checks for the entire floor show of the Rainbow Restaurant, twenty or thirty strapping blondes who crowded around the deathbed, guiding the fountain pen in his failing hand.

Our doleful laughter finally penetrated to the corner where Elmer, the colored boy, had been sitting for days, brooding about his unpaid salary and a pair of field glasses that he wanted to buy for his R.O.T.C. work.

"Mr. Sheer," he murmured, "are you worried about this Caporello? I never did trust him myself, so when I put the bronze in the cab with him I took the driver's number." The atmosphere of the detective story had infected us all.

Mr. Sheer was extremely proud of this quick-wittedness on Elmer's part. "He's a smart nigger," he said. He even paid the boy his salary that Saturday, but was indignant when he learned that Elmer had used it to buy the field glasses, and so he did not pay him again for a long time. "That nigger played on my sympathies," he said. "I thought I was contributing to the support of his poor old mother who does laundry."

The cab driver, whom we reached without difficulty, had been struck by the size of *Custer's Last Stand*, and recalled at once that he had taken Caporello to Tympany's. We telephoned Tympany's and found that the little Italian had sold them the bronze, but was not to receive the check until the following day. Mr. Sheer could just as well have intervened himself, but he wanted, he said, "to have some fun with Caporello," so he sent O'Bannon around to Tympany's to nab Caporello as he came out with the money. The little man was trembling like a drug addict when he arrived, under escort, at the gallery door. He took his hundred dollars' commission and scurried gratefully away, while Mr. Sheer and O'Bannon leaned back on the sofa and had a good laugh.

Now that he had the money, it should have been simple enough to see the girl and get the diamonds. But, frightened and harried as he was, Mr. Sheer still shrank from the direct approach. In the first place, he said, O'Bannon would have to go along, and, in the second place, we would have to get someone to impersonate the owner of the diamonds. But why, I demanded. "You don't understand how to handle these things," he replied. He at length decided that his lady friend, Billie, who was a plump, pasty, semi-genteel matron, would be suitable for the part, and he spent the afternoon rehearsing her in the inner room. It was arranged that the three of them, O'Bannon, Billie, and Mr. Sheer, should confront the girl in her apartment the next morning.

It was almost over. My sense of relief was so great that I bought Billie two cocktails before going to dinner.

But once again, as in the case of Caporello, the human element in the plot he had constructed nearly betrayed Mr. Sheer. At nine-fifteen O'Bannon telephoned that he was sick in Flatbush and would not consider coming to town. Mr. Sheer went out to look for another detective, and the lawyer telephoned to say that he would be at police court at two in the afternoon, swearing out the warrant for Mr. Sheer's arrest. "Without fail," he added with satirical emphasis. Mr. Sheer came back at last with a tall, iron-gray detective who kept asserting that he knew the girl from the Starr Faithful case, and a Negro detective who said nothing but eyed Elmer with steady suspicion. It was at this point we realized that Billie too had failed to appear. The colored detective finally found her, still drunk, in the apartment of an aviator. While we were waiting I told Mr. Sheer about the two cocktails. "It's too bad, Miss Sargent, but you couldn't have known it," he said, mournfully. "She's been on the wagon for two months and she's a perfect lady when she's sober." At one o'clock I saw them all into a taxi, Billie wobbling, her eyes glazed, leaning on the arm of the colored man and trying to repeat her lines, Mr. Sheer admonishing her to try to forget them. "Don't open your mouth, Billie," he was saying. "When we get there, just grab a chair and sit down."

Bierman's lawyer was on his way downtown when they strong-armed their way into an apartment in the Fifties, and found a small, snub-nosed blonde in a maraboued negligee huddled on her bed. The girl began to scream, protesting that she had changed her mind, that five hundred dollars was not enough, that she had never seen Mr. Sheer before. The Negro detective picked her up and slung her over his shoulder, announcing that he was taking her to the Fifty-second Street police station. Billie passed out in her chair. The girl began to struggle, and the negligee slipped off first one shoulder and then the other, and finally fell to the floor. At a sign from the gray-haired man the Negro released her, Mr. Sheer produced the money, and the girl, stark-naked and sobbing, dove under her bed, where about a dozen pairs of shoes lay scattered on the dusty floor. She scrabbled about among them, like a little pug dog, Mr. Sheer said, and began to pull stockings out of the shoes, wildly, at random. With the stockings came a quantity of diamonds, rings, bracelets, pins, and clips. The spectacle so unnerved Mr. Sheer that he could not remember at first which stones were Bierman's. Hazily he selected a few, the Negro detective picked up Billie, who could no longer walk, and they went out, leaving the girl, still weeping, crouched on the floor in the attitude of a Hindu worshiper, before the little pile of diamonds.

"I was so rattled," Mr. Sheer said afterwards, "that it didn't occur to me till we left the building that I should have claimed the whole outfit."

He smiled ruefully, and shook his head.

One morning about a month later a short man with a broken nose came into the gallery.

I had nearly forgotten about the Bierman affair. For a few days after Mr. Sheer had delivered the diamonds, we had discussed it as if it were a party we had gone to. But then a neurotic schnauzer had arrived from the West, and we were back in the dog-crystal business. And when the case was finished, it was utterly finished. We never saw or heard of any of the people again. Mr. Sheer could shut off sections of his life, as a submarine can shut off compartments, and still survive. The effect was so startling as to make you believe that the sections had never been real in the first place, that not only was there no Carew, but there was no girl, there were no diamonds. But this is impossible.

I preferred at the time not to delve into Mr. Sheer's version of the story, but to believe that he had somehow, unintentionally, got himself into a terrible quandary, and that, with my help, he had extricated himself honorably and would never lapse again. All my efforts were bent on keeping Mr. Sheer in a state of grace, and I stood guard over him as fiercely, as protectively and nervously, as if he had been a reformed drunkard. And, like the drunkard's wife, I exuded optimism and respectability.

This particular morning Mr. Sheer was out, but the broken nose and the checked suit the visitor was wearing told me at once that he was not a customer but a friend of Mr. Sheer's. He spoke cordially to Elmer, looked appreciatively at all the things, and asked after business. Business was all right, I said, and my character of the cheerful secretary compelled me to add, "Mr. Sheer has sold quite a few things lately!"

"Yes? I'm in the dog business myself, have been since I left the ring. People aren't buying dogs, so I'm surprised to hear that they're buying anything."

There was an unanswerable skepticism in the man's tone, and I silently began to type a letter. I could hear him walking inquisitively about.

"Say, you don't remember a bronze he used to have? A big thing, *Custer's Last Stand,* what became of it?"

Elmer coughed violently in the corner.

"Oh," I said, happy to find myself on safe ground, "he sold *that* a long time ago."

"That's fine. I hope he got a good price for it."

"Pretty good," I admitted.

He left almost at once, telling me to have Mr. Sheer call him. I was proceeding with the form letter I was typing ("I want you to be among the first to see a tapestry I have just received from abroad. I enclose a photograph, which, of course, can only give you the barest notion of the beauty of the original. This remarkable medieval subject" . . .), when Elmer's voice came weakly from the corner.

"Miss Sargent, I think I better tell you. That man is the owner of that bronze."

My hands dropped from the keys.

"You mean that Mr. Sheer sold it and *then didn't tell him?*"

Elmer nodded.

"It's too bad," he said, "it had to be him. He used to be the welterweight contender."

When he heard the news, Mr. Sheer did not rebuke me. It was bound to happen, he said. But he would have to pay up instantly, and pay not the six hundred dollars he had received for it but eight, which was the value the welterweight contender had originally set on his art treasure.

"Elmer thinks he's going to beat you up," I said.

"No," said Mr. Sheer, and a ruminative smile lit up his pale, sharp face. "You know, Miss Sargent, it's a funny thing, with all the crooked things I've done nobody's ever taken a sock at me. Why do you suppose that is?"

"I don't know, Mr. Sheer," I said sadly.

The word was out at last. I was gratified in a way that

Mr. Sheer had admitted the truth, but depressed by the casual, accidental manner in which it had slipped out, as if that "crooked" were taken for granted by Mr. Sheer, accepted by him as an unalterable part of his personality. My vision of a reformed, transfigured Mr. Sheer began reluctantly to dissolve, as I perceived that there was no possibility of reform because there was no practical basis for it, because, in other words (and now I knew it), there was no merchandise. I saw the nub of Mr. Sheer's business tragedy: he was continually being forced, by the impatience of a creditor, to sell somebody else's property below cost. In order to make good in the Bierman case he had had to sell an eight-hundred-dollar bronze for six hundred, and to make good for the bronze he would have to sell a thousand-dollar tapestry for eight hundred, and to make good for that he would have to sell a twelve-hundred-dollar chalice for a thousand, and so on—in short, every time he sold a picture he not only ran the risk of a jail sentence, but he lost money. Of course, in reality, it was not Mr. Sheer who lost money (since he had none to lose); it was always the last creditor who was the potential loser, and if that chain of debt were ever to break, it would be the ultimate creditor who would have to bear the accumulated losses. Mr. Sheer did not allow himself to imagine that the chain *could* break; rather, he looked forward to a time when by a Big Sale he would loosen it voluntarily; meanwhile he clung to it as a lifebelt. "If I can only keep two jumps ahead of the sheriff, I'll be all right," he said.

But I could not make myself believe in the Big Sale,

and the sheriff, it seemed to me, was gaining. The landlord, the telephone company, the stationers were pressing
in; Elmer had not been paid and he looked sullen and
hungry. We had a gallery full of objects that nobody
wanted, and that, in any case, it would be criminal to sell.
Billie was drunk and telephoning every fifteen minutes,
threatening to commit suicide. Mr. Sheer's jocular brutality ("Go ahead, Billie, I'm glad to hear it; I'll give you a
fine funeral") reminded me of something I had been trying to forget, the picture of a little, white, pug-nosed chorus
girl weeping and struggling in the Negro detective's grip.
The day was hot, the dog's cage needed cleaning, and I
thought that perhaps I had better quit.

But how was Mr. Sheer going to get the eight hundred
dollars to pay for the bronze? I would see him through this
difficulty, I resolved, and then go.

He was walking up and down in front of a very large
Japanese silk screen which showed a deer hunt in progress.
It had started out in life as a hanging and had been cut up
into panels by Mr. Sheer himself, so that, as he said, it would
not take up so much space. In spite of this mutilation, it was
probably the most authentic thing we had, and all summer
we had been asking twelve hundred dollars for it.

"If I marked that down to eight," he said in a meditative tone, "Mrs. La Plante would jump at it."

Mrs. La Plante was the lady with the toy spaniels, the
widow of a theater operator, who always looked as if she
were going through the customs. She dearly loved a bargain, and various merchants had so overstocked her with

possessions that she wore a dozen rings, strung five or six necklaces around her neck, pinned odd bits of priceless lace at her bosom and wrists, and carried two fur stoles even on the hottest summer days. Mr. Sheer could have sold her everything in the gallery, if he had put his mind to it, sold her the things and then kept them on display, since previous purchases had left not an inch of free space in her house, and whenever she made an acquisition nowadays she simply left it with the dealer, dropping in from time to time to enjoy its beauties.

In fact, this fat old lady was the perfect customer. She was passionately hospitable with her comfortable house in Long Beach, where there was plenty to eat, plenty to drink, and a swimming pool to cool off in. Early in the summer Mr. Sheer had spent several week ends there, and it was then that those abortive negotiations for the toy spaniel crystal necklace had taken place. But all at once he had stopped going, and, though Mrs. La Plante would telephone repeatedly, he would always refuse, with a hungry nostalgia in his eyes.

At first I regarded his behavior as perverse, and used to remonstrate with him about it. Mrs. La Plante was just a bargain hunter, he would answer; a dealer had to cheat himself every time he sold her anything. I would conjure up the free meals, the drinks, and he would reply that Mrs. La Plante had too many people on the place. Naturally, Mrs. La Plante was such a Very Good Thing that Mr. Sheer was not the first nor the last to get wind of her, and it was true, as I began to notice, that Mr. Sheer was shy.

He avoided strangers, particularly in large groups, and the volume of our correspondence testified to the fact that he would rather tackle a customer by mail, though this was a notoriously ineffective sales approach, than by telephone or in person. He found it still more comfortable to communicate with a customer through a letter written by someone else; in that way Mr. Sheer hardly figured in the deal at all. It was because I composed the letters that Mr. Sheer considered me invaluable as a stenographer; before my day he used to persuade a couple of elderly *Country Life* journalists to dictate descriptions of the new items to the girl in the office, descriptions which, as I discovered from the files, had had an odd sporting flavor. "This is a champion," a letter would announce of a fine faïence vase.

Nevertheless, I could not believe that it was the fear of meeting all the other gentlemen of the luxury trades that kept Mr. Sheer away from Mrs. La Plante's. Perhaps there had been some question of *quid pro quo,* and he had defended himself as stoutly as Hippolytus.

There was certainly something stoical about his face, as, accepting the loan of the train fare from me, he set out that week end for Long Beach.

He returned on Monday morning, hollow-eyed. Two well-dressed young men with excellent manners escorted him into the gallery. "This is Fred, Miss Sargent, and this is Ernest," he said. "They drove me in." In some indefinable way they seemed like a bodyguard.

"She bought the screen," he announced when we were

alone, "but, Miss Sargent, I'll never do it again. I didn't get
a wink of sleep."

I did not answer. I knew that what Mr. Sheer had done
was absolutely necessary, yet I found myself unable to stifle
my distaste.

"Oh, Miss Sargent, it was terrible," he said, and took a
long breath.

"You don't have to *tell* me about it," I said angrily.

"You mean you could see it?" he asked.

"See what?"

"About the boys . . ."

Mrs. La Plante, Mr. Sheer explained, had lately been
monopolized by three young men—a dress designer, a decorator, and a real-estate operator—who were exploiting the
old lady far more systematically than any previous para-
sites had done. It was the decorator and the real-estate man
I had just met. No one before had ever been able to toler-
ate more than a week end at a time of Mrs. La Plante's
conversation, but the three young men were now living
on the premises, doing needlework, knitting, and playing
with the toy spaniels. They were not gigolos in the ordinary
sense; they were just good company. To Mrs. La Plante
they were her dear boys, and they in turn were fiercely
possessive about the old lady, so possessive that they made
a week-end visit a nightmare for an outsider. A jeweler
had found a garter snake in his bed; a furrier had got a
Mickey Finn; Mr. Sheer had been ducked, wearing one
of his two suits, in the swimming pool—and Mrs. La Plante
had been in a continuous spasm of merriment. "The boys

make me young again," she told Mr. Sheer. One by one,
the ordinary merchants had dropped off. Mr. Sheer had
hung on for a while, but even he could not sustain it.
"They're so petty and malicious, Miss Sargent," he complained. "It broke my heart to see the way they were milk-
ing that innocent old lady." When the boys had begun to
demand commissions on any purchases Mrs. La Plante
made, Mr. Sheer had given up.

This week end Mr. Sheer had been subjected to a more
advanced form of torture. The house was bulging with the
boys and their friends, with the result that Mr. Sheer had
had to share a room with Fred, the decorator.

"In the same bed?" I asked.

Mr. Sheer nodded mournfully. "I was afraid to go to
sleep."

For two nights he had lain tense and watchful while the
decorator tossed restlessly from side to side. In the morning, just as Mr. Sheer was dropping off, the young man had
let all thirty-one toy spaniels into the room. They had
jumped on the bed, and both days Mr. Sheer had waked
up screaming. Mrs. La Plante had come out in a fur-
trimmed dressing-gown and asked him if he had a guilty
conscience.

"I'll never do it again," he repeated, and that afternoon
he took a nap on the velvet sofa in the inner room.

But perhaps, after all, Mrs. La Plante was lonely with
only the boys for company. At any rate, a few days later,
she telephoned Mr. Sheer with a new project for having
the toy spaniels pose in groups. With the bait dangling

before him, Mr. Sheer's resolution wilted. He went out to Long Beach for the night. Then he went out for two week ends in succession. The house was just as crowded; Mr. Sheer's offers to sleep on the couch in the living room were politely brushed aside; so that after each visit Mr. Sheer would have to spend several afternoons napping on our musty sofa. It did not make any difference, though, for during this period, with the exception of Mrs. La Plante, we had no customers.

It was so hot indeed that even Mr. Sheer's creditors slackened in their attentions. Having nothing else to do, Mr. Sheer let his mind play on the problem of the boys. It no longer appeared to him insuperable. His first idea was to make friends with them. They were not necessarily, he said, a closed corporation. Two weeks before he had dismissed them as nauseating creatures; now he took a more tolerant attitude. After all, they could not help it if they were born that way, he said. The effect of the friendship offensive he instantly launched was to demoralize the office. The boys overran the gallery, criticizing the objects, making long-distance calls to their entire acquaintance on the Atlantic seaboard, and harrowing the colored boy with indecent proposals. They had to be taken out to lunch whenever they were in town, and they insisted on either Maillard's or Schrafft's. Finally the little decorator, Mr. Sheer's bedfellow, stole five dollars out of my purse, and I offered Mr. Sheer his choice: them or me. Mr. Sheer advised me absently not to be petty, but he began to relax his attentions to the boys, for it was plain, whatever my feelings, that the friendship offensive was not working out. The boys were using their familiarity with Mr. Sheer's affairs to manufacture new and factually documented slanders for Mrs. La Plante's ears. A short acquaintance with Caporello, who was timidly coming around again, inspired them to say that Mr. Sheer was a silver forger and all his pieces were copies. (So far as I know, this was not true. Certainly many of his attributions were imaginative. He would walk up and down in front of a Japanese lacquer box for a long time, with narrowed eyes, communing with it, and finally he would let a light break on his face and exclaim, perhaps for my benefit, perhaps simply for his own, "Why, that must belong to the Heian period!" From that time on, the box would be dated. But this generous exercise of the critical faculty had little in common with Caporello's artisanship. He would have nothing to do with the modern copies of Queen Anne silver that the Italian brought around from time to time—coffee pots or tankards with the old hallmark skillfully welded on. "You can say what you want, Miss Sargent," he told me once, "but I'd never stoop that low." Apparently, there was some borderline, imperceptible to the normal moral eye, which he would have felt it degrading to cross; and I had hurt his feelings more than once before I learned to watch for it.)

At any rate, the more friendly Mr. Sheer became with the boys, the more chilly Mrs. La Plante's manner grew. Mr. Sheer thought it over. He would take a leaf out of their book, he decided, and expose the boys to Mrs. La Plante. He got hold of a night-club proprietor, a former the-

atrical associate of the dead Mr. La Plante, and primed him
to visit Mrs. La Plante and make her the following speech.
"Mrs. La Plante, it has come to my ears that you are asso-
ciating with Fred So-and-So, Ernest So-and-So, and another
of their ilk. Mrs. La Plante, I could hardly believe it to be
true when my good friend, Mr. Sheer, informed me of the
fact. Mr. Sheer, of course, is an unworldly man, and he
knew nothing against the boys. He told me of your friendship merely as a matter of interest. But I myself am a
worldly man. I have heard of these men, and I tell you,
Mrs. La Plante, Peter La Plante would turn over in his
grave if he knew of this. Why, Mrs. La Plante, those men
are degenerates, those men are homosexuals!"

The night-club proprietor did go out to Long Beach
and faithfully delivered the warning. Unfortunately, the
whole thing fell extraordinarily flat owing to the fact that
Mrs. La Plante did not know what a homosexual was, and,
as the night-club man pointed out later, it was no use at
her age trying to tell her. After this, Mr. Sheer gave up
again. For a second time, the toy spaniel necklace had to be
abandoned, and the office was quiet once more.

It was about this time that the telephone was shut off.
The boys with their long-distance calls had given it the
coup de grâce. We carried on without it, increasing, to
make up for our inaccessibility, the volume of our correspondence. But after ten days of this our stationery was
used up, and the stationers declined to print any more
until the bill had been paid. We were now completely cut
off from the outside world, and, though Mr. Sheer finally

discovered a stationer who would give him credit, a week went by while we waited for the new paper to be finished, a week during which I did nothing—it was September now, but too hot even to read in the office. When at last it came, it did not, as Mr. Sheer said, have the same quality as the old; still, he was prepared to make the best of it. I was just starting on a new series of letters when they came and took the typewriter away.

The typewriter had seemed to me the one solid, permanent object in the gallery, but this, too, did not belong to Mr. Sheer. It had been rented from an agency.

I decided to quit. The means of performing my duties no longer existed; I had been rendered impotent by creditors. Working for Mr. Sheer, moreover, had come to be a luxury for me. I had not been paid for some time, and I was supplying Mr. Sheer with a stream of nickels and dimes which he poured into the pay-telephone box in the lobby of the building. Also I had got to know Mr. Sheer so well that it was impossible for me to leave the gallery at six and carry with me the conviction that he had no way of getting a meal. So, unless one of us had another invitation, I had fallen into the habit of buying his dinner. Mr. Sheer was a connoisseur of the eighty-five-cent *table d'hôte* restaurants. We would eat and he would tell me stories of his past. It was not until much later that I realized how extraordinarily happy Mr. Sheer had been all through that terrible summer. At the time, I was sorry for him in the conventional way, but still I could not afford it. And, in any case, I told myself, it was just a question of time before the pack caught up with Mr. Sheer, and, somehow, I did not want to be in at the kill.

Yet, after I had quit, when I would come back to see him, Mr. Sheer would still be there, the colored boy would still be there, and, as I have said, another girl would be in my place, with another typewriter. I would always scan the building directory downstairs to see if the Savile Galleries were still listed. For a long time they were, but then one day not a week after I had seen Mr. Sheer, the name was gone, and there was no forwarding address. The lifebelt, I presumed, had broken.

But it was not quite over. More than a year later I discovered him by accident in a much larger and more impressive gallery tucked away in an arcade off Forty-seventh Street. He was still wearing the same suit, and the new gallery was like an enlargement of the old. He had taken Elmer and the red and green velvet drapes with him, the rooms were dark, and the priests' robes glimmering down from the walls seemed exactly the same. I noticed a few horse sculptures, which were a departure, and there was a new and curious collection of Louis Quinze love seats, rented, he said, from a theatrical warehouse.

I complimented him on his new surroundings.

"I'll be evicted any day," he whispered.

But he was in buoyant spirits. He showed me a pocketful of summonses as another man might have flashed a bankroll. There must have been twenty of them at least. "I think they've got me this time," he said, and forced his face to assume that funereal expression that he felt the decorum of his predicament required.

"People tell me I ought to go into bankruptcy. But I hate to do it now. Did you see those horse sculptures?" I nodded. "It's a big thing, Miss Sargent, much bigger than the dogs. I've made a lot of wonderful new contacts, and I'd hate to go through court now. You know, Miss Sargent, there are a lot of things I wouldn't like to have come out. Nothing wrong, you know, but . . ."

"Yes," I said.

Two days later he was in jail. He telephoned me from there to ask if I could advance him a hundred dollars. He had failed to meet payments on a judgment against him, and the sheriff had picked him up for contempt of court.

I was sorry, I said, but I really didn't have a hundred dollars.

"I didn't think you would, Miss Sargent. I just thought you'd like to hear about it. There are people here that have been here for years. Mostly alimony cases. You'd get a kick out of it."

If he could wait a day, I said, I would try to raise the money for him.

"No," he answered doubtfully, "I don't want to do that. There's a kind of stigma attached to spending the night in jail. . . ."

The next day he was gone. The debt had been paid at three in the morning, they told me at the jail. I hurried up to the fine new gallery, but he was not there. A furniture van was parked out in front, the gallery door was open, and most of the hangings had been taken off the walls. The phone was ringing through the empty rooms. On an irrational, hopeful impulse I ran to answer it, thinking how providential if now at the ultimate moment this should be the Big Sale that would save him. But it was a sweet-voiced girl from the telephone company asking about the bill. I would speak to Mr. Sheer, I said; it was doubtless an oversight. I waited all afternoon, till the last familiar vase had been carted off, till they took away the chair I was sitting on, but he did not come back, and no one knew where he had gone.

Several years later, as I was coming out of a theater one night, a man touched my elbow. There was something furtive about the gesture, and I turned indignantly. I faced an apotheosis of Mr. Sheer, tall and ruddy, barbered and tailored, exuding a faint, chic fragrance of Caron's "Pour l'Homme." The radiant prosperity of his appearance led me to conclude at once that he had returned to that mysterious underworld from which he had come. There was a pathos of moral defeat about the idea; nevertheless, it was a relief to think that Mr. Sheer had at last ceased to strive.

But he was handing me a card he had selected from his breast pocket, and on it I read the name of a reputable antique dealer, and below it, in smaller letters, the words, I. F. SHEER, THE SPORTSMAN'S CORNER.

It was true. He took me around at midnight to see the place, and there was his private office paneled in knotty pine, his secretary's cubbyhole next to it, and two rooms full of objects of every sort, sculptures in wood and bronze, tapestries, vases, urns, silk panels and screens, rings and earrings, book-ends and doorstops—all of them dealing with a single theme, sport through the ages. There was a Persian horse that anticipated the one that was later shown in the great Persian Exhibition; and in a glass case a gold Cretan dagger with a boar hunt on it. The medieval tapestries and the Japanese cloisonné enamels depicted various aspects of the chase, and a good-sized modern bronze showed a wrestling match in progress. "I've got everything," he said in a jubilant whisper, "except an Egyptian tomb painting." It was true. He had really covered the subject. And what was most remarkable to me was the fact that all these objects had an air of expensive authenticity. I believed in the Persian horse; I could almost believe in the dagger. He showed me over the main gallery, which was even more emphatically, quietly elegant. The collection was miscellaneous—he pointed out a dinner service that had belonged to Franz Joseph, some Pisanello medallions of the Este family, an early rosary, and a prie-dieu that he said had been used by Queen Elizabeth. Yet, ill-assorted as these objects were, they had been tellingly arranged: there was nothing here to suggest the auction room or the second-hand shop. When I had seen the gallery, he had me admire the clothes he was wearing, and they, too, were the McCoy, suit by Tripler, shirt by McLaughlin, tie by Sulka, down to the socks by Saks Fifth Avenue.

Yet there was something about that night in that dark

gallery, lit only by reflectors shining down on tapestries and gold lacquer panels, about Mr. Sheer as he tiptoed from room to room on thick-piled carpets, that made me, following at his heels, feel like a prowler. All the while he was telling me how he came to be there, how the Hermitage Galleries had lifted him out of the gutter and made him a salesman, how he had sold and sold until he was head of his own department, how he would soon become a partner, all that while I had a strong sense that we had no right to be there, I was listening for the knock of the night watchman who would order us away.

His success story seemed to me incredible and I could see, by his excitement in relating it, that he found it so too. Later on, when I saw him in daylight, ingratiating with customers, man-to-man with his partners, authoritative to the office girls, I could believe it and even find reasons to justify it—he had been hired, of course, because in his way he had been a pioneer, selling bric-a-brac to rich dog and horse people who, under ordinary circumstances, could never have been induced to set foot in a dealer's gallery. With his dog crystals he had built up a new sort of clientele, whom he now carried along with him on his great voyage of discovery. And it was precisely his character as a discoverer that endeared him to his clients, gauche and untried themselves in the mysteries of connoisseurship. How, they must have asked themselves, could this man trick us as they say art dealers do; he is too ill-informed, too naïve, in fact too much like ourselves.

But Mr. Sheer did not understand the reasons for his

success, and therefore it made him uneasy. That night I
could see that he, too, felt like a trespasser on those well-
appointed, cultured premises, and this sense of unlawful
entry filled him with both shame and pride. He was moving out of the sporting field, he said; already he was dick-
ering for a tapestry that had been designed by Rembrandt;
in the goldsmith's field there was Cellini; in bronze, Ver-
rocchio and Donatello. And there were even bigger things
to be done. Look at the stuff Hearst had bought, whole
rooms at a time. And this fellow who had made a fortune
selling the Romanoff collection. . . . But as his voice rose
with the great names, there was apprehension in it. The
new merchandise would bring new problems. With the
sporting subjects he knew where he stood: it was easy
enough to demonstrate the points of a hound. But what,
exactly, *were* the points of a Cellini?

He wanted me, he said, to teach him.

I agreed that night to give him lessons in good English,
and in the jargon of art criticism, though I privately felt
that it would be the ruin of his career if he ever learned
how to patronize his customers.

Fortunately for Mr. Sheer, as a student he did not make
rapid progress. Our lessons would take place at lunch, at
dinner, at the theater, or, often, late at night or on Sunday
afternoon, in the dark, empty gallery. I tried to teach him
terms like Byzantine and baroque, but, as I soon discovered, he was chiefly interested in acquiring a string of hy-
perbolical adjectives to describe his stock. And it was
more important to him to learn how to pronounce *Long-*

champs correctly than to memorize the parts of speech.

It was something different from good English, I began to realize, that he wanted from me.

When he passed into the final stage of his business development and became a partner, Mr. Sheer achieved his ambition—to enter a rich man's house by the front door, as a guest. First there had been stag evenings with visiting Middle Western businessmen, but before long, at Aiken, at Palm Beach, on Long Island, Mr. Sheer would now and then be included in the larger cocktail parties. Deeply as he desired these invitations, he could only enjoy them in anticipation and in retrospect. The parties themselves were torture for him. His fear of committing a solecism combined with his shyness in crowds to bleach his conversation to an unnatural neutrality. On the offensive, he restricted himself to the most general statements about politics, the weather, the women's dresses, the state of business; on the defensive, he held off his interlocutor with all the Really's and You-don't-say's and the Well-isn't-that-interesting's of the would-be Good Listener.

Still, this was the apogee of his career, and he knew it. What puzzled him, what at first he could hardly believe, was the fact that he was unhappy. He grew more and more dependent on the evenings we would spend together, exchanging stories of the disreputable old days. "Margaret," he would tell me, "it's a funny thing, but you're the only person I have a good time with any more." He explained this by saying that he could "be himself" with me, but there was more to it than that. For one thing, I was dear to him because I was the only one who *knew*. In my mind he could see as in his own the two Mr. Sheers, the pale, perspiring Mr. Sheer of the past and the resplendent Mr. Sheer of the present. The wonderful, miraculous contrast was alive in me as it was in no one else. What was becoming infinitely saddening to him in his own success story was that he could never allow anyone to know what a success story it was. The old Mr. Sheer had to be kept under cover, and his new friends could only presume that the present Mr. Sheer had sprung full-blown from the head of the Hermitage Galleries.

Moreover, though in the first flush of success, at the time of his greatest happiness, the two Mr. Sheers must have been equally alive and equally vigorous, now in the daily atmosphere of respectability, the old Mr. Sheer was atrophying. Mr. Hyde had turned into Dr. Jekyll, and it required the strongest drugs to get him to go back to his original state. The reminiscences we exchanged were but one of the drugs. Mr. Sheer tried a number of other methods.

In the first place, as I have said, he liked to haunt the gallery out of business hours. Where he had once felt genuinely like a trespasser, he now tried to revive that feeling by imitating the behavior that went with it. But no policeman, no Holmes Protective man, ever halted him, no matter what time of night he came, for now the Fifty-seventh Street police knew him and greeted him with respect.

He produced another imitation of his former character by moving back and forth from one hotel to another. One week he would be at the St. Regis, the next at the Gotham, the next at the Weylin, and so on, until he had made the rounds of the second-string fashionable hotels, when he would start over again. But this elusiveness was synthetic, for now his secretary could always find him. His position as a successful man required that.

In the same way, he would try to inject a little color into his business life by the practice of minor chicaneries. Any large-scale operations were out of the question, for the bookkeeper kept the accounts and handled the money. But he could concoct fabulous histories of the pieces he sold, could suppress an undesirable attribution, could add a signature where none had been before, and happily obliterate what he felt were picayune distinctions between period replicas and originals by a master. He could also reveal business confidences and make promises that were impossible to keep. If he could have had his way, every sale would have been a little conspiracy: in his eyes, the price being equal, it was better to sell a Gobelin tapestry as a Beauvais than to sell it as a Gobelin. I have even watched him trying to persuade himself (and this was the inevitable first step in the process of deception) that a Degas bronze was not a Degas at all, but a Rodin.

Yet, like his personal elusiveness, this slipperiness in business was largely unreal. In the first place, it was unnecessary: he had reached a point in his career where the things he handled could be sold on their merits. In the second place, though it should have been dangerous, though indeed he desired it to be dangerous, his secretary and his partners kept a diligent watch over him to prevent him from hurting himself. They were always ready to intervene with "Mr. Sheer made a mistake, he has so many things on his mind, we will correct the error." He was in the position of a rich kleptomaniac whose family is perpetually on hand to turn her thefts into purchases.

As time passed, it became increasingly difficult for Mr. Sheer to regard his life as an imposture. He still believed that he could "be himself" with me, but actually our conversations were more and more taken up with politics, the weather, the women's dresses, the state of business, till the outlaw Mr. Sheer I dined with was practically indistinguishable from the Mr. Sheer one met at the gallery or at a hunt breakfast somewhere in New Jersey. It was plain, at last, that Mr. Sheer had not imposed on the business world and used it for his own delight, but that the business world had used Mr. Sheer, rejecting the useless or outmoded parts of him. He had not, as he first thought, outwitted anybody, but he had somehow, imperceptibly, been outwitted himself.

Yet masquerade was life to Mr. Sheer. He could not bear to succeed in his own personality, any more than an unattractive woman can bear to be loved for herself. So he began, indirectly, unwittingly, to try to fail. It was distressing to watch him, for even here he was conforming to the conventions of the businessman's world. This Mr. Sheer who had once hunted danger, joyously, down a hundred strange byways, was now walking glumly down a well-trodden road into the jaws of a respectable ruin.

He had a love affair with his best client's wife, and he played the stock market. Both of these ventures he pursued with a terrible listlessness. He could hardly bother to follow his stocks in the newspaper, or to telephone the lady for whom he was risking so much. It was only when his broker sold him out, and when he brought the lady home to her husband with her evening dress wrong-side-out, that his spirits revived, and he would dwell on the two misfortunes with his old rueful delight.

The Hermitage Galleries, however, saw him through, and the client, who had been looking for a pretext to break with his wife, readily forgave him. Mr. Sheer grew more despondent than ever, and his health began to worry him. He had a masseur in the morning, and he went to a gymnasium in the evening; he subjected himself to basal-metabolism tests, urinalyses, blood counts, took tonics to pep him up and bromides to quiet him and was still, unaccountably, tired. Last year they took out his appendix and his teeth; when he recovered, he had not lost that daily, dragging fatigue, but only acquired an appetite for the knife.

I saw him off to the hospital recently to have his gall bladder removed.

"It's a very dangerous operation, Margaret; it may be the death of me," he said.

And for the first time in many weeks he giggled irrepressibly.

THREE   *The Man in the Brooks Brothers Shirt*

THE new man who came into the club car was coatless. He was dressed in gray trousers and a green shirt of expensive material that had what seemed to be the figure "2" embroidered in darker green on the sleeve. His tie matched the green of the monogram, and his face, which emerged rather sharply from this tasteful symphony in cool colors, was blush pink. The greater part of his head appeared to be pink, also, though actually toward the back there was a good deal of closely cropped pale-gray hair that harmonized with his trousers. He looked, she decided, like a middle-aged baby, like a young pig, like something in a seed catalogue. In any case, he was plainly Out of the Question, and the hope that had sprung up, as for some reason it always did, with the sound of a new step soft on the flowered Pullman carpet, died a new death. Already the trip was half over. They were now several hours out of Omaha; nearly all the Chicago passengers had put in an appearance; and still there was no one, no one at all. She must not mind, she told herself; the trip West was of no importance; yet she felt a curious, shamefaced disappointment, as if she had given a party and no guests had come.

She turned again to the lady on her left, her *vis-à-vis* at breakfast, a person with dangling earrings, a cigarette holder, and a lorgnette, who was somebody in the New Deal and carried about with her a typewritten report of the hearings of some committee which she was anxious to discuss. The man in the green shirt crowded himself into a love seat directly opposite, next to a young man with glasses and loud socks who was reading Vincent Sheean's *Personal History*. Sustaining her end of a well-bred, well-informed, liberal conversation, she had an air of perfect absorption and earnestness, yet she became aware, without ever turning her head, that the man across the way had decided to pick her up. Full of contempt for the man, for his coatlessness, for his color scheme, for his susceptibility, for his presumption, she nevertheless allowed her voice to rise a little in response to him. The man countered by turning to his neighbor and saying something excessively audible about Vincent Sheean. The four voices, answering each other, began to give an antiphonal effect, Vincent Sheean was a fine fellow, she heard him pronounce; he could vouch for it, he knew him *personally*. The bait was crude, she reflected. She would have preferred the artificial fly to the angleworm, but still. . . . After all, he might have done worse; judged by eternal standards, Sheean might not be much, but in the cultural atmosphere of the Pullman car, Sheean was a titan. Moreover, if one judged the man by his intention, one could not fail to be touched.

He was doing his best to *please* her. He had guessed from
her conversation that she was an intellectual, and was plac-
ing the name of Sheean as a humble offering at her feet.
And the simple vulgarity of the offering somehow enhanced its value; it was like one of those home-made cakes
with Paris-green icing that she used to receive on her
birthday from her colored maid.

Her own neighbor must finally have noticed a certain
displacement of attention, for she got up announcing that
she was going in to lunch, and her tone was stiff with re-
proof and disappointment so that she seemed, for a moment, this rococo suffragette, like a nun who discovers that
her favorite novice lacks the vocation. As she tugged open
the door to go out, a blast of hot Nebraska air rushed into
the club car, where the air-cooling system had already
broken down.

The girl in the seat had an impulse to follow her. It
would surely be cooler in the diner, where there was not
so much glass. If she stayed and let the man pick her up,
it would be a question of eating lunch together, and there
would be a little quarrel about the check, and if she let
him win she would have him on her hands all the way to
Sacramento. And he was certain to be tiresome. That emblem in Gothic script spelled out the self-made man. She
could foresee the political pronouncements, the pictures of
the wife and children, the hand squeezed under the table.
Nothing worse than that, fortunately, for the conductors
on those trains were always very strict. Still, the whole
thing would be so vulgar; one would expose oneself so to

the derision of the other passengers. It was true, she was always wanting something exciting and romantic to happen; but it was not really romantic to be the-girl-who-sits-in-the-club-car-and-picks-up-men. She closed her eyes with a slight shudder: some predatory view of herself had been disclosed for an instant. She heard her aunt's voice saying, "I don't know why you make yourself so cheap," and "It doesn't pay to let men think you're easy." Then she was able to open her eyes again, and smile a little, patronizingly, for of course it hadn't worked out that way. The object of her trip was, precisely, to tell her aunt in Portland that she was going to be married again.

She settled down in her seat to wait and began to read an advance copy of a new novel. When the man would ask her what-that-book-is-you're-so-interested-in (she had heard the question before), she would be able to reply in a tone so simple and friendly that it could not give offense, "Why, you probably haven't heard of it. It's not out yet." (Yet, she thought, she had not brought the book along for purposes of ostentation: it had been given her by a publisher's assistant who saw her off at the train, and now she had nothing else to read. So, really, she could not be accused of insincerity. Unless it could be that her whole way of life had been assumed for purposes of ostentation, and the book, which looked accidental, was actually part of that larger and truly deliberate scheme. If it had not been this book, it would have been something else, which would have served equally well to impress a pink middle-aged stranger.)

The approach, when it came, was more unorthodox than she had expected. The man got up from his seat and said, "Can I talk to you?" Her retort, "What have you got to say?" rang off-key in her own ears. It was as if Broadway had answered Indiana. For a moment the man appeared to be taken aback, but then he laughed. "Why, I don't know; nothing special. We can talk about that book, I guess."

She liked him, and with her right hand made a gesture that meant, "All right, go on." The man examined the cover. "I haven't heard about this. It must be new."

"Yes." Her reply had more simplicity in it than she would have thought she could achieve. "It isn't out yet. This is an advance copy."

"I've read something else by this fellow. He's good."

"You have?" cried the girl in a sharp, suspicious voice. It was incredible that this well-barbered citizen should not only be familiar with but have a taste for the work of an obscure revolutionary novelist. On the other hand, it was incredible that he should be lying. The artless and offhand manner in which he pronounced the novelist's name indicated no desire to shine, indicated in fact that he placed no value on that name, that it was to him a name like Hervey Allen or Arthur Brisbane or Westbrook Pegler or any other. Two alternatives presented themselves: either the man belonged to that extraordinary class of readers who have perfect literary digestions, who can devour anything printed, retaining what suits them, eliminating what does not, and liking all impartially, because, since they take what they want from each, they are always actually reading the same book (she had had a cousin who was like that about the theater, and she remembered how her aunt used to complain, saying, "It's no use asking Cousin Florence whether the show at the stock company is any good this week; Cousin Florence has never seen a bad play")—either that, or else the man had got the name confused and was really thinking of some popular writer all the time.

Still, the assertion, shaky as it was, had given him status with her. It was as if he had spoken a password, and with a greater sense of assurance and propriety, she went on listening to his talk. His voice was rather rich and dark; the accent was Middle Western, but underneath the nasalities there was something soft and furry that came from the South. He lived in Cleveland, he told her, but his business kept him on the go a good deal; he spent nearly half his time in New York.

"You do?" she exclaimed, her spirits rising. "What *is* your business?" Her original view of him had already begun to dissolve, and it now seemed to her that the instant he had entered the club car she had sensed that he was no ordinary provincial entrepreneur.

"I'm a traveling salesman," he replied genially.

In a moment she recognized that this was a joke, but not before he had caught her look of absolute dismay and panic. He leaned toward her and laughed. "If it sounds any better to you," he said, "I'm in the steel business."

"It doesn't," she replied, recovering herself, making her words prim with political disapproval. But he *knew;* she had given herself away; he had trapped her features in an expression of utter snobbery.

"You're a pink, I suppose," he said, as if he had noticed nothing. "It'd sound better to you if I said I was a burglar."

"Yes," she acknowledged, with a comic air of frankness, and they both laughed. Much later, he gave her a business card that said he was an executive in Little Steel, but he persisted in describing himself as a traveling salesman, and she saw at last that it was an accident that the joke had turned on her: the joke was a wry, humble, clownish one that he habitually turned on himself.

When he asked if she would join him in a drink before lunch, she accepted readily. "Let's go into the diner, though. It may be cooler."

"I've got a bottle of whisky in my compartment. I *know* it's cool there."

Her face stiffened. A compartment was something she had not counted on. But she did not know (she never had known) how to refuse. She felt bitterly angry with the man for having exposed her—so early—to this supreme test of femininity, a test she was bound to fail, since she would either go into the compartment, not wanting to (and he would know this and feel contempt for her malleability), or she would stay out of the compartment, wanting to have gone in (and he would know this, too, and feel contempt for her timidity).

The man looked at her face.

"Don't worry," he said in a kind, almost fatherly voice. "It'll be perfectly proper. I promise to leave the door open."

He took her arm and gave it a slight, reassuring squeeze, and she laughed out loud, delighted with him for having, as she thought, once again understood and spared her.

In the compartment, which was off the club car, it *was* cooler. The highballs, gold in the glasses, tasted, as her own never did, the way they looked in the White Rock advertisements. There was something about the efficiency with which his luggage, in brown calf, was disposed in that small space, about the white coat of the black waiter who kept coming in with fresh ice and soda, about the chicken sandwiches they finally ordered for lunch, that gave her that sense of ritualistic "rightness" that the Best People are supposed to bask in. The open door contributed to this sense: it was exactly as if they were drinking in a show window, for nobody went by who did not peer in, and she felt that she could discern envy, admiration, and censure in the quick looks that were shot at her. The man sat at ease, unconscious of these attentions, but she kept her back straight, her shoulders high with decorum, and let her bare arms rise and fall now and then in short parabolas of gesture.

But if for the people outside she was playing the great lady, for the man across the table she was the Bohemian Girl. It was plain that she was a revelation to him, that he had never under the sun seen anyone like her. And he was quizzing her about her way of life with the intense, unashamed, wondering curiosity of a provincial seeing for the first time the sights of a great but slightly decadent city. Answering his questions she was able to see herself through

his eyes (brown eyes, which were his only good feature, but
which somehow matched his voice and thus enhanced the
effect, already striking, of his having been put together by
a good tailor). What she got from his view of her was a
feeling of uniqueness and identity, a feeling she had once
had when, at twenty, she had come to New York and had
her first article accepted by a liberal weekly, but which had
slowly been rubbed away by four years of being on the inside of the world that had looked magic from Portland,
Oregon. Gradually, now, she was becoming very happy, for
she knew for sure in this compartment that she was beautiful and gay and clever, and worldly and innocent, serious and frivolous, capricious and trustworthy, witty and
sad, bad and really good, all mixed up together, all at the
same time. She could feel the power running in her, like a
medium on a particularly good night.

As these multiple personalities bloomed on the single
stalk of her ego, a great glow of charity, like the flush of
life, suffused her. This man, too, must be admitted into
the mystery; this stranger must be made to open and dis-
close himself like a Japanese water flower. With a messi-
anic earnestness she began to ask him questions, and though
at first his answers displayed a sort of mulish shyness ("I'm
just a traveling salesman," "I'm a suburban businessman,"
"I'm an economic royalist"), she knew that sooner or later
he would tell her the truth, the rock-bottom truth, and
was patient with him. It was not the first time she had
"drawn a man out"—the phrase puckered her mouth, for
it had never seemed like that to her. Certain evenings spent

in bars with men she had known for half an hour came back to her; she remembered the beautiful frankness with which the cards on each side were laid on the table till love became a wonderful slow game of double solitaire and nothing that happened afterwards counted for anything beside those first few hours of self-revelation. Now as she put question after question she felt once more like a happy burglar twirling the dial of a well-constructed safe, listening for the locks to click and reveal the combination. When she asked him what the emblem on his shirt stood for, unexpectedly the door flew open.

"It was a little officer's club we had in the war," he said. "The four deuces, we called ourselves." He paused, and then went on irrelevantly, "I get these shirts at Brooks Brothers. They'll put the emblem on free if you order the shirts custom-made. I always order a dozen at a time. I get everything at Brooks Brothers except ties and shoes. Leonie thinks it's stodgy of me."

Leonie was his wife. They had a daughter, little Angela, and two sons, little Frank and little Joe, and they lived in a fourteen-room house in the Gates Mills section of Cleveland. Leonie was a home girl, quite different from Eleanor, who had been his first big love and was now a decorator in New York. Leonie loved her house and children. Of course, she was interested in culture, too, particularly the theater, and there were always a lot of young men from the Cleveland Playhouse hanging around her; but then she was a Vassar girl, and you had to expect a woman to have different interests from a man.

Leonie was a Book-of-the-Month Club member and she also subscribed to the two liberal weeklies. "She'll certainly be excited," the man said, grinning with pleasure, "when she hears I met somebody from the *Liberal* on this trip. But she'll never be able to understand why you wasted your time talking to poor old Bill."

The girl smiled at him.

"I *like* to talk to you," she said, suppressing the fact that nothing on earth would have induced her to talk to Leonie.

"I read an article in those magazines once in a while," he continued dreamily. "Once in a while they have something good, but on the whole they're too wishy-washy for me. Now that I've had this visit with you, though, I'll read your magazine every week, trying to guess which of those things in the front you wrote."

"I'm *never* wishy-washy," said the girl, laughing. "But is your wife radical?"

"Good Lord, no! She calls herself a liberal, but actually I'm more of a radical than Leonie is."

"How do you mean?"

"Well, take the election. I'm going to vote for Landon because it's expected of me, and my vote won't put him in."

"But you're really for Roosevelt?"

"No," said the man, a little impatiently, "I don't like Roosevelt either. I don't like a man that's always hedging his bets. Roosevelt's an old woman. Look at the way he's handling these CIO strikes. He doesn't have the guts to stick up for Lewis, and he doesn't have the sense to stay out of the whole business." He leaned across the table and added, almost in a whisper, "You know who I'd like to vote for?"

The girl shook her head.

"Norman Thomas!"

"But you're a steel man!" said the girl.

The man nodded.

"Nobody knows how I feel, not even Leonie." He paused to think. "I was in the last war," he said finally, "and I had a grand time. I was in the cavalry and there weren't any horses. But they made me a captain and decorated me. After the armistice we were stationed in Cologne, and we got hold of a Renault and every week end we'd drive all night so we could have a day on the Riviera." He chuckled to himself. "But the way I look at it, there's a new war coming and it isn't going to be like that. God Almighty, we didn't hate the Germans!"

"And now?"

"You wait," he said. "Last time it was supposed to be what you people call an ideological war—for democracy and all that. But it wasn't. That was just advertising. You liberals have all of a sudden found out that it was Mr. Morgan's war. You think that's terrible. But let me tell you that Mr. Morgan's war was a hell of a lot nicer to fight than this new one will be. Because this one will be ideological, and it'll be too damned serious. You'll wish that you had the international bankers and munitions men to stop the fight when things get too rough. I'd like to see this country stay out of it. That's why I'm for Thomas."

"You're a very interesting man," said the girl, tears coming to her eyes, perhaps because of the whisky. "I've never known anyone like you. You're not the kind of business-man I write editorials against."

"You people are crazy, though," he said genially. "You're never going to get anywhere in America with that prole-tariat stuff. Every workingman wants to live the way I do. He doesn't want me to live the way he does. You people go at it from the wrong end. I remember a Socialist or-ganizer came down fifteen years ago into Southern Illinois. I was in the coal business then, working for my first girl's father. This Socialist was a nice fellow. . . ."

His voice was dreamy again, but there was an under-current of excitement in it. It was as if he were reviving some buried love affair, or, rather, some wispy young *tendresse* that had never come to anything. The Socialist organizer had been a distant connection of his first girl's, the two men had met and had some talks; later the Social-ist had been run out of town; the man had stood aloof, neither helping nor hindering.

"I wonder what's become of him," he said finally. "In jail somewhere, I guess."

"Oh no," said the girl. "You don't understand modern life. He's a big bureaucrat in the CIO. Just like a business-man, only not so well paid."

The man looked puzzled and vaguely sad. "He had a lot of nerve," he murmured, then added quickly, in a loud, bumptious tone, "But you're all nuts!"

The girl bit her lips. The man's vulgarity was undeni-able. For some time now she had been attempting (for her own sake) to whitewash him, but the crude raw material would shine through in spite of her. It had been possible for her to remain so long in the compartment only on the basis of one of two assumptions, both of them literary (*a*) that the man was a frustrated socialist, (*b*) that he was a frustrated man of sensibility, a kind of Sherwood Anderson character. But the man's own personality kept popping up, perversely, like a jack-in-the-box, to confound these theories. The most one could say was that the man was frustrated. She had hoped to "give him back to himself," but these fits of self-assertion on his part discouraged her by making her feel that there was nothing very good to give. She had, moreover, a suspicion that his lapses were deliberate, even malicious, that the man knew what she was about and why she was about it, and had made up his mind to thwart her. She felt a Take-me-as-I-am, an I'll-drag-you-down-to-my-level challenge behind his last words. It was like the resistance of the patient to the psychoanalyst, of the worker to the Marxist: she was offering to release him from the chains of habit, and he was standing up and clanking those chains comfortably and impudently in her face. On the other hand, she *knew*, just as the analyst knows, just as the Marxist knows, that somewhere in his character there was the need of release and the humility that would accept aid—and there was, furthermore, a kindness and a general co-operativeness which would make him pretend to be a little better than he was, if that would help her to think better of herself.

For the thing was, the man and the little adventure of

being with him had a kind of human appeal that she kept giving in to against her judgment. *She liked him.* Why, it was impossible to say. The attraction was not sexual, for, as the whisky went down in the bottle, his face took on a more and more porcine look that became so distasteful to her that she could hardly meet his gaze, but continued to talk to him with a large, remote stare, as if he were an audience of several hundred people. Whenever she did happen to catch his eye, to really look at him, she was as disconcerted as an actor who sees a human expression answering him from beyond the footlights. It was not his air of having money, either, that drew her to him, though that, she thought humorously, helped, but it hindered too. It was partly the homespun quality (the use of the word, "visit," for example, as a verb meaning "talk," took her straight back to her childhood and to her father, gray-slippered, in a brown leather chair), and partly of course his plain delight in her, which had in it more shrewdness than she had thought at first, for, though her character was new and inexplicable to him, in a gross sense he was clearly a connoisseur of women. But beyond all this, she had glimpsed in him a vein of sympathy and understanding that made him available to any human being, just as he was, apparently, available as a reader to any novelist—and this might proceed, not, as she had assumed out in the club car, from stupidity, but from a restless and perennially hopeful curiosity.

Actually, she decided, it was the combination of provincialism and adventurousness that did the trick. This man *was* the frontier, though the American frontier had closed, she knew, forever, somewhere out in Oregon in her father's day. Her father, when that door had shut, had remained on the inside. In his youth, as she had learned to her surprise, from some yellowed newspaper clippings her aunt had forgotten in an old bureau drawer, he had been some kind of wildcat radical, full of workmen's compensation laws and state ownership of utilities; but he had long ago hardened into a corporation lawyer, Eastern style. She remembered how once she had challenged him with those clippings, thinking to shame him with the betrayal of ideals and how calmly he had retorted, "Things were different then." "But you fought the *railroads*," she had insisted. "And now you're their lawyer." "You had to fight the railroads in those days," he had answered innocently, and her aunt had put in, with her ineffable plebeian sententiousness, "Your father always stands for what is right." But she saw now that her father had honestly perceived no contradiction between the two sets of attitudes, which was the real proof that it was not he, so much as the times, that had changed.

Yet this man she was sitting with had somehow survived, like a lonely dinosaur, from that former day. It was not even a true survival, for if he was, as he said, forty-one, that would make him thirty years younger than her father, and he would be barely able to recall the Golden Age of American imperialism, to which, nevertheless, he plainly belonged. Looking at him, she thought of other young empires and recalled the Roman busts in the Metropolitan, marble faces of businessmen, shockingly rugged and modern and recognizable after the smooth tranquillity of the Greeks. Those early businessmen had been omnivorous, too, great readers, eaters, travelers, collectors, and, at the beginning, provincial also, small-town men newly admitted into world-citizenship, faintly uneasy but feeling their oats.

In the course of this analysis she had glided all the way from aversion to tenderness. She saw the man now as a man without a country, and felt a desire to reinstate him. But where? The best she could do was communicate to him a sense of his own isolation and grandeur. She could ensconce him in the dignity of sadness.

Meanwhile, the man had grown almost boisterously merry. It was late afternoon; the lunch things had long ago been taken away; and the bottle was nearly empty. Outside the flat yellow farm land went by, comfortably dotted with haystacks; the drought and the cow bones strewn over the Dust Bowl seemed remote as a surrealist painting. Other passengers still paused to look in at the open door on their way to the club car, but the girl was no longer fully aware of them: they existed, as it were, only to give the perspective, to deepen that warm third dimension that had been established within the compartment. The man was lit up with memories of the war, droll stories of horseplay and drinking parties, a hero who was drowned while swimming in a French river, trips to Paris, Notre Dame, and target practice in the Alps. It had been, she could see, an extension of college days, a sort of lower-middle-class Grand

Tour, a wonderful male roughhouse that had left a man such as this with a permanent homesickness for fraternity and a loneliness that no stag party could quite ease.

"I suppose I'm boring you," said the man, still smiling to himself, "but—it's a funny thing to say—I haven't had such a good time since the war. So that you remind me of it, and I can't stop talking. I don't know why."

"*I* know," she said, full of gentle omniscience. (This was her best side, and she knew it. But did that spoil it, keep it from being good?) "It's because you've made a new friend, and you probably haven't made one for twenty years, not since the war. Nobody does, after they're grown-up."

"Maybe so," said the man. "Getting married, no matter how many times you do it, isn't the same thing. If you even *think* you'd like to marry a girl, you have to start lying to her. It's a law of nature, I guess. You have to protect yourself. I don't mean about cheating—that's small potatoes. . . ."

A meditative look absorbed his face. "Jesus Christ," he said, "I don't even *know* Leonie any more, and vice versa, but that's the way it ought to be. A man doesn't want his wife to understand him. That's not her job. Her job is to have a nice house and nice kids and give good parties he can have his friends to. If Leonie understood me, she wouldn't be able to do that. Probably we'd both go to pot."

Tears came to her eyes again. The man's life and her own life seemed unutterably tragic.

"I was in love with my husband," she said. "We understood each other. He never had a thought he didn't tell me."

"But you got a divorce," said the man. "Somebody must have misunderstood somebody else *somewhere* along the line."

"Well," she admitted, "maybe he *didn't* understand *me* so well. He was awfully surprised. . . ." She giggled like a soubrette. The giggle was quite out of character at the moment, but she had not been able to resist it. Besides (she was sure) it was these quick darts and turns, these flashing inconsistencies that gave her the peculiar, sweet-sour, highly volatile charm that was her *spécialité de la maison*.

"Surprised when you picked up with somebody else?" asked the man.

She nodded.

"What happened to that?"

"After I got divorced, I didn't want to marry him any more."

"So now you're on your own?"

The question seemed almost idle, but she replied in a distinct, emphatic voice, as if he were deaf and she had an important message for him.

"No," she said. "I'm going to be married in the fall."

"Are you in love with this one?"

"Oh, yes," she said. "He's charming. And he and I are much more alike than Tom and I were. He's a little bit of a bum and I am too. And he's selfish, which is a good thing for me. Tom was so *good*. And so vulnerable. The back of his neck was just like a little boy's. I always remember the back of his neck."

She spoke earnestly, but she saw that the man did not

understand. Nobody had ever understood—and she herself did not quite know—why this image retained such power over her, why all her feelings of guilt and shame had clustered around the picture of a boyish neck (the face had not been boyish, but prematurely lined) bared like an early martyr's for the sword. "How could I have done it?" she whispered to herself again, as she still did nearly every day, and once again she was suffused with horror.

"He was too good for me," she said at last. "I felt like his mother. Nobody would ever have known it, but he needed to be protected."

That was it. That was what was so awful. Nobody would ever have known. But she had crawled into his secret life and nestled there, like the worm in the rose. How warm and succulent it had been! And when she had devoured it all, she had gone away. "Oh God," she muttered under her breath. It was no excuse that she had loved him. The worm indubitably loves the rose.

Hurriedly, to distract herself, she began to talk about her love affairs. First names, with thumbnail descriptions, rolled out till her whole life sounded to her like a drugstore novel. And she found herself over-anxious to explain to him why in each case the thing had not borne fruit, how natural it was that she should have broken with John, how reasonable that she should never have forgiven Ernest. It was as if she had been a prosecuting attorney drawing up a brief against each of her lovers, and, not liking the position, she was relieved when the man interrupted her.

"Seems to me," he said, "you're still in love with that husband of yours."

"Do you think so really?" she asked, leaning forward. "Why?" Perhaps at last she had found him, the one she kept looking for, the one who could tell her what she was really like. For this she had gone to palmists and graphologists, hoping not for a dark man or a boat trip, but for some quick blaze of gypsy insight that would show her her own lineaments. If she once knew, she had no doubt that she could behave perfectly; it was merely a question of finding out. How, she thought, can you act upon your feelings if you don't know what they are? As a little girl whispering to a young priest in the confessional she had sometimes felt sure. The Church could classify it all for you. If you talked or laughed in church, told lies, had impure thoughts, or conversations, you were bad; if you obeyed your parents or guardians, went to confession and communion regularly, said prayers for the dead, you were good. Protestants, like her father, were neutral; they lived in a gray world beyond good and evil. But when as a homely high-school girl, she had rejected the Church's filing system, together with her aunt's illiterate morality, she had given away her sense of herself. For a while she had believed that it was a matter of waiting until you grew older and your character was formed; then you would be able to recognize it as easily as a photograph. But she was now twenty-four, and had heard other people say she had a strong personality; she herself however was still in the dark. This hearty stranger in the green shirt—perhaps he could really tell whether she was in love with her husband. It was like the puzzle about the men with marks on their foreheads: A couldn't know whether his own forehead was marked, but B and C knew, of course, and he could, if he were bright, deduce it from their behavior.

"Well," replied the man, "of all the fellows you've talked about, Tom's the only one I get a picture of. Except your father—but that's different; he's the kind of a man I know about."

The answer disappointed her. It was too plain and folksy to cover the facts. It was true that she had loved her husband *personally*, for himself, and this had never happened to her with anyone else. Nobody else's idiosyncrasies had ever warmed her; nobody else had she ever watched asleep. Yet that kind of love had, unfortunately, rendered her impotent to love him in the ordinary way, had, in fact, made it necessary for her to be unfaithful to him, and so, in the course of time, to leave him altogether. Or could it not be put in another way? Could she not say that all that conjugal tenderness had been a brightly packaged substitute for the Real Thing, for the long carnal swoon she had never quite been able to execute in the marriage bed? She had noticed that in those households where domesticity burns brightest and the Little Attentions rain most prodigally, the husband is seldom admitted to his real conjugal rights.

But it was impossible to explain this to the man. Already the conversation had dropped once or twice into ribaldry, but she was determined to preserve the decorum of the occasion. It was dark outside now and the waiter was back again, serving little brook trout on plates that had the Union Pacific's crest on them. Yet even as she warned herself how impossible it was, she heard her voice rushing on in a torrent of explicitness. (This had all happened so many times before, ever since, as a schoolgirl, she had exchanged dirty jokes with the college boys from Eugene and seen them stop the car and lunge at her across the gearshift. While all the time, she commiserated with herself, she had merely been trying to be a good fellow, to show that she was sophisticated and grown-up, and not to let them suspect (oh, never!) that her father did not allow her to go out with boys and that she was a neophyte, a helpless fledgling, with no small talk and no coquetry at all. It had not been *fair* (she could still italicize it, bitterly) for them to tackle her like a football dummy; she remembered the struggles back and forth on the slippery leather seats of sports roadsters, the physical awkwardness of it all being somehow the crowning indignity; she remembered also the rides home afterwards, and how the boy's face would always be sullen and closed—he was thinking that he had been cheated, made a fool of, and resolving never to ask her again, so that she would finally become notorious for being taken out only once. How indecent and anti-human it had been, like the tussle between the drowning man and the lifeguard! And of course she had invited it, just as she was inviting it now, but what she was really asking all along was not that the male should assault her, but that he should believe her a woman. This freedom of speech of hers was a kind of masquerade of sexuality, like the rubber breasts that homosexuals put on for drags, but, like the dummy breasts, its brazenness betrayed it: it was a poor copy and a hostile travesty all at once. But the men, she thought, did not look into it so deeply; they could only respond by leaping at her—which, after all, she supposed, was their readiest method of showing her that her impersonation had been convincing. Yet that response, when it came, never failed to disconcert and frighten her: I had not counted on this, she could always whisper to herself, with a certain sad bewilderment. For it was all wrong, it was unnatural: art is to be admired, not acted on, and the public does not belong on the stage, nor the actors in the audience.)

But once more the man across the table spared her. His face was a little heavy with drink, but she could see no lechery in it, and he listened to her as calmly as a priest. The sense of the nightmare lifted; free will was restored to her.

"You know what my favorite quotation is?" she asked suddenly. She must be getting drunk, she knew, or she would not have said this, and a certain cool part of her personality protested. I must not quote poetry, she thought, I must stop it; God help us, if I'm not careful, we'll be singing Yale songs next. But her voice had broken away from her; she could only follow it, satirically, from a great distance. "It's from Chaucer," she went on, when she saw that she had his attention. "Criseyde says it, 'I am myn owene woman, wel at ese.' "

The man had some difficulty in understanding the Middle English, but when at last he had got it straight, he looked at her with bald admiration.

"Golly," he said, "you are, at that!"

The train woke her the next morning as it jerked into a Wyoming station. "Evanston?" she wondered. It was still dark. The Pullman shade was drawn, and she imagined at first that she was in her own lower berth. She knew that she had been drunk the night before, but reflected with satisfaction that Nothing Had Happened. It would have been terrible if . . . She moved slightly and touched the man's body.

She did not scream, but only jerked away in a single spasmodic movement of rejection. This can't be, she thought angrily, it can't be. She shut her eyes tight. When I open them again, she said, he will be gone. I can't face it, she thought, holding herself rigid; the best thing to do is to go back to sleep. For a few minutes she actually dozed and dreamed she was back in Lower Seven with the sheets feeling extraordinarily crisp and clean and the curtains hanging protectively about her. But in the dream her pillow shook under her as the porter poked it to call her for breakfast, and she woke again and knew that the man was still beside her and had moved in his sleep. The train was pulling out of the station. If it had not been so early, outside on the platform there would have been tall men in cowboy hats. Maybe, she thought, I passed out and he put me to bed. But the body next to her was naked, and horror rip-

pled over her again as she realized by the coarseness of the
sheets touching her that she was naked too. Oh my God,
she said, get me out of this and I will do anything you
want.

Waves of shame began to run through her, like savage
internal blushes, as fragments of the night before presented
themselves for inspection. They had sung songs, all right,
she remembered, and there had been some question of disturbing the other passengers, and so the door had been
shut. After that the man had come around to her side of
the table and kissed her rather greedily. She had fought
him off for a long time, but at length her will had softened.
She had felt tired and kind, and thought, why not? Then
there had been something peculiar about the love-making
itself—but she could not recall what it was. She had tried
to keep aloof from it, to be present in body but not in
spirit. Somehow that had not worked out and she had been
dragged in and humiliated. There was some comfort in this
vagueness, but recollection quickly stabbed her again.
There were (oh, holy Virgin!) four-letter words that she
had been forced to repeat, and, at the climax, a rain of
blows on her buttocks that must surely (dear God!) have
left bruises. She must be careful not to let her aunt see her
without any clothes on, she told herself, and remembered
how once she had visualized sins as black marks on the
white soul. This sin, at least, no one would see. But all at
once she became aware of the significance of the sheets.
The bed had been made up. And that meant that the Pullman porter. . . . She closed her eyes, exhausted, unable to

finish the thought. The Vincent Sheean man, the New Deal lady, the waiter, the porter seemed to press in on her, a crowd of jeering material witnesses. If only nobody could know. . . .

But perhaps it was not too late. She had a sudden vision of herself in a black dress, her face scrubbed and powdered, her hair neatly combed, sitting standoffishly in her seat, watching Utah and Nevada go by and reading her publisher's copy of a new *avant-garde* novel. It *could* be done. If she could get back before the first call for breakfast, she might be able to carry it off. There would be the porter, of course, but he would not dare gossip to passengers. Softly, she climbed out of the berth and began to look for her clothes. In the darkness, she discovered her slip and dress neatly hung by the wash basin—the man must have put them there, and it was fortunate, at least, that he was such a shipshape character, for the dress would not be rumpled. On the floor she collected her stockings and a pair of white crepe-de-chine pants, many times mended, with a button off and a little brass pin in its place. Feeling herself blush for the pin, she sat down on the floor and pulled her stockings on. One garter was missing. She put on the rest of her clothes, and then began to look for the garter, but though she groped her way over every inch of the compartment, she could not find it. She sank to the floor again with one stocking hanging loosely down, buried her head in her arms and cried. She saw herself locked in an intolerable but ludicrous dilemma: it was impossible to face the rest of the train with one stocking hanging down; but it was also impossible to wait for the man to wake up and enlist him in retrieving the garter; it was impossible to send the porter for it later in the morning, and more impossible to call for it in person. But as the comic nature of the problem grew plain to her, her head cleared. With a final sob she stripped off her stockings and stuffed them into her purse. She stepped barefooted into her shoes, and was fumbling in her purse for a comb when the man turned over and groaned.

He remembers, she thought in terror, as she saw his arm reach out dimly white and plump in the darkness. She stood very still, waiting. Perhaps he would go back to sleep. But there was a click, and the reading light above the berth went on. The man looked at her in bewilderment. She realized that she had forgotten to buckle her belt.

"Dearest," he said, "what in the world are you doing?"

"I'm dressed," she said. "I've got to get out before they wake up. Good-by."

She bent over with the intention of kissing him on the forehead. Politeness required something, but this was the most she could bring herself to do. The man seized her arms and pulled her down, sitting up himself beside her. He looked very fat and the short hair on his chest was gray.

"You can't go," he said, quite simply and naturally, but as if he had been thinking about it all night long. "I love you. I'm crazy about you. This is the most wonderful thing that's ever happened to me. You come to San Francisco with me and we'll go to Monterey, and I'll fix it up with Leonie to get a divorce."

She stared at him incredulously, but there was no doubt of it: he was serious. His body was trembling. Her heart sank as she saw that there was no longer any question of her leaving; common decency forbade it. Yet she was more frightened than flattered by his declaration of love. It was as if some terrible natural force were loose in the compartment. His seriousness, moreover, was a rebuke; her own squeamishness and sick distaste, which a moment before had seemed virtuous in her, now appeared heartless, even frivolous, in the face of his emotion.

"But I'm engaged," she said, rather thinly.

"You're not in love with him," he said. "You couldn't have done what you did last night if you were." As the memory of love-making returned to him, his voice grew embarrassingly hoarse.

"I was tight," she said flatly in a low voice.

"A girl like you doesn't let a man have her just because she's drunk."

She bowed her head. There was no possible answer she could give. "I must go," she repeated. In a way she knew that she would have to stay, and knew, too, that it was only a matter of hours, but, just as a convict whose sentence is nearly up will try a jail break and get shot down by the guards, so the girl, with Sacramento not far ahead, could not restrain herself from begging, like a claustrophobic, for immediate release. She saw that the man was getting hurt and angry, but still she held herself stiffly in his embrace and would not look at him. He turned her head round with his hand. "Kiss me," he said, but she pulled away.

"I have to throw up."

He pointed to the toilet seat, which was covered with green upholstery. (She had forgotten that Pullman compartments had this indecent feature.) She raised the cover and vomited, while the man sat on the bed and watched her. This was the nadir, she thought bitterly; surely nothing worse than this could ever happen to her. She wiped the tears from her eyes and leaned against the wall. The man made a gesture toward her.

"Don't touch me," she said, "or I'll be sick again. It would be better if I went back to my berth."

"Poor little girl," he said tenderly. "You feel bad, don't you?"

He got out of the berth and took a fresh bottle of whisky from a suitcase.

"I'll have to save the Bourbon for the conductor," he said in a matter-of-fact, friendly voice. "He'll be around later on, looking for his cut."

For the first time that morning the girl laughed. The man poured out two small drinks and handed her one of them. "Take it like medicine," he advised.

She sat down on the berth and crossed her legs. The man put on a dressing-gown and pulled up a chair opposite her. They raised their glasses. The smell of the whisky gagged her and she knew that it was out of the question, physically, for her to get drunk a second time. Yet she felt her spirits lift a little. There was an air of professional rowdyism about their drinking neat whisky early in the morning in a disheveled compartment, that took her fancy.

"What about the porter?"

"Oh," said the man genially. "I've squared him. I gave him ten last night and I'll give him another ten when I get off. He thinks you're wonderful. He said to me, 'Mr. Breen, you sure done better than most.' "

"Oh!" said the girl, covering her face with her hands. "Oh! Oh!" For a moment she felt that she could not bear it, but as she heard the man laugh she made her own discomfiture comic and gave an extra groan or two that were purely theatrical. She raised her head and looked at him shamefaced, and then giggled. This vulgarity was more comforting to her than any assurances of love. If the seduction (or whatever it was) could be reduced to its lowest common denominator, could be seen in farcical terms, she could accept and even, wryly, enjoy it. The world of farce was a sort of moral underworld, a cheerful, well-lit hell where a Fall was only a prat-fall after all.

Moreover, this talk had about it the atmosphere of the locker room or the stag line, an atmosphere more bracing, more astringent than the air of Bohemia. The ten-dollar tips, the Bourbon for the conductor indicated competence and connoisseurship, which, while not of the highest order, did extend from food and drink and haberdashery all the way up to women. That was what had been missing in the men she had known in New York—the shrewd buyer's eye, the swift, brutal appraisal. That was what you found in the country clubs and beach clubs and yacht clubs—but you never found it in the café of the Brevoort. The men she had known during these last four years had been, when you faced it, too easily pleased: her success had been gratifying but hollow. It was not difficult, after all, to be the prettiest girl at a party for the sharecroppers. At bottom, she was contemptuous of the men who had believed her perfect, for she knew that in a bathing suit at Southampton she would never have passed muster, and though she had never submitted herself to this cruel test, it lived in her mind as a threat to her. A copy of *Vogue* picked up at the beauty parlor, a lunch at a restaurant that was beyond her means, would suffice to remind her of her peril. And if she had felt safe with the different men who had been in love with her it was because—she saw it now—in one way or another they were all of them lame ducks. The handsome ones, like her fiancé, were good-for-nothing, the reliable ones, like her husband, were peculiar-looking, the well-to-do ones were short and wore lifts in their shoes or fat with glasses, the clever ones were alcoholic or slightly homosexual, the serious ones were foreigners or else wore beards or black shirts or were desperately poor and had no table manners. Somehow each of them was handicapped for American life and therefore humble in love. And was she too disqualified, did she really belong to this fraternity of cripples, or was she not a sound and normal woman who had been spending her life in self-imposed exile, a princess among the trolls?

She did not know. She would have found out soon enough had she stayed on in Portland, but she had not risked it. She had gone away East to college and never come back until now. And very early in her college life she had got engaged to a painter, so that nothing that happened in the way of cutting in at the dances at Yale and Princeton really "counted." She had put herself out of the running and was patently not trying. Her engagement had been a form of insurance, but the trouble was that it not only insured her against failure but also against success. Should she have been more courageous? She could not tell, even now. Perhaps she *was* a princess because her father was a real gentleman who lunched at his club and traveled by drawing room or compartment; but on the other hand, there was her aunt. She could not find out for herself; it would take a prince to tell her. This man now—surely he came from that heavenly world, that divine position at the center of things where choice is unlimited. And he had chosen *her*.

But that was all wrong. She had only to look at him to see that she had cheated again, had tried to get into the game with a deck of phony cards. For this man also was out of the running. He was too old. Sound as he was in every other respect, time had made a lame duck of him. If she had met him ten years before, would he have chosen her then?

He took the glass from her hands and put his arms around her. "My God," he said, "if this had only happened ten years ago!"

She held herself stony in his embrace, and felt indeed like a rock being lapped by some importunate wave. There was a touch of dignity in the simile, she thought, but what takes place in the end?—Erosion. At that the image sud-

denly turned and presented another facet to her: dear
Jesus, she told herself, frightened, I'm really as hard as
nails. Then all at once she was hugging the man with an
air of warmth that was not quite spurious and not quite
sincere (for the distaste could not be smothered but only
ignored); she pressed her ten fingers into his back and for
the first time kissed him carefully on the mouth.

The glow of self-sacrifice illuminated her. This, she
thought decidedly, is going to be the only real act of charity I have ever performed in my life; it will be the only
time I have ever given anything when it honestly hurt me
to do so. That her asceticism should have to be expressed
in terms of sensuality deepened, in a curious way, its value,
for the sacrifice was both paradoxical and positive; this
was no simple abstention like a meatless Friday or a chaste
Sunday: it was the mortification of the flesh achieved
through the performance of the act of pleasure.

Quickly she helped him take off the black dress, and
stretched herself out on the berth like a slab of white lamb
on an altar. While she waited with some impatience for the
man to exhaust himself, for the indignity to be over, she
contemplated with a burning nostalgia the image of herself, fully dressed, with the novel, in her Pullman seat, and
knew, with the firmest conviction, that for once she was
really and truly good, not hard or heartless at all.

"You need a bath," said the man abruptly, raising himself on one elbow and looking sharply down at her as she
lay relaxed on the rumpled sheet. The curtain was halfway

up, and outside the Great Salt Lake surrounded them. They had been going over it for hours, that immense, gray-brown blighting Dead Sea, which looked, not like an actual lake, but like a mirage seen in the desert. She had watched it for a long time, while the man beside her murmured of his happiness and his plans for their future; they had slept a little and when they opened their eyes again, it was still there, an interminable reminder of sterility, polygamy, and waste.

"Get up," he went on, "and I'll ring for the porter to fix it for you."

He spoke harshly: this was the drill sergeant, the voice of authority. She sprang to attention, her lips quivering. Her nakedness, her long, loose hair, which a moment before had seemed voluptuous to her, now all at once became bold and disorderly, like an unbuttoned tunic at an army inspection. This was the first wound he had dealt her, but how deep the sword went in!—back to the teachers who could smoke cigarettes and gossip with you in the late afternoon and then rebuke you in the morning class, back to the relations who would talk with you as an equal and then tell your aunt you were too young for silk stockings, back through all the betrayers, the friendly enemies, the Janus-faced overseers, back to the mother who could love you and then die.

"I don't want a bath," she asserted stubbornly. "I'm perfectly clean." But she knew, of course, that she had not bathed since she left New York, and, if she had been allowed to go her own way, would not have bathed until she reached Portland—who would think of paying a dollar for a bath on the train? In the ladies' room, where soot and spilt powder made a film over the dressing-tables and the hair receivers stared up, archaic as cuspidors, one sponged oneself hastily under one's wrapper, and, looking at one's neighbors jockeying for position at the mirror, with their dirty kimonos, their elaborate make-up kits, and their uncombed permanents, one felt that one had been fastidious enough, and hurried away, out of the sweet, musty, unused smell of middle-aged women dressing. "I'm perfectly clean," she repeated. The man merely pressed the bell, and when the porter announced that the bath was ready, shoved her out into the corridor in his Brooks Brothers dressing-gown with a cake of English toilet soap in her hands.

In the ladies' lounge, the colored maid had run the bath and stood just behind the half-drawn curtain, waiting to hand her soap and towels. And though, ordinarily, the girl had no particular physical modesty, at this moment it seemed to her insupportable that anyone should watch her bathe. There was something terrible and familiar about the scene—herself in the tub, washing, and a woman standing tall above her—something terrible and familiar indeed about the whole episode of being forced to cleanse herself. Slowly she remembered. The maid was, of course, her aunt, standing over her tub on Saturday nights to see that she washed every bit of herself, standing over her at the medicine cabinet to see that she took the castor oil, standing over her bed in the mornings to see if the sheets were wet. Not since she had been grown-up had she felt this peculiar weakness and shame. It seemed to her that she did not have the courage to send the maid away, that the maid was somehow the man's representative, his spy, whom it would be impious to resist. Tears of futile, self-pitying rage came into her eyes, and she told herself that she would stay in the bath all day, rather than go back to the compartment. But the bell rang in the dressing-room, and the maid rustled the curtain, saying, "Do you want anything more? I'll leave the towels here," and the door swung to behind her, leaving the girl alone.

She lay in the bath a long time, gathering her forces. In the tepid water, she felt for the first time a genuine socialist ardor. For the first time in her life, she truly hated luxury, hated Brooks Brothers and Bergdorf Goodman and Chanel and furs and good food. All the pretty things she had seen in shops and coveted appeared to her suddenly gross, superfatted, fleshly, even, strangely, unclean. By a queer reversal, the very safety pin in her underwear, which she had blushed for earlier in the morning, came to look to her now like a symbol of moral fastidiousness, just as the sores of a mendicant saint can, if thought of in the right way, testify to his spiritual health. A proud, bitter smile formed on her lips, as she saw herself as a citadel of socialist virginity, that could be taken and taken again, but never truly subdued. The man's whole assault on her now seemed to have had a political character; it was an incidental atrocity in the long class war. She smiled again, thinking that she had come out of it untouched, while he had been reduced to a jelly.

All morning in the compartment he had been in a state of wild and happy excitement, full of projects for reform and renewal. He was not sure what ought to happen next; he only knew that everything must be different. In one breath, he would have the two of them playing golf together at Del Monte; in the next, he would imagine that he had given her up and was starting in again with Leonie on a new basis. Then he would see himself throwing everything overboard and going to live in sin in a villa in a little French town. But at that moment a wonderful technical innovation for the manufacture of steel would occur to him, and he would be anxious to get back to the office to put it through. He talked of giving his fortune to a pacifist organization in Washington, and five minutes later made up his mind to send little Frank, who showed signs of being a problem child, to a damn good military school. Perhaps he would enlarge his Gates Mills house; perhaps he would sell it and move to New York. He would take her to the theater and the best restaurants; they would go to museums and ride on bus tops. He would become a CIO organizer, or else he would give her a job in the personnel department of the steel company, and she could live in Cleveland with him and Leonie. But no, he would not do that, he would marry her, as he had said in the first place, or, if she would not marry him, he would keep her in an apartment in New York. Whatever happened she must not get off the train. He had come to regard her as a sort of rabbit's foot that he must keep by him at any price.

Naturally, she told herself, the idea was absurd. Yet sud-

denly her heart seemed to contract and the mood of indulgent pity ebbed away from her. She shivered and pulled
herself out of the tub. His obstinacy on this point frightened her. If he should bar her way when the time came . . . ?
If there should be a struggle . . . ? If she should have to
pull the communication cord . . . ? She told herself that
such things do not happen, that during the course of the
day she would surely be able to convince him that she must
go. (She had noticed that the invocation of her father inevitably moved him. "We mustn't do anything to upset
your father," he would say. "He must be a very fine man."
And tears would actually come to his eyes. She would play
that, she thought, for all it was worth.) Yet her uneasiness
did not abate. It was as if, carelessly, inadvertently, almost,
she had pulled a switch that had set a whole strange factory
going, and now, too late, she discovered that she did not
know how to turn it off. She could have run away, but
some sense of guilt, of social responsibility, of primitive
awe, kept her glued to the spot, watching and listening,
waiting to be ground to bits. Once, in a beauty parlor, she
had been put under a defective dryer that remained on
high no matter where she turned the regulator; her neck
seemed to be burning up, and she could, at any time, have
freed herself by simply getting out of the chair; yet she had
stayed there the full half-hour, until the operator came to
release her. "I think," she had said then, lightly, "there is
something wrong with the machine." And when the operator had examined it, all the women had gathered round,
clucking, "How did you ever stand it?" She had merely

shrugged her shoulders. It had seemed, at the time, better to suffer than to "make a fuss." Perhaps it was something like this that had held her to the man today, the fear of a scene and a kind of morbid competitiveness that would not allow the man to outdistance her in feeling. Yet suddenly she knew that it did not matter what her motives were: she could not, *could not*, get off the train until the man was reconciled to her doing so, until this absurd, ugly love story should somehow be concluded.

If only she could convert him to something, if she could say, "Give up your business, go to Paris, become a Catholic, join the CIO, join the army, join the Socialist Party, go off to the war in Spain." For a moment the notion engaged her. It would be wonderful, she thought, to be able to relate afterwards that she had sent a middle-aged businessman to die for the Republicans at the Alcazar. But almost at once she recognized that this was too much to hope for. The man back in the compartment was not equal to it; he was equal to a divorce, to a change of residence, at most to a change of business, but not to a change of heart. She sighed slightly, facing the truth about him. His gray flannel dressing-gown lay on a chair beside her. Very slowly, she wrapped herself in it; the touch of the material made gooseflesh rise. Something about this garment—the color, perhaps, or the unsuitable size—reminded her of the bathing suits one rents at a public swimming pool. She gritted her teeth and pulled open the door. She did not pause to look about but plunged down the corridor with lowered head; though she passed no one, it seemed to her that she was running the gantlet. The compartment, with its naked man and disordered bed, beckoned her on now, like a home.

When she opened the door, she found the man dressed, the compartment made up, and a white cloth spread on the collapsible table between the seats. In a few minutes the waiter of the night before was back with orange juice in cracked ice and corned beef hash and fish cakes. It was as if the scenery, which had been struck the night before, had been set up again for the matinee. The difference was that the door remained shut. Nevertheless, though there were no onlookers, atmospheric conditions in the compartment had changed; the relationship of the pair took on a certain sociable formality. The little breakfast passed off like a ceremonial feast. All primitive peoples, she thought, had known that a cataclysmic experience, whether joyful or sad, had in the end to be liquidated in an orderly meal. The banquets in Homer came to her mind, the refreshments the Irish put out at a wake, the sweetmeats the Arabs nibble after love, the fairy stories that end And-the-king-ordered-a-great-dinner-to-be-served-to-all-his-people. Upheavals of private feeling, like the one she had just been through, were as incalculable and anti-social as death. With a graceful inclination of her head, she accepted a second fish cake from the waiter, and felt herself restored to the human race.

There was to be no more love-making, she saw, and from the moment she felt sure of this, she began to be a little bit in love. The long day passed as if in slow motion, in desultory, lingering, tender talk. Dreamy confidences were murmured, and trailed off, casual and unemphatic, like the dialogue in a play by Chekhov. The great desert lake out the window disappeared and was replaced by the sagebrush country, which seemed to her a pleasant, melancholy symbol of the contemporary waste land. The man's life lay before her; it was almost as if she could reach out and touch it, poke it, explore it, shine it up, and give it back to him. The people in it grew distinct to her, though they swam in a poetic ambience. She could see Eleanor, now an executive in her forties, good-looking, well-turned-out, the kind of woman that eats at Longchamps or the Algonquin; and then Leonie, finer-drawn, younger, with a certain Marie Laurencin look that pale, pretty, neutral-colored rich women get; then herself, still younger, still more highly organized—and all the time the man, a ludicrous and touching Ponce de Leon, growing helplessly older and coarser in inverse relation to the women he needed and wanted.

And she could see the Brussels carpet in a Philadelphia whorehouse, where he had first had a woman, the old Marmon roadster in which he and Eleanor had made love, and the couch in her father's house where the old man had surprised them, and also the squash court at the club, the aquamarine bathtubs in his house, the barbecue pit, the fraternity brothers, the Audubon prints in his study, the vacuum bottle on the night table. Somehow it had become essential to them both that she should know *everything*. They might have been collaborators, drawing up a dossier for a new *Babbitt*. This is what I am, he was saying:

the wallpaper in the larger guest room is a blue and white colonial design; I go to bed at ten and Leonie sits up and reads; I like kippers for breakfast; we have Hepplewhite chairs in the sitting room; the doctor is worried about my kidneys, and I feel lonely when I first wake up.

There were the details, the realistic "touches," and then there was the great skeleton of the story itself. In 1917 he was a chemistry major, just out of the state university, with a job for the next year teaching science at a high school, and plans, then, for a master's degree, and perhaps a job in the department at Cornell, where he had an uncle in the Agricultural School. The father had been a small business-man in a Pennsylvania coal town, the grandfather a farmer, the mother a little lady from Tennessee. But then there came the Officers' Training Camp, and the brilliant war record, and the right connections, so that the high-school job was never taken, and instead he was playing handball at the Athletic Club in the evenings and working as a met-allurgist for the steel company during the day. Soon he was moved into production, but somehow he was too amiable and easygoing for this, and in the days when he thought he was going to marry Eleanor, he was glad to get out and go into the coal business. When he came back to the steel company, it was as a purchasing agent, and here his shrewd-ness and *bonhomie* were better employed. He became Chief Purchasing Agent and Fourth Vice-President; it was doubtful whether he would ever go further.

For ten years, he confided, he had been visited now and then by a queer sense of having missed the boat, but it was all vague with him: he had no idea of when the boat had sailed or what kind of boat it was or where it went to. If he had married Eleanor? But she was not the type; after eight years they had both seen that and were still good friends. Would he have done better to take the teaching job? It hardly seemed so. Plainly, he was no scientist—the steel company had seen this at once—and, had he taken that other road, at best he would have finished as the principal of a high school or the head of the chemistry department in a small-time state university. No, she thought, he was not a scientist *manqué*, but simply a nice man, and it was a pity that society had offered him no nicer way of being nice than the job of buying materials for a company in Little Steel. The job, she saw, was one of the least compromising jobs he could have held and still made money; by regarding his business life as a nexus of personal friendships he had tried to hold himself aloof from both the banks and the blast furnaces. He was full of fraternal feelings, loyalties, even, toward the tin salesmen and iron magnates and copper executives and their wives who wined him and dined him and took him to the latest musical shows over and over again. ("Don't mistake me," he said, "most of those fellows and their women are mighty fine people.") Still—there was always the contract, waiting to be signed the next morning, lying implacably on the desk.

Here he was, affable, a good mixer, self-evidently a sound guy, and yet these qualities were somehow impeached by the commercial use that was made of them, so that he found himself, as he grew older, hunting, more and more anxiously, for new and non-commercial contexts in which to assert his gregariousness. He refused the conventional social life of Cleveland. At the country club dances, he was generally to be found in the bar, shooting dice with the bartender; he played a little stud poker, but no bridge. In New York, he would stay at the Biltmore or the Murray Hill, buy his clothes at Brooks Brothers, and eat—when Leonie was not with him—at Cavanagh's, Luchow's, or the Lafayette. But the greater part of his time he spent on trains, talking to his fellow-passengers, getting their life stories. ("Golly," he interjected, "if I were a writer like you!") This was one of his greatest pleasures, he said, and he would never go by plane if he could help it. In the three and a half days that it took a train to cross the continent, you could meet somebody who was a little bit different, and have a good long visit with them. Sometimes, also, he would stop over and look up old friends, but lately that had been disappointing —so many of them were old or on the wagon, suffering from ulcers or cirrhosis of the liver. . . .

He spread his hands suddenly. There it was, he indicated; he was sharing it all with her, like a basket lunch. And, as she accepted it, nodding from time to time in pleasure and recognition, supplementing it occasionally from her own store, she knew that the actual sharing of his life was no longer so much in question. During this afternoon of confidences, he had undergone a catharsis. He was at rest now, and happy, and she was free. He would never be alone again, she thought; in fact, it was as if he had never been alone at all, for by a tremendous act of perception, she had thrust herself back into his past, and was settled there forever, like the dear companion, the twin, we pray for as children, while our parents, listening, laugh. She had brought it off, and now she was almost reluctant to leave him. A pang of joy went through her as she examined her own sorrow and found it to be real. All day she believed she had been acting a tragic part in something called *One Perfect Night,* but slowly, without her being aware of it, the counterfeit had passed into the true. She did not understand exactly how it had happened. Perhaps it was because she had come so very, very close—*tout comprendre, c'est tout aimer*—and perhaps it was because she was good at the task he had assigned her: at the sight of his life, waiting to be understood, she had rolled up her sleeves with all the vigor of a first-class cook confronting a brand-new kitchen.

"I love you," she said suddenly. "I didn't before, but now I do."

The man glanced sharply at her.

"Then you won't get off the train . . . ?"

"Oh, yes," she said, for now at last she could be truthful with him. "I'll certainly get off. One reason I love you, I suppose, is because I *am* getting off."

His dark eyes met hers in perfect comprehension.

"And one reason I'm going to let you do it," he said, "is because you love me."

She lowered her eyes, astonished, once more, at his shrewdness.

"Hell," he said, "it's a funny thing, but I'm so happy

now that I don't care whether I ever see you again. I probably won't feel that way after you're gone. Right now I think I can live on this one day for the rest of my life."

"I hope you can," she said, her voice trembling with sincerity. "My dear, dear Mr. Breen, I hope you can." Then they both began to laugh wildly because she could not call him by his first name.

Still, he had not quite relinquished the idea of marrying her, and, once, very late in the afternoon, he struck out at her with unexpected, clumsy ferocity.

"You need a man to take care of you," he exclaimed. "I hate to see you go back to that life you've been living in New York. Your father ought to make you stay home in Portland. In a few years, you'll be one of those Bohemian horrors with oily hair and long earrings. It makes me sick to think about it."

She pressed her lips together, and was amazed to find how hurt she was. It was unthinkable that he should speak of her way of life with such contempt; it was as if he had made a point of telling her that her gayest, wickedest, most extravagant hat was ugly and out of fashion.

"But you fell in love with me because I *am* Bohemian," she said, forcing herself to smile, to take a wise and reasonable tone.

"No," he said, in a truculently sentimental voice. "It's because underneath all that you're just a sweet girl."

She shook her head impatiently. It was not true, of course, but it was hopeless to argue with him about it. Clearly, he took some cruel satisfaction in telling her that she was different from what she was. That implied that he had not fallen in love with her at all, but with some other person: the whole extraordinary little idyl had been based on a misunderstanding. Poor Marianna, she thought, poor pickings, to be loved under cover of darkness in Isabella's name! She did not speak for a long time.

Night fell again, and the little dinner that was presently served lacked the glamour of the earlier meals. The Union Pacific's menu had been winnowed out; they were reduced to steak and Great Big Baked Potatoes. She wished that they were out in the diner, in full view, eating some unusual dish and drinking a bottle of white wine. Even here in the compartment, she had hoped that he would offer her wine; the waiter suggested it, but the man shook his head without consulting her; his excesses in drink and love were beginning to tell on him; he looked tired and sick.

But by ten o'clock, when they were well out of Reno, she had warmed to him again. He had been begging her to let him send her a present; the notion displeased her at first; she felt a certain arrogant condescension in it; she refused to permit it, refused, even, to give him her address. Then he looked at her suddenly, with all the old humility and square self-knowledge in his brown eyes.

"Look," he said, "you'll be doing me a kindness. You see, that's the only thing a man like me can do for a woman is buy her things and love her a hell of a lot at night. I'm different from your literary boy friends and your artistic boy friends. I can't write you a poem or paint your picture.

The only way I can show that I love you is to spend money on you."

"Money's your medium," she said, smiling, happy in this further insight he had given her, happy in her own gift of concise expression.

He nodded and she gave her consent. It must, however, be a very *small* present, and it must not, on any account, be jewelry, she said, not knowing precisely why she imposed this latter condition.

As they moved into the last hour of the trip, the occasion took on an elegiac solemnity. They talked very little; the man held both of her hands tightly. Toward the end, he broke the silence to say, "I want you to know that this has been the happiest day of my life." As she heard these words, a drowsy, sensuous contentment invaded her; it was as if she had been waiting for them all along; this was the climax, the spiritual orgasm. And it was just as she had known from the very first: in the end, he had not let her down. She had not been wrong in him after all.

They stood on the platform as the train came into Sacramento. It was after three in the morning. Her luggage was piled up around them; one suitcase had a missing handle and was tied up with a rope. The man made a noise of disapproval.

"Your father," he said, "is going to feel terrible when he sees *that.*"

The girl laughed; the train slowed down; the man kissed her passionately several times, ignoring the porter who waited beside them with a large, Hollywood-darky smile on his face.

"If I were ten years younger," the man said, in a curious, measured tone, as if he were taking an oath, "I'd never let you get off this train." It sounded, she thought, like an apology to God.

In the station the air was hot and thick. She sat down to wait, and immediately she was damp and grubby; her stockings were wrinkled; her black suede shoes had somehow got dusty, and, she noticed for the first time, one of the heels was run over. Her trip home seemed peculiarly pointless, for she had known for the last twelve hours that she was never going to marry the young man back in New York.

On the return trip, her train stopped in Cleveland early in the morning. In a new fall suit she sat in the club car, waiting. Mr. Breen hurried into the car. He was wearing a dark-blue business suit and had two packages in his hand. One of them was plainly a florist's box. She took it from him and opened it, disclosing two of the largest and most garish purple orchids she had ever seen. He helped her pin them on her shoulder and did not appear to notice how oddly they harmonized with her burnt-siena jacket. The other box contained a bottle of whisky; *in memoriam,* he said.

They had the club car to themselves, and for the fifteen minutes the train waited in the station he looked at her and talked. It seemed to her that he had been talking ever since she left him, talking volubly, desperately, incoherently, over the long-distance telephone, via air mail, by Western Union and Postal Telegraph. She had received from him several pieces of glamour-girl underwear and a topaz brooch, and had been disappointed and a little humiliated by the taste displayed. She was glad now that the train stopped at such an outlandish hour, for she felt that he cut a ridiculous figure, with his gifts in his hand, like a superannuated stage-door Johnny.

She herself had little to say, and sat passive, letting the torrent of talk and endearment splash over her. Sooner or later, she knew, the law of diminishing returns would begin to operate, and she would cease to reap these overwhelming profits from the small investment of herself she had made. At the moment, he was begging her to marry him, describing a business conference he was about to attend, and asking her approval of a vacation trip he was planning to take with his wife. Of these three elements in his conversation, the first was predominant, but she sensed that already she was changing for him, becoming less of a mistress and more of a confidante. It was significant that he was not (as she had feared) hoping to ride all the way to New York with her: the business conference, he explained, prevented that.

It never failed, she thought, to be a tiny blow to guess that a man is losing interest in you, and she was tempted, as on such occasions she always had been, to make some gesture that would quicken it again. If she let him think she would sleep with him, he would stay on the train, and let the conference go by the board. He had weighed the conference, obviously, against a platonic interlude, and made the sensible decision. But she stifled her vanity, and said to herself that she was glad that he was showing some signs of self-respect; in the queer, business-English letters he had written her, and on the phone for an hour at a time at her father's house, he had been too shockingly abject.

She let him get off the train, still talking happily, pressed his hand warmly but did not kiss him.

It was three weeks before he came to see her in her New York apartment, and then, she could tell, he was convalescent. He had become more critical of her and more self-assured. Her one and a half rooms in Greenwich Village gave him claustrophobia, he declared, and when she pointed out to him that the apartment was charming, he stated flatly that it was not the kind of place he liked, nor the kind of place she ought to be living in. He was more the businessman and less the suitor, and though he continued to ask her to marry him, she felt that the request was somewhat formal; it was only when he tried to make love to her that his real, hopeless, humble ardor showed itself once more. She fought him off, though she had an inclination to yield, if only to re-establish her ascendancy over him. They went to the theater two nights, and danced, and drank champagne, and the third morning he phoned her from his hotel that he had a stomach attack and would have to go home to Cleveland with a doctor.

More than a month went by before she saw him again. This time he refused to come to her apartment, but insisted that she meet him at his suite in the Ambassador. They passed a moderate evening: the man contented himself with dining at Longchamps. He bought her a large Brie cheese at the Voisin down the street, and told her an anti-New-Deal joke. Just below the surface of his genial manner, there was an hostility that hurt her. She found that she was extending herself to please him. All her gestures grew over-feminine and demonstrative; the lift of her eyebrows was a shade too arch: like a *passée* belle, she was overplaying herself. I must let go, she told herself; the train is pulling out; if I hang on, I'll be dragged along at its wheels. She made him take her home early.

A little later she received a duck he had shot in Virginia. She did not know how to cook it and it stayed in her icebox so long that the neighbors complained of the smell.

When she got a letter from him that had been dictated to his stenographer, she knew that his splurge was over. After that, she saw him once—for cocktails. He ordered double Martinis and got a little drunk. Then his friendliness revived briefly, and he begged her with tears in his eyes to "forget all this red nonsense and remember that you're just your father's little girl at heart." Walking home alone, trying to decide whether to eat in a tearoom or cook herself a chop, she felt flat and sad, but in the end she was glad that she had never told him of her broken engagement.

When her father died, the man must have read the account in the papers, for she got a telegram that read: SIN-CEREST CONDOLENCES. YOU HAVE LOST THE

BEST FRIEND YOU WILL EVER HAVE. She did not file it away with the other messages, but tore it up carefully and threw it into the wastebasket. It would have been dreadful if anyone had seen it.

FOUR   *The Genial Host*

WHEN he telephoned to ask you to do something he never said baldly, "Can you come to dinner a week from Thursday?" First he let you know who else was going to be there: the Slaters, perhaps, and the Berolzheimers, and John Peterson, the critic. And he could not leave this guest-list to speak for itself, but would annotate it at once with some short character sketches. "Peterson's a queer fellow," he would say. "Of course, he's moody and right now he's too much interested in politics for his own good, but I hope he'll get back soon to his book on Montaigne. That's his real work, and I wish you'd tell him that. You may not like him, of course, but underneath it all John is a marvelous person." He was deferential, ingratiating, concerned for your pleasure, like a waiter with a tray of French pastry in his hand. This one had custard in it and that one was mocha; the chocolate-covered one had whipped cream, and the little one on the side was just a macaroon. With Pflaumen you were always perfectly safe—you never had to order blind.

In a way, it was a kindness he did you, putting it like that. Other acquaintances made the opposite error, calling up to demand, "Are you free Thursday?" before disclosing whether they wanted you to picket a movie house, attend a lecture at the New School, buy tickets for a party for Spain, or go and dance at a new night club. Nevertheless, there was something too explicit about Pflaumen's invitations that made you set down the telephone with a feeling of distaste, made you dress hurriedly, though carefully, for his parties, as if you were going to keep some shameful assignation, made you, stepping out of your door in the new clothes you had bought, look furtively up and down the street before starting for the subway. Pflaumen had taken the risks out of social life, that was the trouble; and you felt that it was wrong to enjoy an evening without having paid for it with some touch of uncertainty, some tiny fear of being bored or out of place. Moreover, behind those bland and humble telephone calls, there was an unpleasant assumption about your character. Plainly Pflaumen must believe that you went out at night not because you liked your friends and wanted to be with them, but because you were anxious to meet new people, celebrities, to enlarge your own rather tacky social circle. No doubt this was at least half true, since with your real friends you seemed to prefer those whose spheres of interest were larger rather than smaller than your own—or at any rate to see more of them, if you could—but in those cases you were able to be sure that you *liked them for themselves*. With Pflaumen, unfortunately, there was never any question of that. Yet every time you accepted one of his invitations you entered into a conspiracy with him to hide the fact that he was a foolish, dull man whom nobody had much use for. And though some of his friends—the rich ones, perhaps— could feel all right about sitting at his table (after all, *they* were doing *him* a favor), you poor ones knew that he had bought your complaisance with his wines and rich food and prominent acquaintances, and you half-hated him before your finger touched his doorbell.

Standing there in the apartment-house corridor, you listened for voices that would mean that other guests had arrived and you would not be alone with him and the unmentionable secret. If you heard nothing, you hesitated, considered hurrying back downstairs and walking round the block till someone else should get there; but perhaps *he* had heard the elevator stop, heard your heels click on the stone floor, and was even now on the other side of the door silently waiting to admit you. You rang, and by the length of time it took him to answer, you knew that he had been in his bedroom after all. He came to the door in a maroon-colored smoking jacket, evening trousers, and black patent-leather shoes; he was newly shaved and scrubbed and powdered, and there was a general odor of Mennen's about him. His whole stocky, carefully exercised body was full of energy: well-directed arrows of delight and welcome shot at you out of his black eyes, and his mouth curved downwards in a strenuous, sickle-shaped smile that gave his face an expression of cruelty.

How ill-suited he was, you thought, to his role of *élé-*

gant! What a tireless struggle he must wage against his own physical nature! Looking at him, so black and broad and hairy, you saw that his well-kept person must appear to him like a settler's plot triumphantly defended against the invading wilderness. No wonder he took such pride in the fit of his coat, the shine of his nails, the whiteness of his sharp, jagged teeth. You saw the lines his body ought to have followed; he had the regular merchant's build; though he was not yet thirty-five, you looked for the crease in the waistcoat, but it was always just absent. Whenever you really noticed Pflaumen, you became aware of an additional person, a comfortable, cigar-smoking, sentimental family man, a kind of ancestral type on which the man-about-town had been superimposed, so that his finished personality came out as a sort of double exposure that was very disconcerting. If you were in a sympathetic mood, you might think what a pity it was he had not given in to his real self, had not married some nice girl and had some children, and reproduced in modern terms that atmosphere of bay rum, whisky, spilled ashes, poker chips, potted plants, kindness, and solid comfort that must have been his father's personal climate. How nice he could have been under those circumstances! But if you looked at him hard again, you realized that something else was being held in check, something that did not fit at all with this picture of easygoing German-Jewish family life—something primitive and hungry and excessively endowed with animal vitality. Though it was true that his figure had a mercantile cast to it, in other ways he did not look like a German Jew, but like a member of some early barbarous tribe, a Scythian on a Greek vase. In his habits he was soft and self-indulgent; yet you felt there was a furnace of energy burning in him, and you drew back from the blast. It was this energy that had made it possible for him to discipline his body and his manners into patterns so unnatural to him; and, ironically, it was at the same time this energy that undid him as a society man by making him over-demonstrative, over-polite, over-genial, like a comedian who produces an effect of fatigue in his audience by working too hard at putting his gags across.

He held out his arms to help you with your coat, and what might have been an ordinary service became a tableau of politeness. Your hands shook, missing the buttons, for you felt that the coat was getting too much of the lime-light. It would have been kinder to whisk the shabby thing inconspicuously into a closet. If you did not yet know him well, you did not realize that he loved you for that patched fur, It signified that you were the *real thing*, the poet in a garret, and it also opened up for him charming vistas of What He Could Do For You. He led you into his bedroom, where a new novel by one of his friends and a fine edition or two lay open on a table. A lamp with a pale-amber shade (better for the eyes) was burning beside them, and the cushion in the easy chair by the table was slightly mussed. An impression of leisure and the enjoyment of fine things was readily engendered, though you knew that he could not have been back from his office for more than an hour, and that he must have bathed, shaved, dressed, and arranged the final details during that time. Yet he was not a hypocrite, so undoubtedly he had been reading. Five minutes with a book was as good as an hour to him anyway, for he took literature like wine-tasting: you can get all the flavor in the first sip; further indulgence might only blunt your palate. The room was furnished in a half-monastic style; the bed was narrow, with a monkscloth cover. On the walls were pictures by Kunyoshi and Reginald Marsh, some George Grosz water colors and the reproduction of a detail from a mural by Rivera. You sat down behind his desk, a good piece, a little too heavy for the room, in black walnut; it had a great many fancy paper-weights on it, and a large marble cigarette-lighter, gifts, obviously, from clients in the patent law business. He got out the cocktail shaker, and said, "Let's try it before the others come."

He was disappointed, always, if you pronounced it perfect. He wanted to tinker with it a little, add a dash of Cointreau or Curacao at your suggestion. "You're absolutely right," he would agree at once. "I knew it needed something," and, picking up the shaker, he would hurry out to the bar he had installed in what had once been a linen closet. When he came back the drink would taste exactly the same to you, but Pflaumen's satisfaction in it would be somehow deepened. The process was familiar to you. You had gone through it with other people, at dress rehearsals, at fittings with a tailor or a dressmaker, in a painter's studio, till you had become expert at discovering and pointing out some trifling flaw that in no way invalidated the whole, a prop that was out of place, a coat that wrinkled imperceptibly across the shoulders, sleeves that were a quarter of an inch too short on a dress, a foreground that seemed a little crowded. Once you had made your criticism, everybody would be very happy. It was a form of exorcism: some minor or totally imaginary error is noted and corrected, symbolically, as it were, with the idea that all real and major imperfections have thereby been dealt with—as if by casting out some impudent small devil you had routed Beelzebub himself. Perhaps, also, there was a hope of dispersing responsibility; that cocktail was not Pflaumen's any longer, but yours and his together, as it would never have been if you had merely given it your approval. By arriving early, you had become his hostess, and, all at once, you were sure that Pflaumen had intended this to happen.

Yet this conviction did not disturb you. On the contrary, you felt slightly uplifted, like one of those "good" bums who voluntarily chops half a cord of wood for the lady of the house to square her for the meal she has just put in front of him. Pflaumen rarely gave you a chance to repay his benevolence, so that generally you were uncomfortable with him, dangerously over-stored, explosive, a living battery of undischarged obligations. There were, for example, those letters of introduction, a great pile of them now, lying unopened, gathering dust on your desk. If only you had not drunk too much that one night when you had first known Pflaumen! If you had not let him see that you were frightened because you had no job and almost no money left! Above all, if you had not cried about it! The next morning he had sent you a sheaf of letters of introduction, and you had been touched and a little amused by the lack of judgment behind them. But you had presented them all. You had interviewed a brassière manufacturer in Ozone Park, a crank lawyer downtown who wanted someone to ghostwrite a book on the sunspot theory of economics, an advertising executive who needed some soap slogans, a hotel man, a brilliantine manufacturer. When it was over you were relieved, for somehow you had never felt so out of step, so unwanted, so drably unemployed, as in these offices Pflaumen had sent you to.

But the next week there was a new batch of letters, some of them signed by people you had never heard of, friends of Pflaumen's whom he had got to recommend you for a job; and while you were delivering these, still more letters came in, taking you on errands that grew more and more bizarre. There was a loft in the garment district with AMERICAN RESEARCH printed on the door and inside three large rooms that contained nothing but a filing cabinet and a little man with a cigar—you had never found out what his research consisted of. Then there was a bald man on the seventeenth floor of the St. Moritz hotel who wanted a girl to go round the world with him—he, too, was writing a book, on occultism.

After that, you had presented no more letters, but they kept coming in as relentlessly as bills, and there was Pflaumen's voice on the telephone, patient at first, then hurt and puzzled, but always mysteriously complacent. Had you gone to see the man in the Squibb Building? No? Really,

it was impossible to understand you. He had been under
the impression that you *wanted* a job. You made explanations at first, halting and shamefaced (after all, you supposed, he was trying to help you). Finally, you had quarreled with him; but your rudeness had only added to your
debt, and your air of bravado and Bohemian defiance had
quickened his admiration. (Such indifference to the question of survival was impractical, of course, but somehow,
he knew, in awfully good taste.) You were for him, you
discovered, the perfect object of charity, poor but not be-
draggled, independent, stubborn, frivolous, thankless, and
proud. He could pity you, deplore you, denounce you, display you, be kind to you, be hurt by you, forgive you. He
could, in fact, run through his whole stock of feelings with
you. A more grateful beneficiary would have given him no
exercise for his masochistic emotions; a more willing one
would have left his sadism unsatisfied. He was not going to
let you go if he could help it. You stood to him in the relation of Man to God, embraced in an eternal neurotic mystery compounded out of His infinite goodness and your
guilt.

When the others came, you all went into the living
room, which was done in honey beige. There were pieces
of sculpture by Archipenko and Harold Cash, and the head
of a beautiful Egyptian queen, Neferteete. Everybody
praised the cocktail, and Pflaumen's old friends, of whom
there were always a pair, complimented him on a new acquisition—a painting, a vase, a lamp—he had made. All

Pflaumen's friends lived on terms of intimacy with his possessions; if someone did not notice a new object, it was as mortifying a slip as a husband's failure to notice his wife's new hat. Indeed, Pflaumen, opening the door of his apartment, often wore that look of owlish mystery that says, "What's new about me?" and the guests, being warned by it, examined the premises sharply till they found the single ornament that was responsible for the host's elation. This acquisitiveness of Pflaumen's was, you thought, just another way of making it easy for his friends to appear to like him. He was giving them something they could honestly admire, and if the objects could be viewed as extensions of Pflaumen's personality, why, then, it followed that his friends admired Pflaumen. It was on such questionable but never questioned syllogisms that his social life was built.

By the time the maid announced dinner and the party moved down to a refectory table set in the foyer, Pflaumen's eyes were damp with happiness. Everything was going well. Voices had risen in lively controversy over the new play, the new strike, the new Moscow trials, the new abstract show at the Modern Museum. Nobody was incoherent; nobody made speeches; nobody lost his temper. Sentences were short, and points in the argument clicked like bright billiard balls. Everyone felt witty. Pflaumen made a great bustle of seating the guests, and finally plumped himself down at the head of the table and beamed at them all as if to say, "Isn't this cozy?" The steak came in, with an orange and sherry sauce, and everyone exclaimed over it. Pflaumen himself kept casting joyous sheep's eyes up at his maid, commending her for the success of "their" dish. (He had put into circulation a dozen anecdotes designed to prove that this Scotchwoman who worked for him, like the maids of all really smart people, was a Character, full of sweet crotchets, *bons mots,* and rough devotion. Nobody, however, had seen the slightest sign of this, and tonight, as usual, she paid no attention to her employer, but continued to make her rounds with a stony face.) Peas were served, new ones cooked in the French style in their pods, and then the wine was brought in, a Château Latour Rothschild.

This was Pflaumen's apogee. Having tapped on his glass to get the table's attention, he read aloud the Château and the year, and then uncorked the bottle himself, standing up to do it. Somebody at the end of the table, a man with a hearty voice, called, "Look out, there, George Arliss may come out of that bottle!" Pflaumen, pouring a little into his own glass, laughed with the others, but he was not quite pleased—it was the sort of joke he was capable of making himself. "Give us a speech, about the wine," said one of the ladies obligingly. "The way they do at gourmet dinners." "Why," said Pflaumen, still standing at the head of the table with the bottle in his hand, "it's not one of the great Bordeaux. . . ." "I prefer the word 'claret,'" someone else put in, "it's so full of English history." "You mean," retorted Pflaumen, "English history is so full of *it.*" He waited for the laugh, which came reluctantly—it was said that Pflaumen had "a pretty wit," but there was something chilling about it; he had never learned how to throw a line away. "Anyway," he went on, with a little laugh, so that no one should think he took all this too seriously, "it's a nice brisk wine, on the astringent side. I thought it would do well with the steak." "Perfect!" exclaimed a lady, though the glasses were still empty. "Of course I think it's silly," continued Pflaumen, starting to go round the table with the bottle, "to be too pedantic about what you drink with what. I'll take a good Burgundy with a broiler and a Rhine wine with a kidney chop any time I can get it." Murmurs of approval greeted this unconventional statement, and Pflaumen passed on down the line, carefully decanting the wine into each glass.

Across the table from you someone refused, and all the rest raised their heads with an identical look of worry. It was the young Russian Jew, the instructor in law at Columbia, who wore a rather quizzical, sardonic expression on a pure Italianate face. His Marxist study of jurisprudence had created a stir. Still, perhaps Fleischer had made a mistake in him. Was it possible that he was not an eccentric but a crank? This act of abstention was a challenge to everyone at the table, an insult to the host. For almost a full minute nobody spoke, but muscles tightened with hostility. In different circumstances the young man might have been lynched.

"You don't *drink*?" said a woman at last in a loud, bewildered voice.

"I drank a cocktail," he admitted. "It went to my head. If I took any more I might make a fool of myself." He twisted his head and looked up at Pflaumen with a disarming boyish grin. "You'll have to give me a course in the art of drinking. That's one subject that was left out of my proletarian education." He pronounced the last words mildly, with a sort of droll self-mockery that deprecated, ever so faintly, his innocence, his poor Russian parents, his studiousness, the Talmudic simplicity of his life. There was a burst of relieved laughter, and after that everyone liked him. Thank God, was the general feeling, he had turned out not to be one of those Marxist prigs!

Once the wine was poured, Pflaumen took very little part in the conversation. He leaned back in his chair with the air of a satisfied impresario, embracing all his guests in a smile of the most intense and proprietary affection. Now and then, this look of commendation would rest particularly on you; whenever this happened, it was as if, in his delight, he had reached over and squeezed you. From time to time, his cup of bliss would appear to run over, and the smile would break into a short high giggle. When the spasm was over, he would take out his handkerchief and carefully wipe his eyes, and the old-fashioned masculinity of this gesture made a strange contrast with the schoolgirl-ish sound he had just produced. Sitting at his left hand, you looked down at your plate until this display was finished. There was something androgynous about Pflaumen, something not pansy, but psychically hermaphroditic that was always disconcerting you. It was as if the male and female strains in his personality had never blended, but were engaged in some perennial household spat that you were obliged to eavesdrop on. For, when you came to think of it, the Jewish paterfamilias was not the only figure that kept hovering behind your host's well-padded shoulder; there was also a young girl, newly married to a man already coarse and comfortable, a young girl playing house all by herself in a fine establishment full of wedding presents that both astonished and saddened her. Most Jewish men were more feminine than Gentile men of similar social background. You had noticed this and had supposed, vaguely, that it was the mark matriarchy had left on them, but looking at Pflaumen you saw the whole process dramatically. The matriarch had begun by being married off to a husband who was prosperous and settled and older than herself, and her sons she had created in her own image, forlorn little bridegrooms to a middle-aged bride.

In most of the men, the masculine influence had, in the end, overridden or absorbed the feminine, and you saw only vestigial traces of the mother. There might be a tendency to hypochondria, a readiness to take offense, personal vanity, love of comfort, love of being waited on and made much of; and, on the other hand, there would be unusual intuitive powers, sympathy, loyalty, tenderness, domestic graces and kindnesses unknown to the Gentile. But with Pflaumen it was not a question of the survival of a few traits. Two complete personalities had been preserved in him, as in a glacier. Half of him was a successful businessman and half of him was playing house. These dinners of his were like children's tea parties, and in this lay their strength and their weakness. They had the sort of perfection that can only be achieved in miniature. The groaning board was not in Pflaumen's style at all: one exquisite dish, one vegetable, a salad and some cheese were what you got, rarely a soup, never a dessert. You thought of your little electric stove, your cambric tea or hot chocolate and your *petits fours* from the caterer. But more important than the perfection of the appointments was the illusion of a microcosm Pflaumen was able to create, the sense of a little world that was exactly the same as the big world, though it had none of the pain or care.

Each of Pflaumen's guests had been selected, as it were, for his allegorical possibilities, and every dinner was presented as a morality play in which art and science, wealth and poverty, business and literature, sex and scholarship, vice and virtue, Judaism and Christianity, Stalinism and Trotskyism, all the antipodes of life, were personified and yet abstract. Tonight there was John Peterson, who stood for criticism and also for official Communism. There was Jim Berolzheimer, a bright young man in one of the great banking houses, who represented capitalism, and his wife who painted pictures and was going to have a baby, and was therefore both art and motherhood. There was Henry Slater, the publisher, very flirtatious, with a shock of prematurely white hair, who was sex, and his wife, an ash-blond woman with a straight bang, who kept a stable full of horses and had no opinions and was sport. There was a woman psychoanalyst who got herself up in a Medici gown and used a cigarette holder. There was a pretty English girl named Leslie who worked on *Time*. There was the young Jew, Martin Erdman, who did not drink. There was Pflaumen himself, who stood for trade marks and good living, and you, who stood for literature and the Fourth International. After dinner there might be others: a biologist and his wife, a man who was high up in the Newspaper Guild, a matronly young woman who wore her hair in a coronet around her head and was active in the League of Women Shoppers, a Wall Street lawyer, a wine dealer, a statistician.

And here was the striking effect produced by Pflaumen's dinners: you truly felt yourself turning into an abstraction of your beliefs and your circumstances. Contradictions you had known in yourself melted away; challenged by its opposite, your personality hardened into something unequivocal and defiant—your banners were flying. All the guests felt this. If you asserted your Trotskyism, your poverty, your sexual freedom, the expectant mother radiated her pregnancy, the banker basked in his reactionary convictions, and John Peterson forgot about Montaigne and grew pale as an El Greco saint in his defense of Spanish democracy. Everybody, for the moment, knew exactly who he was. Pflaumen had given you all your identity cards, just as a mother will assign personalities to each of her brood of children: Jack is hard-working and steady, Billy is a flash-in-the-pan, never can finish anything he starts. Mary is dreamy, Helen is practical. While it lasted, the feeling was delightful; and at the dinner table everyone was heady with a peculiar, almost lawless excitement, like dancers at a costume ball.

It was only when you caught a glimpse of the author of

your happiness, ensconced there, so considerate, so unobtrusive, at the head of his table, that your conviction wavered. To the others, too, he must have been a disturbing
factor, for throughout the meal there was a tacit conspiracy
to ignore the host, to push him out of the bright circle he
had so painstakingly assembled. Once the dinner got under
way, nobody accorded him more than a hasty glance. If he
dropped a pun or a platitude into the conversation, it was
just as if he had dropped a plate: there would be a moment of frozen silence, then the talk would go on as before.

Pflaumen did not appear to mind this; in fact, he seemed
to accept it as natural. Here in this apartment, all the rules
of ordinary politeness were suspended; and at first you
were so caught up in your own gaiety that you hardly
noticed this, and it seemed to you, too, perfectly natural
that no one should speak to the host. But gradually, as in
a dream, you became aware that the laws of the normal
world were not operating here, that something was wrong,
that nothing was what it seemed to be, that the church bell
you were listening to was really the alarm clock. And, just
as in a dream, the exhilaration continued for a little, but
underneath it ran distrust and terror. You knew that it was
not what it pretended to be, this microcosm of your host's,
for if it were actually so fine and first-rate, Pflaumen himself would not be in it, even on sufferance. He was the clue
in the detective story, the piece of thread, the thumbprint,
the bullet in the wainscoting, that stares up at the bright
detective and tells him that the well-arranged scene before
him is the work, not of Nature, but of Man. You had only

to look at him to know that the morality play was just a puppet show, that the other guests did not represent the things they were supposed to, that they could be fitted into this simulacrum of the larger world precisely because they were small, unreal figures, and with growing anxiety you asked yourself, "Why am I in it too?"

The conversation around you began to sound peculiarly flat. "Cultivate your own garden is what I told her," the publisher was saying. "She'll never understand politics." "She'd do better to cultivate her gardener—like Lady Chatterley," put in the English girl. Next to her, John Peterson went on talking through her joke. He was a little tight. "This back-stabbing that goes on here makes me want to vomit," he said. "I can't listen to it after what I've seen in Madrid. I've heard La Pasionara sing. What do these petty political squabbles mean to her? She's got a heart as big as the Spanish earth."

Suddenly you knew that you must cut yourself off from these people, must demonstrate conclusively that you did not belong here. You took a deep breath and leaned across the table toward John Peterson. "God damn you," you said in a very loud voice, such as you had once heard a priest use to denounce sinners from the pulpit, "God damn you, what about Andres Nin?" You felt your body begin to shake with stage fright and the blood rush up into your face and you heard the gasp go around the table, and you were gloriously happy because you had been rude and politically unfashionable, and really carried beyond yourself, an angel warrior with a flaming sword. Surely, there could be no doubt that you had put yourself beyond the pale. But when you looked up you saw that Pflaumen was beaming at you again, his eyes wetter than ever, as proud as if you had just spoken your first word to an audience of aunts.

"Meg is a violent Trotskyist," he said tenderly. "She thinks the rest of us are all GPU agents." The publisher, who had been concentrating on the English girl, looked across the table at you, sizing you up for the first time. "My God," he said, "you're certainly spirited about it." Martin Erdman was watching you, too. He clapped his hands twice in pantomime and gave you a long, ironic smile. You bent your head and blushed, and, though you were excited, your heart sank. You knew that you were not a violent Trotskyist, and Erdman must know it too. It was just that you were temperamentally attracted to unpopular causes: when you were young, it had been the South, the Dauphin, Bonnie Prince Charlie; later it was Debs and now Trotsky that you loved. You admired this romantic trait in yourself and you would confess humorously: "All I have to do is be *for* somebody and he loses." Now it came to you that perhaps this was just another way of showing off, of setting yourself apart from the run of people. Your eyes began to fill with tears of shame; you felt like Peter in the Garden, but yours was, you knew, the greater blasphemy: social pressure had made Peter deny the Master; it had made you affirm him—it was the difference between plain and fancy cowardice.

You held your eyes wide open to keep the tears from

falling. The others, staring at you, must certainly think that your brimming eyes testified to the depth of your feeling for the murdered Nin. You tossed your head slightly and the tears began to settle.

"You *are*," you said, "a lot of you, GPU agents. The trouble is you're such idiots you don't even get paid for it."

It was a harsh joke, but it was a joke, and it was your peace offering. There was a cackle of laughter, and then everyone but John Peterson and Erdman was looking at you fondly, as if they were all much older than you were. Peterson cast you a malignant glance from his pale eyes, but he did not say anything. He was not too drunk to know that though the others actually agreed with him about Nin (or else did not care), temporarily, in some way, you had got them on your side. Erdman did not speak either; he nodded his head twice in the same tempo he had clapped his hands in, and kept smiling at you with that strange, mocking, affectionate expression.

You saw how profitable that exchange had been for you: it had earned you an enemy and, you thought, a lover. The first thing made you feel good, and the second saddened you. The next morning the phone would wake you and you would reach out and take it dreamily and it would be Erdman speaking very softly, asking you to have tea with him. You could see how it would all be. You would go to bed with him finally, but it would not last long, because you had both been compromised at this dinner party, and you had both understood this and understood each other. "Have you seen Pflaumen lately?" he would ask from time to time, and you would not be able to meet his eyes when you answered yes or no. He would not pursue the subject (you would never dare discuss Pflaumen together), but both of you would be silently asking the same question: what weakness, what flimsiness of character, what opportunism or cynicism had put the other into Pflaumen's hands?

On the other hand, you would treat each other gently, with a special tenderness, as though you were both wounded. For if, in one way, your love would be full of doubt, in another, it would be over-full of comprehension, lacking in mystery, like the grave dreary love between brother and sister. You had recognized him in the scene about the wine; he had recognized you in the scene about Nin. You would have liked, both of you, to play a lone hand; but you had not been strong enough for it. In each case, your war of independence had been an inglorious *Putsch ("Excuse me, Officer, I was only fooling.")*

While the coffee and liqueurs were being served, new people came in, and the party broke up into smaller units. The publisher whispered in the English girl's ear; the banker talked Bermuda with the publisher's wife. John Peterson, glassy-eyed, exhorted the woman psychoanalyst—"But surely in his later years Freud played into Hitler's hands." You stood beside Martin Erdman, not talking, listening to the others, sharing an ironic smile between you. Pflaumen sat on a sofa beside the expectant mother; he was telling her about a new product he had just had trademarked, while she went through a pantomime of congratu-

lation. Only she could afford to be polite, for she had nothing to gain now from social intercourse, and, being easily
fatigued, nothing much to give. She was comfortable with
Pflaumen; he took her hand and she let him hold it; he was
one of her oldest friends.

What had happened to you with Erdman was happening
with others all over the room. Men were taking out address
books or repeating phone numbers in low voices. There
was a slight shuffle of impatience; nothing more could be
done here; it was time to go and yet it was much too early.

People got up and shifted around, like people in a rail-
road station when the stationmaster has come in to announce that the train will be forty minutes late. New combinations were formed. The publisher was sitting on the
arm of your chair now, asking if you would like to write
an opinion on a manuscript. You agreed, and for you, too,
now the party was over. You had got everything you came
for—a new lover and some work to do. Pflaumen came and
sat at your feet on the floor. "You were wonderful," he
said, looking up at you with that over-energetic expression
of delight. You had an unaccountable impulse to kick him
exactly where the paunch should have been. "The Berolzheimers are crazy about you," he went on, ignoring your
angry look, putting it down to "temperament," an inesti-
mable commodity. "They want me to bring you to dinner
next Wednesday." You raised your eyebrows into circles
of surprise; yet you had known, ever since that scene at the
table, that the Berolzheimers would invite you. They were
pleasant and they would have a nice house with good food,

and there would be new people there; it would be interesting to see the world through a banker's eyes.

"Are you having fun?" asked Pflaumen, drawing his knees up and hugging them with his arms in a real ecstasy of coziness.

"Yes," you said. "It's a very gay party."

"Erdman is interesting . . ." he began tentatively.

You don't miss a trick, you thought, but you answered him impassively. "Is he?" you said. "I can't really tell. I haven't talked much to him."

Pflaumen looked hurt.

"Of course," he said, "it's none of my business . . ."

"I don't know what you mean," you said, in a stubborn childish voice.

The warm, twosey smile had died on his lips, but he revived it with an effort.

"Personally," he went on, "I should have thought Peterson was more in your line. I asked him specially because I thought he could do you some good . . ."

He paused. The unresolved sentence hung coaxingly in the air, begging your denial, your explanation, your attention. But cruelly you ignored it, and leaned back in your chair, as if to catch the words of the neighboring conversation. "Did you hear that?" you said finally. "They are picketing *The Tsar to Lenin.*"

Pflaumen glanced up at you, refusing the diversion. "Oh Meg," he murmured reproachfully, "I thought we were such friends."

"Don't be tiresome!" you exclaimed. "Why don't you get

me another highball?" You put your glass in his hand with a decisive gesture.

"All right," he acceded, scrambling to his feet. You thought you had won. At a single sharp word that hungry ego had scuttled back into the shell of function, where friendship and hospitality were identical and every highball was a loving cup. But he had taken only a few steps toward the bar, when he stopped, as if he had forgotten something, and turned back to you with an anxious face. "You're not drinking too much, are you?" he asked, in a true stage whisper. Several people, including Erdman, turned their heads.

At last, you thought, the bill had come in. The dinners, the letters of introduction, the bottle of perfume, the gardenias, the new Soviet film, the play, the ballet, the ice-skating at Rockefeller Plaza had all been invoiced, and a line drawn underneath, and the total computed. How recklessly you had accepted, like a young matron with a charge account ("Take two, madam; the bill will not go out till after the first of the year"). Now, when you looked at it, the total was staggering; it was more than you could pay.

You remembered suddenly all the warning signs. How deep Pflaumen always was in the confidence of his friends, how offended if two of them should meet in his absence! How careful people were to serve the whisky Pflaumen's client made—you recalled how a young husband had hurried out, unshaved, to the liquor store, so that the label on the bottle should be right when Pflaumen arrived for highballs; you remembered another husband pouring wine into a decanter so that Pflaumen should not know that it came from his client's competitor. And how fond Pflaumen was of talking about loyalty! "It's the only thing I expect of my friends," he would say, sententiously. Loyalty, you now perceived, meant that Pflaumen should never be left out of anything. He was like an x that you can never drop out of an equation no matter how many times you multiply it or add to it this side of infinity. All at once, you saw how he could be generous and humble and look predatory at the same time; the hawklike mouth was not deceptive, for he was a true bird of prey: he did not demand any of the trifles that serve as coin in the ordinary give-and-take of social intercourse; he wanted something bigger, he wanted part of your life.

For the first time, you understood why it was that this apartment of Pflaumen's affected you so unpleasantly, why you went there almost surreptitiously, not telling anyone, so that your closest friends were hardly aware that you knew Pflaumen. You saw that it was indeed a house of assignation, where business deals, friendships, love affairs were arranged, with Pflaumen, the promoter, taking his inevitable cut. When you had refused to tell Pflaumen about Erdman—though, so far, there was nothing really to tell—you had violated the code. You had tried to cheat him of his rightful share; you had been guilty of disloyalty. And he was going to crack down on you; he had, in fact, already begun.

When he came back from the bar with your glass in his hand, he was smiling, but the down-curved lips were strained and angry. You took the glass and set it down;

Erdman in a cheap tweed coat was making his way toward you, ready to say good-bye. You smiled at him faintly, knowing that Pflaumen was watching you, and knowing, too, with a certain vindictive happiness, that of all the things about Erdman, Pflaumen was most envious of that baggy Kollege Kut coat with its raglan collar. You thought of your own poor coat, and you could see the two of them hanging side by side in Pflaumen's closet, like two pairs of shoes outside a hotel room in a naughty French movie, sentinels to a private, serious world that Pflaumen could never—even vicariously—invade.

The two men were shaking hands. "Come again," said Pflaumen, "and I'll get Farwell from the Yale Law School to meet you. And bring your wife," he added, in an emphatic voice. "You ought to meet her, Meg."

"Yes," you said thinly. "I didn't know Mr. Erdman was married."

"He tries to keep it dark," said Pflaumen, suddenly very jovial. He slapped Erdman on the back and began to propel him toward the door.

You went quietly into the bedroom and took your coat out of the closet. By the time Pflaumen returned from the elevator, you were ready to go.

"You're not leaving?" he said, looking alarmed. "If you wait till the others go, I'll drive you."

"Don't bother," you said. "I'm used to the subway."

"But what about the Berolzheimers?" he asked breathlessly, in a sort of panic. Clearly he had not intended that things should go quite so far. "Next Wednesday?"

You had forgotten about the Berolzheimers. Now you hesitated, weighing the invitation. Sooner or later you would break with him, you knew. But not yet, not while you were still so poor, so loverless, so lonely. "All right," you said, "you can pick me up at my place."

The time after the next, you promised yourself, you would surely refuse.

FIVE *Portrait of the Intellectual as a Yale Man*

To look at him, you would never have believed he was an intellectual. That was the nice thing about Jim Barnett. With his pink cheeks and sparkling brown eyes and reddish brown hair that needed brushing and well-cut brown suit that needed pressing, he might have been any kind of regular young guy, anywhere in America. He made you think of Boy Scouts and starting a fire without matches and Wesley Barry and skinning the cat and Our Gang comedies and Huckleberry Finn. If he had ever been hard up, he could have been a photographic model, and one would have seen his pleasant, vaguely troubled face more often in *The Saturday Evening Post* than in *Esquire*. He might have done very well as the young man who is worried about his life insurance, the young man who is worried about dandruff, the young man whose shirts won't fit him, the young man who looks up happily from his plate of Crunchies, saying, "Gee, honey, I didn't know breakfast food could taste so good!"

In real life, his concerns were of a different order. The year he came down from Yale (where he could have been Bones but wouldn't), he was worried about Foster and Ford and the Bonus Marchers and the Scottsboro Boys. He had also just taken a big gulp of *Das Kapital* and was going around telling people about how he felt afterwards. He would buttonhole a classmate after a few sets of tennis down at the old Fourteenth Street Armory. "You know, Al," he would say, twisting his head upwards and to one side in the characteristic American gesture of a man who is giving a problem serious thought (the old salt or the grizzled Yankee farmer scanning the sky for weather indications), "you know, Al, I never thought so at college, but the Communists *have* something. Their methods over here are a little operatic, but you can't get around their analysis of capitalism. I think the system is finished, and it's up to us to be ready for the new thing when it comes." And Al, or whoever it was, would be doubtful but impressed. He might even go home with a copy of the *Communist Manifesto* in his pocket—in that period, the little socialist classic enjoyed something of the popularity of the *Reader's Digest*: it put the whole thing in a nutshell, let a fellow like Al know just what he was up against. Later that evening Al might remark to his wife that maybe it would be a good idea (didn't she think?) to lay in a stock of durable consumers' goods—in case, oh, in case of inflation, or revolution, or anything like that. His wife would interpret this in terms of cans and leave a big order for Heinz's baked beans, Campbell's tomato soup, and somebody else's chicken à la king with the grocer the next day. This was the phenomenon known as the dissemination of ideas.

In much the same tone (that of a man in an advertisement letting another man in on a new high-test gasoline) Jim began to write about his convictions in articles and book reviews for the liberal magazines. Capitalism was on the skids, and everybody ought to know about it. He could never have written, "Capitalism is doomed," any more than he could have talked about "the toiling masses." At Yale, elevation in speech had been held to be quite as barbarous as eccentricity in dress or the wrong sort of seriousness in study; and if Jim had committed an unpardonable breach of manners in interesting himself in Marxism, his rough-and-tumble vocabulary was a sort of apology for this, a placatory offering to the gods of decorum, who must have appeared to him in the guise of football players. Certainly, his vocabulary had something to do with the enthusiasm his work excited. The ideas he put forward, familiar enough when clothed in their usual phraseology, emerged in his writing in a state of undress that made them look exciting and almost new, just as a woman whom one has known for years is always something of a surprise without her clothes on. And, in the end, it was not the ideas that counted so much, as the fact that Jim Barnett held them.

This was the thing that nobody, including Jim himself, could ever quite get over. Now and then someone would be frank enough to ask him how it had happened, and he

would laugh and say that it had been an accident: he had
had a roommate at college who was literary, and once you
got started reading one thing led to another. But modest
men, like boasters, are never believed, even when they
speak the exact truth; and in 1932 everyone on the left
was convinced that this "accident" was really a miracle,
a sign from heaven or history that the millennium was at
hand. Most men had come to socialism by some all-too-
human compulsion: they were out of work or lonely or
sexually unsatisfied or foreign-born or queer in one of a
hundred bitter, irremediable ways. They resembled the
original twelve apostles in the New Testament; there was
no real merit in their adherence, and no hope either. But
Jim was like the Roman centurion or Saint Paul; he came
to socialism freely, from the happy center of things, by a
pure act of perception which could only have been
brought about by grace; and his conversion might be interpreted as a prelude to the conversion of the world.

And, like all miracles, this particular one served to
quicken the faith of the stragglers, the tired workers, and
the worldlings. Silly people who had gone a little to the
left and then begun to wonder whether they had not, after
all, made a mistake, had only to look at Jim Barnett to
feel reassured. Nobody could possibly object to socialism
if it were going to be run by earnest, undogmatic Yale
men—some of them out of Shef, to take care of the technical side. On the other hand, serious middle-aged men
who had been plugging Marxism for years in little magazines that owed the printer money and never came out on

time would have a conversation with Jim and feel heart-
ened, even inspired. If a nice, average boy like that could
tumble into the movement, surely the old ideas must be
bankrupt at last. When capitalism, intellectually speaking,
could no longer feed her favorite children, the end could
not but be very, very near.

By simply being the way he was, Jim Barnett made a
great many people on the left feel happy, almost sentimental. He was a mascot, a good-luck piece; and there was
perhaps some superstition behind the fact that very little
was demanded of him—you must not ask too much of a
talisman or the power will go out of it, and it is better not
to look a gift horse in the mouth. At any rate, unlike most
converts of that period, he was not expected to follow the
Party line, even on a long leash. From the very first, Jim
was an independent in politics, siding now with the Communists, now with the Lovestoneites, now with the
Trotskyists, now with the group of middle-class liberals he
had known at college who were trying to build a Farmer-
Labor party of their own. In anybody else, such behavior
would have been politically suspect: the man would have
been damned as a careerist, on the one hand, or a dilettante
on the other. Yet neither of these allegations was ever
made against Jim. His heterodoxy was received by all
factions with paternal indulgence. "Let the boy have his
head," was the feeling. "A wild oat or two won't hurt
him."

With Jim himself it was a point of honor that he should
never agree completely with anyone or anything. He had

never swallowed Marxism whole, he used to say in a slightly boastful tone, as if he had achieved a considerable feat of acrobatics. It was true; he never swallowed any doctrine whole. Like a finicky eater, he took pride in the fact that he always left something on the plate. There was something peculiarly American and puritanical about this abstemiousness of his; in other countries children are taught that it is bad manners not to finish everything that is set before them. But at Yale a certain intellectual prodigality had been cultivated in the students; it was bad taste to admire anything too wholeheartedly. They thought "bad taste" but they meant "dangerous," for the prodigality was merely an end product of asceticism: you must not give in to your appetites, physical or spiritual; if you did, God knows where it would land you, in paganism, Romanism, idolatry, or the gutter. Like all good Yale men, Jim feared systems as his great-grandfather had feared the devil, the saloon, and the pope.

Naturally, for boys brought up under these influences, systems of thought had a certain wanton, outlawed attractiveness; and Marxism was to become for Jim's generation what an actress had been for the youths of the Gilded Age. During the first years of the New Deal, there were many flirtations, many platonic friendships with the scarlet woman of the steppes. Jim, being courageous, went farther than most. And, at first glance, that balkiness of his, that hesitation, that unwillingness to take the final step, might have appeared to be merely a concession to tradition, another bone thrown to the Eli bulldog, who was always extraordinarily hungry.

Actually, it was deeper and more personal than that. If other people on the left stood in superstitious awe of Jim, Jim also stood in awe of himself. It was not that he considered that he was especially brilliant or talented; his estimation of his qualities was both just and modest. What he reverenced in himself was his intelligent mediocrity. He knew that he was the Average Thinking Man to whom in the end all appeals are addressed. He was the man that Uncle Sam points his finger at in the recruiting posters, that political orators beseech and ad-writers try to frighten; he was the stooge from the audience that the magician calls up on the stage, the foreman on the Grand Jury, the YOU in "This means YOU." He was a walking Gallup Poll, and he had only to leaf over his feelings to discover what America was thinking. There was something sublime about this, but there were responsibilities, too. The danger was that you would lose your amateur standing. It was essential to remain—not aloof, exactly, for that implied some aristocratic hauteur—but accessible, undecided. It was so easy, so fatally easy, to become a professional innocent; one day you were a bona fide tourist, and the next you were a shill in a Chinatown bus. If you were not remarkably alert, you might never know it had happened.

Jim Barnett, however, *was* alert, and he took every possible precaution. His mind and character appeared to him as a kind of sacred trust that he must preserve inviolate. It was as if he were the standard gold dollar against which the currency is measured. It would be wrong to debase it with lead, but it would be equally wrong to put more than the specified amount of gold into it. The dollar was supposed to be impure in certain unalterable proportions: you could not change that without upsetting the whole monetary system. Jim's function, as he saw it, was to ring the new ideas against himself, and let the world hear how they sounded. It was his duty, therefore, to "be himself," and his virtues and his weaknesses were alike untouchable. On the one hand, he could not drop into the life of a Communist front man, because this would have involved a suspension of individual judgment, a surgical sterilization of the moral faculty that was odious to him; on the other hand, he could not lift himself into the world of Marxist scholarship, because, to put it frankly, this might have overtaxed his powers, might (who knows) have crippled him for good.

It did not occur to him, or, indeed, to anyone else, that he was taking the line of least resistance. This state of being unresolved, on call, as it were, was painful to him, and he used to envy his friends who, as he said, were "sure." The inconsistencies he found whenever he examined his own thoughts troubled him a good deal. He found, for example, that he liked to drink and dance and go to medium-smart night clubs with medium-pretty girls. Yet he believed with Veblen that there was no greater folly than conspicuous consumption, and his eyes and ears told him that people were hungry while he had money in his pocket. This was a problem all well-to-do radicals had to face, and there were any number of ways of dealing with it. You could stop being a radical, or you could give your money away. Or you could give a little of it away and say, "I owe something to myself," or give none of it away, and say, "I'm not a saint, and besides I have something more important than money to contribute." The Communist Party in those years did its best to settle this delicate question gracefully for prosperous fellow-travelers. It was reported that Browder had declared that there was nothing worse for the movement than what he called "a tired radical," and that men and women would be better workers for the cause if they let themselves go and enjoyed life once in a while. This pronouncement was widely quoted—over cocktails in the Rainbow Room, and sometimes (even) over a bottle of champagne in more intimate *boîtes;* it was believed that this showed "the human side" of the Party leader, and gave the lie to those perpetual carpers (tired radicals, undoubtedly) who kept talking about Communist inflexibility. The example of Marx and Engels was also cited: they had had great Christmas parties and had called the young Kautsky a mollycoddle because he would not drink beer. (And how right their judgment had been! Forty years later Kautsky had betrayed the revolution by voting war credits in the German Reichstag, and Lenin had called him, among other things, an old woman.) Jim Barnett tried all these formulas on his conscience, but stretch them as he would, he could not make them cover the abyss between the theory and the practice.

He decided, at last, to let the abyss yawn, and in the course of time he fell into it.

The second year Jim was in New York, he went to work as assistant editor on one of the liberal weeklies. The whole staff was instantly delighted with him, from the septuagenarian editor and publisher down to the red-haired telephone girl. He brought a breath of fresh air into the office, the women told each other, while the old man muttered happily about "young ideas," and the men of forty-odd, Harvard graduates who remembered Jack Reed and who were rather dried and historical themselves, they, too, welcomed Jim Barnett in their own way, shaking their heads over him and prophesying with a certain relish that he would soon lose his illusions and resign himself, as they had done, to the world. The gratitude and joy everyone felt translated itself at once into action. The magazine began—with an alacrity that was almost fatuous—to smarten itself up. The advertising manager had herself an expensive permanent, Labor and Industry took to using mascara, the library got a set of modernistic chairs, some of the new lamps with indirect lighting, and a thick-piled gray rug from a neo-cubist furniture store on Eighth Street. Tea was served in the afternoons; a new format was planned for the magazine; the switchboard girl began to listen in to phone calls; and the managing editor asked a well-known Marxist hothead to do a series of articles on the New Deal.

All this attention embarrassed Jim a little. It did not

go to his head. He even opposed some of the changes, in
the manner of a small boy who says, "Aw, Ma, you're
taking too much trouble." There was talk of moving the
paper uptown, but Jim squelched this by insisting that
the old-fashioned offices had a quaint integrity of their
own, that the very editorial policy might be imperiled by
a move to more glittering quarters. He perceived that the
editors were ready to do anything he wanted—and he did
not like it at all. It was true, he was anxious to put over
his ideas, but he saw himself accomplishing this by argument, not by ingratiation. In his eyes, there was something
ugly about the fact that these seasoned liberals should go
to such lengths to please him. It·was like having a girl
give in too quickly; you felt that she did not take you, as
an individual, seriously—she only wanted a man. At the
back of his mind he was aware of a contempt for the
Liberal's editorial board, like the contempt he had felt
for the easy makes, the town girls in New Haven; and it
was a contempt that was restless and full of fear, since
the idea that kept pushing itself in was, "They would
have done it for any young guy. They have no political
respect for me as a person." This was one of the penalties
of being the Average Man, that you were never sure
whether people were not mixing you up with someone
else. Sometimes you did not feel average so much as
anonymous. Jim could never understand quite why it was,
but whenever anyone talked about losing yourself in a
cause, or in the Common Will, a thrill of horror would
go through him, and he would recall the lost feeling, the

tangled-up feeling, he got in a certain recurrent dream he had, where he could not find out who he was.

In the editorial staff of the *Liberal,* Jim sensed a great aching unspecific need for somebody, anybody, to think by and live by, as a mother lives by her son. Only the old man, with his long black coat and pompous manners and his eyeglasses on a black ribbon, seemed to be exempt from this necessity, and it was only with him in his private office that Jim felt truly comfortable. The others wanted to be bullied or taken by storm; the old man merely wanted to talk. He was interested in what Jim had to say, while the others, Jim felt, did not so much listen to his remarks as eavesdrop on them, waiting for him to express a preference they could gratify, or a decision they could concur with. It was like walking down Fifth Avenue with your mother or your girl during the Christmas shopping season: you did not dare pause for an instant before a tennis racket, an English sweater, or a toilet case in a store window; if you showed the faintest flicker of interest she would buy the thing for you, whether you wanted it or not. With the old man, however, Jim felt safe. He could say whatever came into his head and know that it would not appear, in a slightly garbled form, in one of the lead paragraphs on the following Wednesday. The two of them would sit in the old man's room, facing each other on a pair of squeaky swivel chairs, and discuss the AAA, the court-packing plan, the Kirov assassination and the execution of the hundred White Guards.

On all of these subjects the old man held opinions that

were in the eyes of most of his staff and many of his readers an indication of failing powers. Mr. Wendell was uncompromisingly against what he called, in a public-auditorium voice, this new spirit of bureaucracy, this specter that was haunting the world under the name of progressivism or communism. He believed in socialism, but he held out for an economy of abundance, for a free judiciary, and trial by jury. He stood for inviolable human rights rather than plans or programs; and no plan, he declared, was worth a nickel that would sacrifice these rights at the first hint of trouble. Years later, Jim decided that time had, in each of these instances, proved the old man right. At the moment, he was not so sure. He did not quite agree with his friends who considered Mr. Wendell a tiresome old fuddyduddy. Still, he thought that you could probably trust Mr. Roosevelt and Comrade Stalin to abrogate liberty only just so much as was absolutely necessary— and always in the right direction, that is, to abrogate your opponent's liberty rather than your own. When he told the old man that he was making a fetish of civil liberties, that the liberties were for the people and not the people for the liberties, Mr. Wendell replied that Jim was making a fetish out of socialism. Jim had to smile a little ruefully, conceding the point.

One day a new argument occurred to him, one he had heard the Communists advance. After all, he said, there has to be a limit to everything. Nobody can be allowed to practice freedom at the expense of everybody else. The government, for instance, has to protect itself against sedition and

against the betrayal of state secrets in wartime. He looked
up at the old man expectantly, wondering what he could
answer. "Doesn't it?" he asked earnestly, when Mr. Wendell remained silent. "I don't believe in war," the old
man answered calmly, and Jim blushed. He did not
believe in war, either; at least he said he didn't, not in
imperialist war anyway; but the words he had just spoken
seemed to show that he did, that he believed in it more
than anything else, more than free speech, more than the
right to agitate against the government. He was so deeply
chagrined by this discovery that the thread of the debate
slipped from his hands, and it did not occur to him until
he lay in bed that night that the old man had not answered
the question but only parried it, and in such a way as to
assert his moral superiority, to remind Jim of his long
and heroic career as a fighter for peace. Jim laughed to
himself, and turned over, contentedly. Of course there
had to be certain restrictions on liberty; anybody but an
anarchist would admit that. Of course there would have
to be policemen, even in a classless society. "I'm too much
of a realist," Jim said to himself proudly, "to imagine that
anywhere, at any time, a state could be run on the honor
system." Yet there *was* a problem. People said that you
must never forget that the Soviet Union was moving
toward greater democracy all the time; you had to look
at a thing like this Kirov business *historically*: if you
remembered the Czarist repression and the hated Okhrana,
you would see that the execution of a few White Guards
was a step forward—there were merely a hundred or so of

them after all. But that, Jim thought, was like patting a
mass killer on the head because this time he had only
committed one little murder. "No!" he heard himself say,
loudly and defiantly into the darkness. It was wrong to
condone an affair like these executions. So far the old man
was right. But there must be some middle ground. You
ought to hate the sin and love the sinner. That was very
difficult in practice, but everything was difficult. At least,
he congratulated himself, he had faced the problem, even
if he had not solved it. He settled himself comfortably
on the horns of the dilemma and fell asleep.

When he married Nancy Hodges, he invited everybody
on the *Liberal* to the wedding. Some of the older women
looked a little dowdy and were inclined to be skittish
about the champagne, but Mr. Wendell made a distinguished appearance, and, in any case, Nancy's parents,
good, well-to-do Connecticut people, were not precisely
streamlined themselves. The women, on their side, were
faintly disappointed in Nancy. She was pretty, everyone
conceded that; she had a straight, short nose and blond
hair and sweet, direct, blue eyes. Yet somehow, they
thought, she was not very *exciting*. She looked too much
like her mother, which was a very bad thing in a girl.
If Jim had to marry, they felt, it should have been somebody like an actress or a fast society girl or a painter or a
burning-eyed revolutionary, somebody out of the ordinary.
For Jim to have chosen such a humdrum little person as
Nancy was, it seemed to them, a reflection on themselves.

Around the office he had been so very careful: a cheerful word and a joke for everybody, but never a lunch or a dinner alone with a female member of the staff. They had not permitted themselves to feel resentment because they knew from the phone operator that there was a girl in the picture; and they had, one and all, persuaded themselves that she must be infinitely more beautiful and glamorous than they were. In this way, their own charms were not called into question. If a man prefers, say, Greta Garbo to you, it does not mean that you are not perfectly all right in your own style, not perfectly adequate to any of the usual requirements. The sight of Nancy in her wedding dress dispelled these comforting illusions. Every moderately young woman on the *Liberal* looked at Nancy and was affronted. "Why not me?" they all thought, as they clasped her small, plump hand, and murmured an appropriate formula.

"I'm afraid it's going to be one of those Dos Passos situations," the literary editor said to the managing editor on the way back on the train. "You know. She won't let him see his friends or do or think anything that her father wouldn't approve of. She'll make him buy a house in the country, and they'll live exactly like all the neighbors. She looks sweet, but like all those women she probably has a will of her own."

Jim, however, had been alert enough to consider these possibilities for himself. Nancy was conventional in many ways, but she was not ambitious or priggish or socially insecure. Nancy believed that you ought to have children and that they ought to have good doctors and good schools and plenty of fresh air and wholesome food. She believed that it was nice to go dancing on Saturday nights, and that it was nice to take a vacation trip once a year. She wanted to have big comfortable chairs in their apartment, and a big comfortable colored maid who came in by the day, and the first thing she bought was the very best Beautyrest mattresses for them to sleep on, and the very best box springs for their twin beds. Later, they got a good radio and phonograph combination, and they collected the choicest classical records they could find. Nancy was, from the beginning, careful with Jim's money and she put most of it into things that did not show, like the box springs, or a good plain rug, or life insurance. She subscribed to Consumer's Union, and to the hospitalization plan. She bought her clothes at Best's or Lord and Taylor's, and if she had fifteen dollars to spare from her household budget, she would put it into a new electric mixer for her maid rather than into an after-dinner coffee service for herself.

On the other hand, Nancy gave money to beggars in the street. She was tender-hearted, and she had majored in sociology in college. She knew that conditions under capitalism were horrifying, and she would always sign a check for a worthy cause. Her father showed a tendency to snort over Jim's activities; but Nancy handled this difficult situation perfectly: she took Jim's side but she did not argue; she merely patted her father on the cheek and told him he was an old fogy. "Do you mean to tell me you believe in this communistic talk of his?" the old man would ask. "I don't believe in *all* of it," she would answer with dignity, "but I believe in Jim." The phrasing was a little trite, but the sentiment was unimpeachable, for Nancy's father, like everyone else, believed in Jim, too. He could not help it.

Nancy was limited, but she was good. And she expected things of Jim. This was what drew him. Unlike the people in the *Liberal* office, unlike the radicals of all groups that he had been hobnobbing with, Nancy did not want Jim on any old terms. Nancy was not exacting, and yet there was an unwritten, unspoken contract between them. If she, on her side, had renounced all dreams of fortune and large success, he, on his side, was renouncing the right to poverty, loneliness, and despair. She was not to goad him up the social ladder, but he must never, never let her down. It was understood that he should not be pressed to go against his convictions; it was also understood that she must not go hungry. When he thought about them in the abstract, it seemed to him, now and then, that these guarantees were mutually incompatible, that Clause B was in eternal obstinate contradiction to Clause A. In practice, however, you could, if you were sufficiently agile, manage to fulfill them both at once. The job on the *Liberal* kept his conscience clean and brought the bottle of Grade A to the door every morning. Many a discord, he thought, which cannot be resolved in theoretical terms, in real life can be turned into perfect harmony; and his own marriage demonstrated to him once again the superiority of pragmatism to all foreign brands of philosophy.

Still, he had misgivings. Sometimes it appeared as if his relation with Nancy were not testing his convictions so much as his powers of compromise. Their wedding had been a case in point. Nancy's parents had wanted a church wedding, and Jim had wanted City Hall. What they had had was a summer wedding on the lawn with a radical clergyman from New York officiating. It was the same way with their choice of friends. Park Avenue and Fourteenth Street were both ruled out. The result was that the people who came to their cocktail parties, at which Nancy served good hors d'oeuvres and rather poor cocktails, were presentable radicals and unpresentable conservatives— men in radio, men in advertising, lawyers with liberal ideas, publishers, magazine editors, writers of a certain status who lived in the country. Every social assertion Nancy and Jim made carried its own negation with it, like the Hegelian thesis. Thus it was always being said by Nancy that someone was a Communist but a terribly nice man, while Jim was remarking that somebody else worked for Young and Rubicam but was astonishingly liberal. Every guest was a sort of qualified statement, and the Barnetts' parties, in consequence, were a little dowdy, a little timid, in a queer way (for they were held in Greenwich Village) a little suburban. For some reason, nobody ever came to the Barnetts' house without his wife, unless she were in the hospital having a baby. They came systematically in pairs, and, once in the apartment, they would separate, as though by decree, and the men would talk, standing up, against the mantelpiece, while the women chattered on the sofa. The same people behaved quite differently at other parties; but here it was as if they were under a compulsion to act out, in a kind of ritualistic dance, the dualism of the Barnetts' household, the dualism of their own natures.

Jim recognized that his social life was dull, but he did not object to this. He worked hard during the day; he was alert and gregarious; he had a great many appointments and a great many duties. There were people who believed that he used Nancy as a sedative, to taper off his day, as some men take a boring book to bed with them, in order to put themselves to sleep. Yet this theory, which was popular in the *Liberal* office, was not at all true. Jim loved Nancy with an almost mystical devotion, for Nancy was the Average Intelligent Woman, the Mate. If there was narcissism in this love, there were gratitude and depend-ence, too, for Jim had a vague notion that Nancy had saved him from something, saved him from losing that precious gift of his, the common touch, kept him close to what he called the facts. Some businessmen say humor-ously of their wives, "She keeps my nose to the grind-stone." Of Nancy, Jim was fond of saying, "She keeps my feet on the ground." The very fact that his domestic life was wholesome and characterless, like a child's junket, was a source of satisfaction to him. He had a profound conviction that this was the way things ought to be, that this was life. In the socialist millennium, of course, every-thing would be different: love would be free and light as air. Actually, this aspect of the socialist millennium filled Jim with alarm; he hoped that in America they would not have to go so far as to break up the family; it would be enough if every man could have the rock-bottom, durable, practical things, the things Nancy cared about so very, very much.

Moreover, the insipidity of his domestic life was, in a sense, its moral justification. Jim could think of the poor and the homeless now, and conscience no longer stabbed him, for he had purchased his immunity in the true American Way. Unable to renounce money, he had renounced the enjoyment of it. He had sold his birthright to gaiety for the mess of pottage on the dinner table and the right to hold his head up when he walked through the poorer districts in his good brown suit. Christ could forgive himself for being God only by becoming Man, just as a millionaire can excuse his riches by saying, "I was a poor boy once myself." Jim, in a dim, half-holy way, felt that with his marriage he had taken up the cross of Everyman. He, too, was undergoing an ordeal, and the worried look he had always worn deepened and left its mark around his eyes, as if anxiety, hovering over him like a bird, had at last found its natural perch, its time-ordained foothold in bills and babies and dietary disturbances.

Jim was quite sure that his marriage was "real." It pinched him now and then, and that, to his mind, was the test. What disturbed him at times was the fact that it had been so extraordinarily easy to reconcile his political beliefs with his bread and butter. There ought to have been a great tug of war with Nancy at one end and Karl Marx at the other, but the job on the *Liberal* constituted a bridge between the opposing forces, a bridge which he strode across placidly every day, but which he nevertheless suspected of insubstantiality. There was something unnatural about a job that rewarded you quite handsomely for expressing your honest opinions; it was as if you were being paid to keep your virtue when you ought to be paid to lose it. More and more often it seemed to Jim that, if he was "facing facts" at home, in the office he was living in a queer fairy-tale country where everything was comfortable and nothing true. He might, however, have smothered this disquieting notion if he had not heard somebody else put it into words.

It happened at tea in the library one afternoon, when Jim had been married only a short time. Jim did not ordinarily come in for tea, but there was a new girl in the office, an assistant to the literary editor, and at four o'clock, the managing editor had poked her head in at Jim's door and said in a sprightly voice, "You must come and meet our gay divorcee." Jim had no interest in divorcees, and it seemed to him that the managing editor was being a little corny, as he put it, about the facts of life; nevertheless, he obeyed. When he shambled into the library, the girl was sitting across the room in a wing chair, with a cup of tea in her lap. She was telling anecdotes about Reno in a rather breathless voice, as if she were afraid of being interrupted, though everyone in the room was listening to her in fascinated silence. There was something about the scene that Jim did not like, and he went over to the shelves and took down a book.

He had seen the girl before—he knew this at once—somewhere, in a bright-red evening dress that looked too old for her. It must have been at a prom or a football dance at Yale. Suddenly he remembered the whole thing—he had noticed her and thought that she was good-looking and a little bit fast (she had worn long gold earrings), and he had cut in on her without being introduced, just to see what she would say. To his astonishment, she had talked to him about poetry; the mask of the enchantress had dropped from her face and she had seemed excited and happy. In the middle of it, the man she had come with had tapped him on the shoulder with a grumpy air, and danced off with her. Jim had watched her from the sidelines for a little while, admitting to himself that she was having too good a time, or rather, that she was having the wrong kind of good time: she was not floating from man to man as a proper belle should, but talking, laughing, posing, making part of the effort herself. He ought not to have cut in on her without asking her man or some other person to introduce him; yet she had created the sort of lawless atmosphere that provoked such behavior. He did not cut in on her again, and he had never been able to make up his mind whether he liked her or not.

Here she was again, looking rather prettier and younger, almost virginal, he thought, in a black dress with a white organdy ruffle at the neck; and yet again she was somehow out of bounds, and here in the library as on the dance floor she was having too much of a success.

"This is Miss Sargent," the managing editor said, taking his arm and leading him up to the girl's chair.

Jim smiled vaguely.

"I liked your last article," she said, "the one about the smooth-paper magazines."

"Speaking of that," said Labor and Industry, "do you know that Trotsky has been writing for *Liberty?*"

"Writing against Russia," put in the foreign-news man, who was sympathetic with the Communist party.

The managing editor bit her lips. "Oh, dear," she exclaimed plaintively, like a mother who has lost control of her children, "I wish he wouldn't do that! It's such a shame to divide our forces now, when we need unity so badly."

The cup rattled on the new girl's saucer. When Jim looked down he could see that she had spilled her tea. There was a brown pool in the saucer, and her cup dripped as she picked it up again.

"It was just an historical piece," she said stiffly.

Several of the women exchanged smiles. "She's supposed to be a Trotskyist," the advertising manager, who was good-looking, whispered to Jim.

"Is that all?" said the foreign-news man. "It's simply a funny coincidence, I suppose, that it appeared in the place where it could furnish the most ammunition to the enemies of the Soviet Union?"

"You would have been delighted to run it in the *Liberal*, of course," said the girl with an ironical smile.

The managing editor cut in. "Well, no, we wouldn't. We *have* published things by Trotsky, but I think he goes too far. Solidarity on the left is so important at this moment. We can't afford self-criticism now."

"What do you think, Jim?" said Labor and Industry.

Jim cocked his head and considered the question. "I don't agree with Helen," he said finally, nodding toward the managing editor. "Any movement that doesn't dare hear the truth about itself hasn't got much on the ball, in my opinion. But I *would* say that you have to be careful where you print that truth. You want it to be read by your friends, not by your enemies. I think we should have published Trotsky's piece in the *Liberal*. On the other hand, I think Trotsky made a mistake in giving it to *Liberty*. He might just as well have given it to Hearst."

The girl drew a deep breath. She looked stubborn and angry. All at once, Jim was sure that he liked her, for she was going to fight back, he saw, and it took courage to do that on your first day in a new job. He wondered, inspecting her clothes and trying to price them, whether she needed the money.

"It's a delicate problem," she began, speaking slowly, as if she were trying to control her feelings and, at the same time in that stilted way that the Trotskyists had, as if they all, like the Old Man, spoke English with an accent, "and it's a problem that none of you, or I, have had to face, because none of us are serious about revolution. You talk," she turned to Jim, "as if it were a matter between you and God, or you and your individual, puritan conscience. You people worry all the time about your integrity, like a debutante worrying about her virginity. Just how far can she go and still be a good girl? Trotsky doesn't look at it that way. For Trotsky it's a relation between himself and the masses. How can he get the truth to the masses, and how can he keep himself alive in order to do that? You say that it would have been all right if he had brought the piece out in the *Liberal*. It would have been all among friends, like a family scandal. But who are these friends? Do you imagine that the *Liberal* is read by the masses? On the contrary, *Liberty* is read by the masses, and the *Liberal* is read by a lot of self-appointed delegates for the masses whose principal contact with the working class is a colored maid."

"The trade-union people read the *Liberal*," said the managing editor, her square, plump face flushing indignantly.

"Who? Dubinsky? Sidney Hillman?" She pronounced the names contemptuously. "I don't doubt it. The point is, though, that you—" she turned again to Jim—"you admit that Trotsky is telling the truth, but you think that nobody is good enough to hear it except a select little circle of intellectuals and *Liberal* readers. What snobbism! Naturally," she went on, "you have to be careful about how you write the article. You have to write it so that anybody who reads it with the minimum of attention will see that what you are saying to them about the Soviet Union

is quite a different thing from what the editors of *Liberty*
have been saying to them. You know, you might not think
so, but it's quite as possible for a revolutionist to make
use of Hearst as it is for Hearst to make use of a revolutionist. Lenin went through Germany in a sealed train:
the Germans thought they were using him, but he *knew*
he was using the Germans. This *Liberty* business is the
same thing on a smaller scale. The reactionaries have
furnished Trotsky with a vehicle by which he can reach
the masses. What would you have him do? Hold up his
hands like a girl, and say, 'Oh no! Think of my reputa-
tion! I can't accept presents from strange gentlemen!' " Jim
laughed out loud, and one or two of the older men
snickered. "Besides," she continued, dropping her voice a
little, "there's the problem of survival. The liberal magazines haven't shown any desire to stake Trotsky to an orgy
of free speech; his organization is poor; would you like it
better if he starved?"

She had finished, and she let her breath out in a tired
exhalation, as if she had reached the top of a long flight
of stairs. Nobody answered her, and after a moment she
picked up her tea cup and began to drink with an air of
intense concentration. This ostrich maneuver was classi-
cally unsuccessful, for everyone in the room continued to
watch her, knowing, just as Jim did, that the tea must be
stone-cold. At last, one of the older men spoke.

"Well," he said, with a sort of emaciated heartiness,
"Trotsky must be a better man than I gave him credit for,
to have such a pretty advocate." The remark dropped like

a stone into the pool of silence, setting up echoes of itself, little ripples of sound that spread and spread and finally died away.

Jim stopped her on her way out of the office.

"Ride down in the elevator with me," he said.

"I've been thinking," he began as they stood waiting for the car, "you were absolutely right this afternoon. But you won't last long here."

"I know it," she said wryly, getting into the elevator. She shrugged her shoulders.

"Is it true," he asked, "that you're a Trotskyite?"

The girl shook her head.

"I'm not even political," she said.

"But why—?"

"Oh, I don't know. I do admire Trotsky. He's the most romantic man in modern times. And you all sounded so smug." She paused to think. They were standing on the street in the autumn twilight now. "Working on a magazine like the *Liberal* does make you smug. You keep patting yourself on the back because you're not working for Hearst. It's like a lot of kept women feeling virtuous because they're not streetwalkers. Oh yes, you're being true to your ideals; and the kept women are being true to Daddy. But what if Daddy went broke, or the ideals ceased to pay a hundred and a quarter a week? What then? You don't know and you'd rather not think about it. So when something like Trotsky's writing for *Liberty* comes up, it makes you nervous, because it reminds you of the whole problem, and you are all awfully quick to say that *never*, under *any* circumstances, would you do that."

"Yes," Jim said, "I see what you mean. But aren't you being a little romantic? Aren't you trying to say that we all ought to starve for our convictions?"

Miss Sargent smiled.

"I won't say that, because if I said it, then I ought to go and do it, and I don't want to. But I do think, somehow, that it ought to be a little bit harder than it is for you *Liberal* editors. It generally is, for people who are really independent. Society makes them scramble in one way or another. The thing is, Mr. Wendell did scramble, not financially, because he inherited money, but morally and probably socially, a long time ago. And you people are living off the moral income of that fight, just as you are living off his money income."

"What about you?" said Jim.

"Oh, me, too," said the girl. "But as you say, I won't last long. Neither will you, I hope. The *Liberal* is all right as a stopgap, or as a job to support you while you're writing a book; but the *Liberal* is not a way of life. If you begin to think that, you're finished."

"What about Mr. Wendell?" said Jim. "It's a way of life for him."

"Oh, Mr. Wendell! Mr. Wendell is a crusader. Of course, it's a way of life for him. An honorable one. But the *Liberal* puts him in the red every year, while it puts you and me in the black. That's one reason he's managed to be serious for seventy years—every word costs him something. The good things in life are not free."

"Public opinion is against you there," said Jim.

"Maybe. Well, I must go." She hesitated a moment. "How does the old man feel about the paper?"

"Worried."

"Yes," she said. "Like a self-made man who's tried to give his children all the advantages he didn't have. And then they turn out badly, and he can't understand it. You prove my point for me. Well, good-bye."

He walked to the subway with her, and all the way home he thought about the conversation. He was very much excited and disturbed. At home he told Nancy what had happened.

"She is going to stir up a lot of trouble," said Nancy calmly.

"Yes," Jim answered, smiling, "that's the kind of girl she is. A troublemaker."

"There must be something wrong with her."

"Yes," said Jim. "I suppose there is."

It was queer, he thought, lying in bed that night (for he still did his thinking, like a boy, with the lights out), it was queer that Nancy had hit on it instantly. *There must be something wrong with her.* On the surface, it might appear that she had everything—looks and brains and health and youth and taste—and yet in a strange way she went against the grain. She was too tense, for one thing. It was as if she lived on excitement, situations, crises, trouble, as Nancy said. And she was not one of those happy trouble-makers who toss the apple of discord around as though it were a child's ball. On the contrary, this afternoon in the library, she had been scared stiff. In one way, he was sure, she had not wanted to speak up for Trotsky at all; she had had to force herself to it, and the effort had left her white. You had to admire her courage for undertaking something that cost her so much; but then, he thought, why do it, why drive yourself if it doesn't come easy? Nothing had been gained; Trotsky was no better off for her having spoken; and she herself, if she went on that way, would lose her job. For the spectator there had been something horrible about the scene; it was like watching a nervous trapeze artist performing on the high bars without a net: if the performer did not have iron nerves, he ought to get out of the business. "The coward dies a thousand deaths," he murmured. "The brave but one."

"What did you say, dear?" asked Nancy from the other bed.

"I didn't know you were awake."

"I've got those cramps in my legs again."

She was seven months pregnant.

"I'm sorry," he said. "I was just thinking out loud."

"About that girl, I bet," she said cheerfully.

"Yes."

"Watch out!" said Nancy in a bantering voice.

"Hell," Jim answered, and his reply had more distaste in it than he had intended to put there. "I wouldn't have her for anybody's money. Besides," he went on, "she's

supposed to be engaged. She divorced her husband to
marry some other guy. Though when I left her this evening, she looked to me like a girl who didn't have a date.
She lingered, you know . . ."

"Yes," said Nancy. "Well, I guess you're safe."

Two months later, en route between a cocktail party
and a political dinner, he kissed Miss Sargent in a taxi.
Nancy was in the hospital with a new baby girl, and as he
leaned down toward his companion, it seemed to him that
this fact justified the kiss, lent it indeed the stamp of
orthodoxy—young husbands were supposed to go slightly
on the loose when their wives were in the hospital having
babies; it was the Yale thing, the manly thing, to do. Yet
he had hardly framed the excuse to himself when he heard
his own voice speaking, a little thick with Martinis and
emotion.

"I love you," he said, and listened to the words with
surprise, for this was not on the cards at all, and he did not
even know if it were true.

"I know," she whispered, and as soon as he heard her
say this he was convinced that it *was* true, and he began to
feel joyfully unhappy.

"Ever since that Shef dance," he continued. "You wore
a red dress." Now he believed (for he was a little tight and
every love must have its legend) that he had been fatefully
in love with her for years, but that there had been some
barrier between them; yet at the same time, kept, as it
were, in the cold-storage compartment of his heart, was
the certainty that the only barrier that had ever existed

was the faint distaste he felt for what was extreme and headstrong and somehow unladylike in her nature.

"I didn't think you remembered," she said. "Why didn't you cut in on me again?"

"You terrified me," he said, knowing, all at once, that this too was true.

The taxi had drawn up to the door of a third-rate hotel that was frequently used for left-wing, money-raising evenings.

"Do you want to go in?" he said.

"Of course," she answered, and raised her head for him to kiss her.

He was disappointed. He had half-expected her to say something foolish and passionate like, "Let's keep on driving around all night," or something sultry like, "Come home with me." Her equanimity angered him, for what good was a girl like this unless she *was* foolish and passionate and sultry? He did not kiss her again, but gave her shoulder a slight, friendly push toward the doorman who was waiting to open the cab door. She evaded the doorman's hand and jumped out. By the time Jim had finished paying the cab, she had disappeared into the hotel.

Jim was at the speakers' table, though he was not scheduled to give a formal talk. From where he sat he could see the girl, eating with some people he did not know. He counted them carefully; the number was uneven; unquestionably, she was the extra girl. The discovery gave him a strange kind of satisfaction: she was free, and the evening was not over; anything could still happen; on the other hand, the fact that she was so patently free, dangling there at her table under his eyes, made it easy for him to relinquish her in his mind. He had already decided to go home early and call Nancy the first thing in the morning to tell her how much he loved her, when he looked down at the girl's table and found that she was gone. Her friends were still there; there was only a single empty chair pushed back from the table, as if it had been abandoned in a hurry. He was filled with despair. His prudent, saving self told him that at least he could still call Nancy with a clear conscience—that much had been salvaged from the evening —but the notion no longer pleased him; there is something savorless about a profit that has not been made at somebody else's expense. He began to move about restlessly on his chair, and at the first break between the speeches, he went out to the bar.

She was there, standing beside a fat, middle-aged radical who had his arm around her waist. She was drinking a Scotch and soda and laughing at what the man was saying. The man reached out and tapped Jim on the shoulder as he passed by.

"Hello," he said, with a slight German accent. "The speeches are terrible."

The girl turned and saw Jim.

"Now I know," she said, "why you wanted to pass this up. Can you imagine," she added to the man, "I thought it was my personal charm."

Jim smiled uncomfortably. This Dorothy Parker act

rubbed him the wrong way. Especially after what had happened.

"Would you like to go somewhere and dance?" he said.

The girl looked inquiringly at her companion.

"What about it?" she asked.

"I didn't invite Leo," Jim said, trying to make his voice sound light, knowing that he was behaving foolishly, that Leo was a gossip, and that Nancy would probably hear of this.

"Oh, but *I* invite him," said the girl.

"I don't dance," Leo said. "You young bourgeois go along."

In the end, Leo went with them. The two men bought the girl gardenias on a street corner, and there was a great deal of joking competition as to whose gardenia was the biggest and most perfect. They went to a French place on the West Side that had a small orchestra and was not too capitalistic. Jim and the girl danced, and Leo sat at the table like a German papa and made Marxist witticisms about them. The girl did not dance so well as Nancy, but she carried herself as if she were the belle of the evening. When it was time to go home, there was more joking about who should be dropped first, but it was finally agreed that Leo's place was obviously the first stop. As soon as the cab door closed on Leo's stout figure, Jim kissed the girl again.

"I love you," he said.

"It was better to bring Leo along," she murmured as if in answer. "I'm an expert conspirator. I know."

Jim felt a slight chill run through him.

"I don't like conspiracies," he said.

"Oh, neither do I," she said quickly. "But sometimes they're necessary."

Her tone, he thought, was precisely that of an army officer who professes to hate war.

"This time," he said, "they *won't* be necessary, Margaret."

She looked up at him. As they passed a street light, he thought he could see her lips quiver slightly.

"It's funny," she said, "whenever a man starts to tell you he's going to break with you, he uses your first name, even if he's never used it before."

"I wasn't . . ." said Jim.

"Oh yes," she said. "Yes, you were. Well, I'm going to be nice. I'm going to help you out. I'm going to say all the proper things." She took a breath and began to recite. "There is no future in this, it can't lead anywhere, it would only hurt us both, it wouldn't be any good unless it were serious and under the circumstances it can't be serious; if we once loved each other, we might not be able to stop, so we had better stop now. Or I could say," her voice dropped, "if we once loved each other, we *would* be able to stop, so let's stop before we find that out."

The taxi drew up in front of her apartment, which was on a street with a quaint name, in the Village.

"Good night," she said. "Please don't see me to the door." She jumped out of the taxi with a kind of exaggerated lightness, just as she had done at the hotel. She ran up the steps and opened the outer door.

"Where to?" said the driver.

Jim could still see her in the entryway, searching in her purse for the key.

"Go on across Seventh Avenue," he said.

The next afternoon he took her home from work on the subway. They went up to her apartment, where they made love. After dinner, he had to leave her to go to see Nancy in the hospital. He stopped and bought some flowers on the way.

It was fortunate, all things considered, that he was called to Washington the following morning. When he got back, Nancy was ready to come home with the baby. Naturally, under the circumstances, there could be no thought of continuing the affair. Miss Sargent, he told himself, was an intelligent girl; she would surely understand . . . the impossibility, et cetera, better to kill the thing quickly . . . more painless in the long run . . . no need to talk about it . . . why stir up the embers? These serviceable phrases rose readily to his mind; it was as if he had memorized them long ago for just such an occasion. The only difficulty was that he could not imagine looking Miss Sargent in the eye and uttering a single one of them.

From her demeanor he could make out whether she was suffering. It seemed to him sometimes that she was waiting, waiting with a kind of maddening self-control for the word of explanation, the final phrase with which to write off the affair. But it was quite possible that this notion was purely subjective with him, that it arose from his own sense of owing her an explanation and had no basis in fact. It was possible that she had already written off the affair, that she had never expected anything of him, that he was just a guy she had gone to bed with one afternoon, when she had no other engagement. After all, she had never said she loved him. It was he, he thought with a groan, who had said all those things; she had merely said "I know" in a sweet, wise voice. Recalling his declarations in the taxi that night, he ground his teeth in shame and anger.

"Why the hell did I do it?" he muttered to himself. He considered what alternatives there had been. If he had not let her run away that night? If he had followed her and taken the key from her hand and opened her door? He could imagine himself climbing the stairs behind her. He could see them coming into her small room and turning to face each other, bulky and absurd in their winter coats. Her face would have had that strange, white look, as if she were going to faint. They would have clung to each other just as they were, and he would have pushed her gently down on the couch. He could not see clearly what would have happened afterwards, when they would have begun to talk again; but it would have been something desperately serious. He would have promised to leave Nancy. Suddenly he felt utterly sure that that was what he would have done; and even now, in his office, his mind turned a somersault of terror at the very idea. It was a premonition of this that had made him, in the taxi, acquiesce in her dismissal of him, accept her formulation of why it could not be. He had ridden home in a mood of mournful exaltation, in which a sense of heroic resignation had mingled with relief and joy, as if he had come out of some terrible catastrophe alive.

But when he woke up the next morning, this peculiar happiness, half-elegiac, half-prudent, had vanished, and he was on fire with lust. He knew that he had had a narrow escape, but he knew also that he could not leave the thing as it was. He had an implacable conviction that the affair must be finished off somehow, and he had not been at the office half an hour before he had decided that it was absolutely essential to his peace of mind for him to sleep with the girl. He could not read a manuscript or write a letter; he could not listen when anyone spoke to him; later, when he went out to lunch, he could eat nothing but the quartered pickle that lay beside the sandwich he had ordered. There was no longer any question of love or high tragedy; he had given the girl up the night before; and he saw no reason now to change his mind. He was going to give her up, of course, but he must have her first, and indeed it seemed to him that if he did not have her he could not give her up. All his feelings about her had hardened into a physical need which he endured like a pain, believing from moment to moment that he could not stand it any longer. He said to himself that if he could only bear it for a day or two, it would diminish and finally be dissipated altogether; but, though he knew from observation and experience that this was true, he did not believe it, or rather it seemed irrelevant to him, for, like all sufferers, he had lost the sense of time.

Shortly after lunch, he knew that he had passed the threshold of tolerance, and just as a desperate patient will reach up and deflect the surgeon's arm, no longer caring what the surgeon or the nurse or the attendants think of him, he leapt up from his desk and strode into the literary editor's office. "I'll take you home at five," he said in a grim voice. Both of the women stared at him. "You sound as if you were going to murder her," exclaimed the literary editor, but Jim had already turned and was on his way out.

Immediately, he felt better. His excitement was succeeded by a frozen calm. He was able to go on with his work, able to think about the girl with detachment, able even to feel a premature remorse, as if he had already committed the adultery, and were now doing penance for it. The girl no longer appeared to him so desirable; he could toy with the notion of *not* sleeping with her; in fact, he nearly persuaded himself that he was going to sleep with her somehow against his inclination and only because he had told her he would take her home. It was as if he had made a contract with her which he would be glad to wriggle out of, but which seemed, alas, binding.

Riding uptown on the subway beside her, he began to dislike her. If only she would flirt or be demure or pretend that she did not know what was going to happen! Then he could feel free to choose her all over again. But she did not speak, and when he looked into her face, he saw there an expression that was like a tracing made with

fine tissue paper of his own feelings, an expression of suffering, of resignation, of stoical endurance. It was as if she
were his sister, his twin, his tormented Electra; it was as if
they were cursed, both together, with a wretched, un-
quenchable, sterile lust that "ran in the family." Once she
turned her head and smiled at him disconsolately, but
though he felt a touch of pity, he could not smile back; he
had lost the ability to make any human gesture toward her.

In the apartment, he took her twice with a zeal that was
somehow both business-like and insane, and then rolled
over on his back and sighed deeply, like a man who has
completed some disagreeable but salutary task. He no
longer wanted her; he knew he would never want her
again. As if she, too, knew that it was finished, she got up
at once, with an air of apology for being naked in unsuitable circumstances. She picked her clothes off the floor
where he had tossed them, and went into the bathroom.
When she came out, she was dressed. Without a word, he
took his own clothes off the chair and went on into the
bathroom.

Why the hell, he said to himself now, had he not at least
taken her to a decent restaurant for dinner and bought her
cocktails and a bottle of wine? "I could have taken her to
Charles," he murmured once. "It was right around the
corner." He banged his fist on the desk until it hurt him.
Instead, they had gone to a Japanese tearoom, where they
had eaten the seventy-five-cent dinner and talked lamely
of office politics. He had called for the check before she had
quite finished her chocolate sundae.

Much later, when his career had been achieved, that afternoon assumed for Jim an allegorical significance. Here, surely, had been the turning-point; here the hero had been chastened and nearly laid low; here had been the pit, the mouth of hell, the threat of oblivion, the gleam of redemption. Or, to put it more vaguely, as he did himself, this unfortunate love affair had somehow been "necessary": he had had to go through it in order to pass on to the next stage of his development. It was like one of those critical episodes in the autobiographies of great businessmen, as ghostwritten for *The Saturday Evening Post*—the moment of destiny when the future E. W. Sears or Frank Woolworth is fired by his employer for daydreaming or incompetence, and thus awakened to the necessity of carving his own niche, a moment the elderly tycoon reverts to in print with tireless gratitude: "If he had not fired me, I would be a clerk today." In later years, Jim came to have this same kind of feeling about Miss Sargent, and, once, when he was tight at a party, he tried to tell her about it. "Oh, thank you," she had exclaimed, widening her eyes. "I'll have a brass plaque made to hang around my neck, saying, 'Jim Barnett slept here.'" And he had burst out laughing at once, saying, "Ouch" loudly, because there was no real vanity in him.

It was a long time, however, before he took this view of the affair, a long time, indeed, before he could think of it without the most excruciating remorse. The odd thing was that this remorse seemed to have no connection with Nancy. He did not feel that he had betrayed Nancy with the girl in the office; he saw it, in fact, the other way around. He could almost believe that with Nancy and the new baby he was enjoying an idyllic and respectable liaison, while Miss Sargent was the neglected wife. He found that he was avoiding her around the office, fearing a showdown in an empty corridor, fearing equally a kiss or a snub. He came in softly, at odd hours, like a married man in a comic strip creeping up the dark stairs with his shoes in his hand. At the same time, he found that he was trying to appease her politically. At editorial conferences, he began to reveal certain ultra-leftist tendencies; he would make long, earnest speeches, stuttering slightly in the Yale style, and then raise his eyes furtively for her approval. But still she gave no sign, and as time passed and she continued to behave with impenetrable self-possession, as they never met in the elevator or the library, he began to desire the showdown as greatly as he had feared it. Now he arranged occasions to be alone with her; and he was startled to discover, after several failures, that *she* was avoiding *him.* She came to the office late and left early; the telephone operator reported that she was engaged to a new man. Late that summer she went away, out West somewhere, where she came from; it was understood in the office that she was to get up some articles for the paper and at the same time secure her father's blessing for her second marriage.

As soon as she was gone, Jim felt light and happy again, and the other women in the office told him that he was "more like himself." He threw himself into the job of getting out a special election supplement. This was the sort of work he was well suited to, for he took the election with intense seriousness, regarding his vote as a sum of money which was not to be invested lightly. Unlike the other members of the staff, who were hysterically predisposed in Roosevelt's favor, Jim could look at the array of candidates with the impartial sobriety of the ideal consumer attempting to choose between different brands of soap. He was not deceived by labels, and he saw at once that Landon was not a tory, Lemke was not a fascist, Browder was not a communist, and Roosevelt was not a socialist. He was sent to interview each of the candidates, and he wrote a series of informal character sketches that astonished everyone with their perspicacity and good humor. In the end, he decided to vote for Roosevelt, though he had an uneasy feeling about Norman Thomas, whom Mr. Wendell, alone on the paper, was supporting. The war in Spain, however, seemed to clinch the matter; in times like these, a protest vote was a luxury, and that was enough to outlaw it in Jim's eyes.

He was never sure, afterwards, whether or not it was Miss Sargent's letter that changed his mind. This was a reply to an election questionnaire the paper had sent out to its contributors; Jim came upon it one afternoon in August. She would vote, she wrote, for the Socialist-Labor candidate, whose name she could not remember—would someone in the office please find out for her? Jim stared at the familiar angular handwriting, and felt himself flush with anger. It must be a joke, he said to himself; it was something she had thought up to annoy the managing

editor; in fact she could not even have thought it up for
herself; her friend Leo must have egged her on to it.
"What a damn silly thing to do!" he exclaimed out loud,
and he was tempted to destroy the letter to save the girl's
face. Then suddenly a large sense of chivalry displaced his
annoyance: he was determined to protect her from the
consequences of her frivolity. He could announce that he
was supporting the Socialist-Labor candidate himself, write
an article on that tiny, fierce, incorruptible sect. Something
might be done about De Leon and the American socialist
movement. But almost immediately he realized that the
idea was too outlandish; he could not bring himself to cut
so fantastic a figure. Why, for God's sake, couldn't she vote
for Thomas, he muttered, and then it came to him as a
happy thought that *he* could vote for Thomas: in some
indefinable way this would cover her, make a bridge between her and the rest of the staff.

A fine exhilaration quickly took possession of him, and
he perceived that he had wanted to vote for Thomas all
along. The Roosevelt bandwagon had been far too comfortable—that fact alone should have been a warning to
him. He could predict for himself a long talk with Nancy
and a short wrangle with the managing editor, but already
he could see the article that would appear in next week's
issue, "Why I Think I'll Vote for Thomas," by James Barnett. It would be an honest, dogged, tentative, puzzled
article that would invite the reader into the author's mind,
apologize for the furniture, and beg him to make himself
quite at home. In the end, the reader might not be per-

suaded, but he would be able to leave with the assurance that, however he voted, there would be no hard feelings. With each of Jim Barnett's articles, that, somehow, became the main object. He was like a happy-go-lucky, well-mannered salesman who seems to the prospect delightfully different from other salesmen—as, indeed, he is, since in his eagerness to please he loses sight of his purpose and sells nothing but himself. The born political pamphleteer, like the born salesman, is usually a slightly obnoxious person. Inescapably, Jim had noticed that the two qualities often went together, but it did not appear to him in the light of a general law, but rather as an unhappy accident, a temporary disagreeable state of things which could, with patience, be remedied. And, for a long time, he considered himself the exception which disproved the rule. When it came to him at last that he was not exceptional but irrelevant, when he was, so to speak, *ruled out* as immaterial, having no bearing, incompetent in the legal sense, the shock was terrific.

It was the Moscow trials that made him know, for the first time, that he did not really "belong." Miss Sargent came into his office one day in the fall with a paper for him to sign. (She was back from the Coast and—mysteriously—no longer engaged to be married.) Clearly, the document in her hand was of deep significance for her, and as Jim read it over, his heart swelled with magnanimity, for he saw that he was going to be able to grant her the first request she had ever made of him, and grant it easily, largely, without a second thought, like a millionaire signing a check for a sister of Charity. The statement demanded a hearing for Leon Trotsky, who had been accused in the trials in Moscow of numberless crimes against the Soviet state. It demanded, also, what it called (rather pompously, he thought) the right of asylum for him. Jim had never believed for a moment that Trotsky was guilty of the charges, and this disbelief remained to the bitter end profound and unshakable. Other people wavered, were frightened or coaxed or bribed to resign from the Trotsky Committee; Trotskyites of long standing would wake sweating in the night to ask, "What if Stalin were right?" but Jim was serene and jocular through it all, and the strength of his skepticism came, not from a knowledge of the evidence, nor a sense of Trotsky's integrity, nor an historical view of the Soviet Union, but simply from a deficiency of imagination. Jim did not believe that Trotsky could have plotted to murder Stalin, or to give the Ukraine to Hitler, because he could not imagine himself or anybody he knew behaving in such a melodramatic and improbable manner. People did not act like that; it was all like a bad spy picture that you hissed and booed and applauded (ironically) from the gallery of the Hype in New Haven. And indeed the whole Russian scene appeared to Jim at bottom to be the invention of a movie writer; his skepticism included not only the confessions of the defendants but the *fact* of the defendants' existence. How could there be such people as Romm and Piatakov and the GPU agent, Holtzman? How indeed could there be such a dark and terrible organization as the GPU? It was all so very unlikely. And, in some strange way, Europe itself was unlikely. Jim always had the greatest difficulty in making himself see that Hitler was real, and one reason he had never subscribed to the Popular Front was that whenever he tried to conjure up the menace of fascism, somewhere deep down inside him a Yale undergraduate snickered.

So that it was no problem at all for him to put his signature below Miss Sargent's. Aside from everything else, there was a purely sporting question involved: you don't accuse a man without giving him a chance to answer for himself. Of course Trotsky should be heard. He said as much to Miss Sargent and she smiled at him, and their Anglo-Saxon sense of fair play was warm for a moment between them—he could feel it in his stomach like a shot of whisky. All the shame of that other afternoon was gone suddenly, and he thought what a hell of a nice, straight, clear-eyed girl she was, after all.

This sense of recognition, this spiritual handclasp, lasted only an instant, however, for as soon as she began to speak, her words tripped over each other, and he saw, with disappointment, that she was being intense about the matter. She said something about his "courage," and he reddened and blinked his eyes and twisted his head from side to side, disavowing the virtue. Why, he thought impatiently, was it necessary for Marxists to talk in this high-flown way? There was no question of courage here; it was just a matter of common sense. And he anticipated no trouble. There was never any trouble if you handled these controversies in the right way, kept your head, took it easy, did not let the personal note intrude. It was unfortunate, he had been saying for years, that the radical movement had inherited Karl Marx's cantankerous disposition together with his world-view. The "polemical" side of Marxism was its most serious handicap; here in America, especially, it went against the grain. He was not so simple as to subscribe to the mythology of the conference table (the class struggle was basic, inadjudicable), but surely on the left itself, there could be a little more friendliness, a little more co-operativeness, a little more give-and-take, live-and-let-live and let-sleeping-dogs-lie. And it was really so easy. Take his own case: he had friends of every shade of opinion, argued with them freely, pulled no punches, but never had a quarrel. There had been the time when he had been obliged to throw a classmate out of his apartment for telling an anti-Semitic story, but the guy had come back the next day, sober, and apologized, and they had shaken hands on it, and the incident was forgotten. It only went to show. Unfortunately, however, the bad side of Marxism was precisely what attracted warped personalities of the type of Miss Sargent, who had long lists of people she did not speak to, and who delighted in grievance committees, boycotts, and letters to the editor. So that the evil multiplied a thousandfold. It was like an hereditary insanity that is perpetuated not only through the genes but by a process of selection in which emotional instability tends to marry emotional instability and you end up with the Jukes family. Or you begin with Marx's carbuncles and you end with the Moscow trials.

"Take it easy," he said to the girl, patting her shoulder in token of dismissal.

"I'll try," she answered, lightly enough, but as she turned to go, she flung at him that same sad, desperate smile that she had given him on the subway just before— He closed the door hastily behind her. For an instant it was as if he, too, had heard the chord that announces the return of a major theme, a sound heavy with dread and expectation. *It was all going to begin again*, the same thing, disguised, augmented, in a different key, but irrefragably the same thing. His stomach executed a peculiar drop, and this sensation, also, he remembered. It was the feeling you have on a roller-coaster at Coney Island, when the car has just started and you are sitting in the front seat, and you know for sure (you have been wondering up to this moment) that you do not want to ride on it. After the first dip, you lose this certainty (you would unquestionably die if you kept it), you may even enjoy the ride or suggest a second trip, become an *aficionado* of roller-coasters, discriminate nicely between the Cyclone at Palisades Park and the Thunderbolt at Revere Beach. You are, after all, a human being, with a hundred tricks up your sleeve. But at the very beginning you *knew*.

However, there seemed at first no cause for alarm. The whole *affaire Trotsky*, as somebody called it, was going off according to schedule. Miss Sargent would come to the office every morning in a fever of indignation: mysterious strangers telephoned her at midnight, she received anonymous letters and marked copies of the *Daily Worker*, a publisher went back on a verbal agreement he had made with her, people cut her on the street, an invitation to a summer writers' conference had been withdrawn. Jim listened to these stories with a tolerant smile: this was the usual sectarian hysteria. No doubt some of these things had actually happened to her (he would not go so far as to say she had made them up), but certainly she exaggerated, colored, dramatized, interpreted, with very little regard for probability. Nothing of the sort was happening to him. He was on the best of terms with his Stalinist friends, who even kidded him a little about his association with Trotsky; several publishers were after him to do a book; and he got an offer to join the staff of a well-known news magazine. If anything, his open break with the Party had enhanced his value.

Moreover, he was enjoying himself enormously. He had the true American taste for argument, argument as distinguished from conversation on the one hand and from oratory on the other. The long-drawn-out, meandering debate was, perhaps, the only art form he understood or relished, and this was natural, since the argument is in a sense our only indigenous folk-art, and it is not the poet but the silver-tongued lawyer who is our real national bard. The Moscow trials seemed admirably suited to the medium, and at any cocktail party that season, Jim could be found in a corner, wrangling pleasantly over Piatakov and Romm, the Hotel Bristol in Copenhagen and the landing field at Oslo.

However, here, as in the other arts, there were certain conventions to be observed: statistics were virtually *de rigueur,* but rhetoric was unseemly; heat was allowed, but not rancor. Jim himself obeyed all the rules with a natural, unconscious decorum, and in his own circle he felt perfectly secure in advocating Trotsky's cause. It was at the Trotsky committee meetings that he had misgivings. An ill-assorted group of nervous people would sit in a bare classroom in the New School or lounge on studio couches in somebody's apartment, listening to Schachtman, a little dark lawyer, demolish the evidence against the Old Man in Mexico. Schachtman's reasoning Jim took no exception to (though it was, perhaps, almost *too* close); what bothered him was the tone of these gatherings. It seemed to him that every committee member wore an expression of injury, of self-justification, a funny, feminine, "put-upon" look, just as if they were all, individually, on trial. They nodded with emphasis at every telling point, with an air of being able to corroborate it from their own experience; ironical smiles of vindication kept flitting from face to face. And not only, Jim thought, did they behave like accused persons; they also behaved like guilty persons; the very anxiety of their demeanor would have convicted them before any jury. Watching them all, Jim would wish that he was the only guy in the world who took Trotsky's side, and he would feel a strong sympathy with Leibowitz, who, at Decatur during the Scottsboro case, was supposed to have told the Communists to get the hell out of town. Sometimes, even, listening to Novack read aloud a fiery letter from the Old Man, he would wish that Trotsky himself could be eliminated, or at least held incommunicado, till the investigation was over. The Old Man did not understand Americans.

And after the meeting had broken up, over coffee or highballs, the committee members would exchange anecdotes of persecution, of broken contracts, broken love affairs, isolation, slander, and betrayal. Jim listened with an astonished, impatient incredulity, and he and Nancy used to laugh late at night in their living room over the tales he brought home of Trotskyist suggestibility. They laughed kindly and softly—so as not to wake the baby—over their Ritz crackers and snappy cheese, and Nancy, full-bosomed, a little matronly already in her flowered house coat, seemed to Jim, by contrast with the people he had just left, a kind of American Athena, a true presiding deity of common sense.

Yet occasionally, when he was alone, when an engagement had fallen through and he was left unoccupied, when Nancy was late getting home in the afternoon, he wondered. What if all these stories were true? What if even some of them were true? How did it happen that he was exempt from this campaign of terror? He had not compromised; he had spoken his mind. Did the others, the Stalinists, hope that he would "come around"? Or did they believe that terroristic methods would not work with him? This thought was pleasing and he would hold it at arm's length for a moment, contemplating it, in a kind of Boy Scout daydream of torture and manly defiance, of Indians and the Inquisition, and the boy with his finger in the dike. But humor inevitably challenged this view; the dream dissolved; he was left puzzled. Sometimes, a sort of mild panic would follow. He would be overwhelmed by a sense of trespassing on the Trotsky case. It was as if he had come to dinner at the wrong address and the people were very polite and behaved as if he were expected; out of good breeding they would not allow him to explain his mistake, nor would they set him on his way to the right house. Or it was as if he were an extra who had got onto the stage in the wrong scene: the actors went on acting as if he were not there, and nobody furnished him with a pretext for an exit.

Before long, he began to notice in himself a desire to compete, to have some hair-raising experience of his own and vie in martyrdom with the other members. He was ashamed of this wish; at the same time, it confirmed his skepticism. Here, he felt, was the key to the whole business; nobody wanted to be left out of a thing like this; it was the phenomenon that had been noted again and again at spiritualistic séances: people unconsciously began to co-operate with the medium and with each other, so that no one should seem to be deficient in psychic powers.

This shrewd explanation might have satisfied him—if it had not been for John Dewey. . . . The adherence of the dean of American philosophy, which ought to have reassured Jim, worried him profoundly. It never failed to violate Jim's sense of fitness to see this old man, the very apotheosis of the cracker-barrel spirit, deep in conversation with Schachtman or Stolberg, nodding his white head from time to time in acquiescence to some extravagant statement, smiling, agreeing, accepting, supporting. It was like finding your father in bed with a woman. And the most painful thing about it was that the old man should be so *at home* here, so much more at home than Jim could ever be. *He takes to it like a duck to water*, committee members would say, proudly and affectionately to each other, and Jim could not deny that this was so. Dewey truly appeared to have no reservations; you could not call that mild irony a reservation, for it was a mere habit, like his Yankee drawl, that was so ingrained, so natural, that it seemed to have no specific relation to the outside world, but only to his own, interior life. Whenever Jim heard that dry voice swell out at a mass meeting in anger and eloquence, he squirmed in his seat, not knowing whether to feel embarrassed for Dewey or for himself. The very kinship he felt with the old man served to deepen and define his own sense of alienation, as in a family the very resemblance that exists between the members serves to make more salient the individual differences. It was impossible, moreover, to doubt Dewey's judgment, and when Jim saw that Dewey believed the stories of persecution (he had indeed been a little bit persecuted—"annoyed," Dewey put it, himself), Jim, unwillingly, began to believe too.

Now the ground was cut from under him. This was perhaps the first time in his life that he was subscribing to something which he could not check against his own experience or psychology, which his own experience and psychology seemed, in fact, to contradict. There was no sub-jective correlative; he was no longer his own man. Yet once he had conceded the point, the evidence began rushing in at him. A hundred incidents that he had forgotten or ig-nored or discounted marshaled themselves before his eyes. He remembered the prominent names that had dropped off the committee's letterhead, the queer, defamatory sto-ries he had encountered everywhere about members of the committee, the books unaccountably rejected by publish-ers. What was more devastating, he saw now (a thing he had denied a month before) that the Stalinist campaign of intimidation had already had its effect on the *Liberal's* policy.

He read down the contributors' column one day and found it a roster of new names—youngsters just out of col-lege, professors from obscure universities, elderly, non-political writers who had been boasting for years that they did not "take sides" and who were now receiving their re-ward. It was hard to know exactly when they had come in, but suddenly they were all there. The whole complexion of the magazine had unobtrusively changed. It was not, precisely, that it had become Stalinist; rather, like some timid and adaptive bird, it was endeavoring to make itself as neutral-colored as possible and fade discreetly into the surrounding landscape. The whole process, he saw, had been a negative one. A few months earlier, Mr. Wendell had resigned—on account of his age, it was said officially. The paper had been made two pages shorter, there were more cartoons, more straight reportage. Shorter articles **in** larger type, not so much political and aesthetic theory. Articles had been limited to two thousand words apiece; the book-review section had been cut in half and a humorous column had been added. Nothing you could put your finger on, yet by these innocent measures the paper had effectively purged itself of Trotskyism, for the fact was that the Trotskyists, anarchists, and other dissidents *did* run to political and aesthetic theory, to articles more than two thousand words long, to book reviews of unpopular novelists and poets.

That same afternoon, he observed for the first time the machinery of exclusion. He came into the literary editor's office; it was her day for seeing book reviewers. A young anti-Stalinist reviewer was standing despondently in front of the shelves, which usually overflowed with books (for the literary editor was rather inefficient about getting things reviewed on time), but which were now unwontedly, desolately empty. Eight or nine popular novels with garish jackets leaned against each other in one corner. The young man had been asking for a new book—Jim did not catch the name. The literary editor shook her head; unfortunately the book had just gone out to a professor at Northwestern. He mentioned another title; that, too, had been assigned—to an instructor at Berkeley. He mumbled something about an article on Silone; the literary editor was not encouraging; she wondered whether you *could* do justice to Silone in fifteen hundred words; the paper was not printing many general articles; she could not promise anything.

She got up from her desk and wandered toward the shelves, gesturing vaguely at the popular novels. "Do us a note of a hundred words on one of these—if you feel like it," she said negligently. The young man shook his head and shambled out of the office; it was perfectly clear that he would not return. The literary editor murmured something pettish about the insularity of New York intellectuals, and Miss Sargent, who had been sitting all the while with averted head, looked up.

"On Broadway they call that the brush-off," she said.

The literary editor affected not to hear.

Miss Sargent continued, looking straight at Jim, speaking in a louder voice.

"Have you heard? I'm being transferred to Labor and Industry. On account of the curtailment of the book-review section—which we all deplore—my duties are being assumed by a stenographer."

"Oh, Margaret," said the literary editor, "you're becoming perfectly impossible. I should think you'd be glad to be out of this. I know I would."

The girl did not answer, but kept on looking at Jim. It was impossible to misread her gaze, which held in it something challenging and at the same time something feminine and suppliant. He met her eyes for an instant, then shook his head hopelessly.

"You girls," he began, intending to say something humorous and pacific, but he could not finish his sentence. He shook his head again, and retreated from the office. As soon as he got into the corridor, however, the truncated conversation continued in his mind. That book reviewer, said a firm light soprano, that unfortunate boy, with his bad complexion, his blue mesh shirt open at the throat, was Stalin's victim just as surely as the silicosis sufferers who had recently been displayed at a Congressional investigation were the victims of industrial capitalism. What the hell, his own voice answered, the young man was probably no great shakes as a writer (he looked like a punk); it was not a question of life and death; the kid was on the WPA and the *Liberal*'s check could do no more than buy him a few beers at the Jumble Shop. Ah yes, the first voice resumed, martyrs are usually unappetizing personally; that is why people treat them so badly; for every noble public man, like Trotsky, you must expect a thousand miserable little followers, but there is really more honor in defending them than in defending the great man, who can speak for himself. His own voice did not reply, and a visual illusion succeeded the auditory one. He saw the figure of the book reviewer splashed on a poster, like the undernourished child in the old Belgian relief stickers; underneath a caption thundered: WHAT ARE YOU GOING TO DO ABOUT IT?

That was the first time. Soon it became a regular thing with Jim to talk to Miss Sargent in his mind. The moment the lights were out at night, the cool, light voice would begin its indictment, and his own voice, grumbling, expostulating, denying, would take up the defense. And in the daytime, Jim would find himself thinking up arguments, saving them, telling himself, "I must be sure to mention this," just as if it were a real conversation he was going home to. He remembered enough of his psychology courses to know that he was not having hallucinations. Though the voice sounded perfectly natural, he did not hear it with his physical ear, but only with his mind. Moreover, the conversations were, in some sense, voluntary; that is, he did not like them, he did not want to have them, yet they did not precisely impose themselves on him, for it was he, unwillingly, of his own free will, who was making them up.

Nevertheless, he was alarmed. It was screwy, he told himself, to spend your time talking to someone who was not there. At the very least, it showed that the person had a hold on you—a disagreeable, unnerving idea. In Jim's world, nobody had a "hold" on anybody else. Yet the fact was (and he had to face it) he was not in the driver's seat any more. For almost as long as he could remember there had been two selves, a critical principled self, and an easygoing, follow-the-crowd, self-indulgent, adaptable self. These two characters had debated comfortably in bed, had "taken stock," defined their differences, maintained an equilibrium. But it was as if, during the Moscow trials, the critical principled self had thrown up the sponge; it had abdicated, and a girl's voice had intruded to take over its function. At some point in those recent months, Jim had ceased to be his own severest critic, but criticism, far from being stilled, had grown more obdurate. When we pass from "I ought to do this" to "You *think* I ought to do this," it seems to us at first that we have weakened the imperative; actually, by externalizing it, we have made it unanswerable, for it is only ourselves that we can come to terms with. And where Jim had once had to meet specific objections from his better nature, he was now confronted with what he imagined to be a general, undiscriminating hostility, a spirit of criticism embodied in the girl that was capricious, feminine, and absolutely inscrutable, so that he went about feeling continually guilty without knowing just what it was he had done. It haunted him that if he could anticipate every objection, he would be safe, but there was no telling *what* this strange girl might find fault with, and the very limitation of his knowledge of her made the number of possible objections limitless.

He longed to act, he told himself, yet the vague enormity of his situation furnished an apparently permanent excuse for inaction. He believed that he was waiting for an issue big enough to take a stand on, but now all issues seemed flimsy, incapable of supporting his increasing weight. In a curious way, his ego had become both shrunken and enlarged; his sense of inadequacy had made him self-important. He began to talk a good deal about "petty" squabbles, tempests in teapots, molehills and mountains. If he were to resign from the *Liberal*, he said to himself, he would have to do so in his own way, for his own reasons. To resign on behalf of some Eighth Street intellectual would be to accept that intellectual as his ally, to step off the high ground of the *Liberal* into the noisome marsh of sectarian politics. And, above all, Jim feared that terrible quicksand, which would surely, he thought, swallow him up alive, if he so much as set a foot over the edge. Here was the paradox: though his immunity from the Stalinist attacks was the immediate cause of his sense of shame (to be spared, ostentatiously, in a general massacre is a distinction reserved for spies, old men, children, and imbeciles), Jim nevertheless found it temperamentally impossible to venture directly into the melee. What he sought was some formula by which he could demonstrate his political seriousness without embroiling himself in any way—a formula which would, in fact, perpetuate his anomalous situation. It was an irony that Jim did not perceive. He only knew that he must postpone action (for the moment, at least), while he yearned at the same time to be acted *upon*.

If the managing editor would only fire him, for example, he would be free, and nothing he did afterwards could be held against him. He might get a job in an advertising agency, or on one of the news magazines; he would be quit at last of leftist politics, and no one could blame him. "Jim Barnett lost his job over that Trotsky business," they would say. "The poor guy is working for *Newsreel* now." The picture of himself as a victim of circumstances, an object of public sympathy, did not displease him; in fact what his heart cried for was some such outcome for his dilemma, an outcome in which his own helplessness should be underlined.

The managing editor, however, seemed not at all disposed to give him this friendly push, and his self-regard would not permit him simply to disengage himself from the struggle as he might have done from a street brawl. In some way, he felt, he was condemned to "stick it out," perhaps indefinitely, and to pay for his non-intervention by sleeplessness, indigestion, and outbursts of irritability with Nancy.

Nevertheless, when the moment came, Jim found it perfectly simple to quit. The managing editor came into his office one afternoon and told him that in accordance with the magazine's new budget, Miss Sargent would have to go. It was purely a matter of seniority; she was the newest employee; it was only fair that she should be the first, et cetera.

"I wish it hadn't worked out that way," she continued, biting her lips and speaking in a confidential tone. "You know how excitable she is, Jim. She'll be sure to think that it has something to do with politics. That letter, you know . . ."

Jim smiled grimly. The *Liberal,* after months of silence, had endorsed the Moscow trials, and "that letter" was a denunciation of the magazine. It had been signed by Miss Sargent, by a number of ex-contributors to the *Liberal,* and by Jim himself.

"But, of course," the managing editor went on, "I forgot! You signed it too. So that shows . . ." She spread out her hands, leaving the sentence unfinished. "You know I would never deny anybody the right of criticism. I'm glad you spoke out if you felt that way. And Miss Sargent, of course, too. And the fact that *you're* continuing on the paper speaks for itself. Still . . ." She paused. "It's the effect on her I'm worried about. She's too bitter already. There's too *much* bitterness in the radical movement. I think we agree about that."

She was silent for a moment. Jim waited.

"Oh, Jim," she burst out at length. "I wish *you* would break it to her. Explain it to her. She'd take it all right coming from you, since you agree with each other politically. You could make her understand . . ."

"You go to hell, Helen," Jim said. The words came as naturally as a reflex and even in his first joy, Jim found time to tell himself that it had been morbid to worry about the matter beforehand. You waited until the right time came and then you acted, without thought, without plan, and your character—your character that you had suspected so unjustly—did not betray you.

The managing editor gasped. Jim took his brown coat and hat from the stand and walked deliberately out of the office. He went down the street to a bar he knew and ordered a Scotch and soda. When he was halfway through the drink, he stepped into the phone booth and called up Miss Sargent at the office.

"Come on down here," he said, "and help me write a letter of resignation."

He went back to wait for her at his table, and suddenly he found himself thinking of a book he would like to write. It would deal with the transportation industries and their relation to the Marxist idea of the class struggle. He thought of the filling stations strung out over America, like beads on the arterial highways, and of the station attendants he had seen in the Southwest, each man lonely as a lighthouse keeper in his Socony or his Shell castle: how were you going to organize them as you could organize workers in a factory? He thought also of the chain-store employees as the frontiersmen of a new kind of empire: The Great Atlantic and Pacific Tea Company—the name had the ring of the age of exploration; it brought to mind the Great South Sea Bubble. Monopoly capitalism was deploying its forces, or, rather, it was obliging its historic enemy, the workers, to deploy theirs. As financial and political power became more concentrated, industry was imperceptibly being decentralized. The CIO might find the answer; on the other hand, perhaps the principle of industrial unionism was already superannuated. There was a great book here somewhere, an important contribution, and now he would have the time to write it. It would have been out of the question of course, had he stayed on the *Liberal.* . . .

"Oh boy!" he said to himself, revolving the book in his mind, marveling at it, accepting it as a sort of heavenly tip for services rendered. He clacked his tongue appreciatively against the roof of his mouth. The bartender looked over at him in surprise, and Jim chuckled to himself. He was tremendously elated. He could hardly wait to get home to tell Nancy, and at the same time, he felt a large tenderness toward the girl who was even now making her way toward him through the snowy streets. He owed it all to her, *of course*. Hadn't she told him from the very beginning that the *Liberal* was a dead end, that if he wanted to make anything of himself, he would have to get off it? And it was on account of her, in the end, that he had been able to do it. If they had not decided to fire her, he might never have . . . He stopped short in his reverie, momentarily sobered. In his excitement he had almost forgotten that she had lost her job. Here he was, ready to begin his real work, but for her the prospect was not bright. No doubt she would be glad to hear that she had made such a nuisance of herself that the managing editor could brook it no longer; there would be the surge of leftist piety, the joy of self-immolation. But, practically speaking, it was going to be hard on her. He himself had money saved, and, with Nancy's income, he could get along well enough. The girl was not so fortunately equipped: he could guess without asking that she had not saved a cent (she was probably in debt), and it would not be easy for her to find another job. *She is going to have a tough time,* he said to himself. And she was not going to like it. She would dramatize her position for a week or so, but when it came down to it, she was not going to enjoy being poor, for Trotsky or anybody else. The thought of the discomfort she would have to endure bit into his happiness; it annoyed him that she should behave with such irresponsibility. She had no right, he told himself, to play for high stakes when she could not afford to lose; it was not ethical; it made the other players at the table uncomfortable. Already, *in absentia,* she had robbed him of a little of his joy.

With a slight effort he brought himself back to the projected book. The excitement revived as he imagined the gray winter afternoons in the public library, the notes on white cards in the varnished yellow box, the olive-green filing cabinet he would install in the spare room. "A second *Das Kapital*," a voice within him murmured, but though he stilled it peremptorily, he could not help but grin in an awkward, lopsided way, as though someone had paid him an absurd, delicious compliment. The strange thing was, it was the girl's voice that had spoken; perhaps, he thought, in years to come, she would read the book and *would* say that to him. By the time the door swung open and she stepped quickly into the bar, he felt very much pleased with her.

He rose to meet her; she extended her hands. He seized them both; they were very cold.

"I lost my gloves," she said.

How feminine of her, he thought, how ungrammatical, how charming! In the last few weeks he had been very unfair to her. This was no Zetkin, no Luxemburg. If the truth were known, she was probably as much out of her depth in sectarian politics as he was. He squeezed her hands.

She sat down.

"Well," he said. "You've lost your job."

"Oh," she murmured, looking grave for an instant. Then she shrugged her shoulders. "I suppose it was about time. But you—" He watched her get the idea. "Did you——?"

"I walked out," he said.

He stared into his glass and hoped that she was not going to be effusive. When he finally looked up at her, however, he saw that she was blushing slightly.

"Thank you very much," she said. "I suppose I ought to tell you that you shouldn't have done it."

"Never mind," he said. "It was a good thing to do, anyway. I feel wonderful. I'm going to write a book. It all just came to me while I've been sitting here, though I guess the idea must have been in the back of my mind for quite a while."

He told her about the book.

"It's a very good idea," she said at last.

"You ought to write a book yourself."

She shook her head.

"A fortune teller told me I was born to fritter away my talents. I wouldn't want to go against my destiny."

He grinned at her. It was a silly remark, and characteristic, too, but it was no longer within her power to make him angry. He could barely recall a time when he had wrestled with her all night in a terrible ideological embrace, though it was not yet twenty-four hours since Nancy had spoken from the next bed and begged him to go into the living room if he could not stop tossing.

She went on talking excitedly and he ordered two more drinks. He had forgotten about the letter of resignation, and he did not want her to go. He had gradually become aware that he would like to sleep with her, but he did not know how to broach the suggestion. The fact that it would not be the first time made it more difficult. All those months in which he had not wanted to sleep with her would have to be wiped out with some brief, tactful sentence, but no satisfactory one occurred to him, partly because he was puzzled as to why, on the one hand, he should want to sleep with her now, and why, on the other, he should not have been sleeping with her all along, since she was undoubtedly an attractive girl.

"I was not free . . ." he muttered, experimentally, to himself. But it would not do. She might want to know in what sense he was free now, and had not been before. In relation to Nancy, he was still tied. Did he mean that his time was now his own, that an afternoon of love could—without too much difficulty—be occasionally slipped into his new schedule? No, he thought decidedly, he did not mean that. The idea of a systematic infidelity was offensive to him; the very notion of assignations, trysts, affected him in much the same way that the notion of crop rotation affects the American farmer. It would not be right, he told himself. You oughtn't to plan a thing like that. Besides, he would be too busy. The new book would need all his energies. It was just this once that he wanted her. "I was not free," he repeated, troubled by these words that had risen to his mind, feeling that they were true in some way that he had not put his finger on. It was as if he had paid off a nagging creditor, a creditor whom for months he had not dared to face, but to whom he could now open the door with the utmost geniality, knowing that there was nothing the man could do to him, knowing that his former fears had been groundless, that the creditor was just a human being like himself.

"You really are a sweet girl," he said, "even if you do act like a Trotskyite dragon."

After the third drink he took her home in a taxi. He decided not to say anything but merely followed her up the stairs and kissed her as she stood in the doorway. She put her hands on his shoulders and pushed him back with a look of astonishment; for a moment, he thought she was going to bar the way to him. She dropped her hands, however, and went on into the apartment. She sank into a chair. He shut the door behind him and waited.

"I'm sorry, Jim," she said. "I'd like to celebrate your resigning and the book and everything, but I just can't."

"It's not a question of a celebration," he said stiffly.

"Well . . ." she conceded, as if not disposed to argue. Her whole aspect was vague and weary. There was a look of strained kindness about her, as she sat in the chair, her coat falling loosely about her; she might have been a schoolteacher kept after hours.

"Margaret," he said, "I can't explain, but the set-up wasn't right before. Working in the same office . . ."

"Yes," she agreed. "It would have been a terrible mess." She smiled.

"It hasn't been any picnic for me, Margaret," he said in an aggrieved tone. "I still feel the same way about you."

"That's wonderful," she said with her first touch of sharpness. "I would like to feel the same way about you (I really would), but I can't. I don't seem to be able to bank my fires. That's a man's job, I suppose."

He frowned. There was some ugly implication in that metaphor of hers, something he did not want to examine at the moment.

With a dim idea of being masterful, he strode across the room and half-lifted her to her feet. He attempted a long close kiss, pressing her body firmly against his. In a moment, however, he let her go, for, though she kissed him back, he could feel no response at all. It was not that she was deliberately stifling her feelings (if he could have believed that, he would have been encouraged to go on); rather, she seemed preoccupied, bored, polite. It was like kissing Nancy when she had toast in the toaster.

She walked to the door with him.

"Good-bye," she said. "Good luck with your book. And don't think I don't appreciate . . ."

"Forget it," he said.

He closed the door behind him, feeling slightly annoyed. In some way, he thought, he had been given the run-around. When you came right down to it, he had quit his job for her sake. What more did she want? "The hell with her," he said, dismissing her from his mind. "After all, she knew I was married." The thought of Nancy brought him up short. Under a street lamp he drew out his watch. If he took a taxi, he would still be in time for dinner. And after dinner, he promised himself, he would make love to Nancy. He would have her put on her blue transparent nightgown, the one he had given her for Christmas and she had only worn once. Making love to her would be more fun than usual because he was still steamed up about that girl. He sensed at once, as he raised his hand for a taxi, that this sexual project of his was distinctly off-color; yet his resolution hardly wavered. In the first place, Nancy would never know; in the second place, he was entitled to some recompense for the moral ordeal he had been through that day. Later on, in bed, his scruples served him well; where a thicker-skinned man would have known that he was simply sleeping with his wife, Jim's active conscience permitted him to see the conjugal act as a perverse and glamorous adultery, an adultery which, moreover, would never land him in a divorce court or an abortionist's waiting room.

No one could ever understand, afterwards, what happened about that book. When his resignation from the *Liberal* was made public, all sorts of people congratulated Jim. Literary columns in the newspapers reported that he was at work on a study of the transportation industries which promised to revise some of the classical conceptions of Marxism. Several publishers wrote him letters, hoping that he would allow them to be the first to see . . . It was felt in general that he was coming into his manhood, that his undeniable talents were at last to be employed in a work of real scope. Jim himself began the task with enthusiasm. He did six months of research in the public library, and amassed a quantity of notes. Then he wrote two chapters. He worked over them diligently, but somehow from the very first sentence, everything was wrong. The stuff lacked punch. Jim saw it at once, and the publishers he sent the chapters to saw it also. It did not sound, they wrote him reluctantly, like the real Barnett. On the other hand, it did not sound (as he had hoped it would) like a major work. It was solemn enough but it was not momentous. What was missing was the thing Jim had found in Marx and Veblen and Adam Smith and Darwin, the dignified sound of a great calm bell tolling the morning of a new age. Jim reread these masters and tried to reproduce the tone by ear, but he could not do it. He became frightened and went back to the public library; perhaps, as someone had suggested, the material was under-researched. He could not bring himself to go on with the writing, for that would be sending good money after bad. When he got an offer from the illustrated magazine *Destiny*, the businessman's *Vogue*, as someone called it, to do an article on rural electrification, he accepted at once. Traveling with a photographer all over America, he would have the chance, he thought, to see his own subject at first hand. He could do the piece for *Destiny*, and then return to his own work, refreshed from his contact with living reality. However, when the article was done he took a job with *Destiny*, promising himself that he would work on his book over the week ends. He started at ten thousand a year.

The job took more of his time than he had expected, and his friends eventually stopped asking him about his book. Once in a while someone would question Nancy, and she would contract her brows in a little worried frown. He was working much too hard, she would say. He had counted on a vacation to get back to the book, but when the time came, he was on the verge of nervous exhaustion and she had had to take him to Havana for a rest. "You have no idea," she was fond of exclaiming, "what a terrific toll *Des-*

tiny takes of its writers. It burns them right out. If Jim didn't keep up his tennis, and get away to the country every possible week end, he'd be in the hospital right now."

Everyone sympathized with Nancy on this point. The research girls in the *Destiny* office worried a good deal about Jim, and they, too, thought it was a great pity that he did not have time to do his own writing. Jim himself took a certain pride in being overworked, especially since he was not underpaid—the original ten thousand had been raised several times and he got a handsome bonus at Christmas every year. The truth was that he enjoyed working on *Destiny*. Outsiders imagined that his radicalism kept him in hot water there, but this was not true. He wrote about American youth, farm security, South America, musical comedy, and nylon. He said what he pleased, and if the article seemed too "strong," it was given to someone else to modify. He was not obliged to eat his own words. Now he was not so much a writer as a worker on an assembly line. He did his own task conscientiously, and since the finished product was always several removes away from him, it was, in a certain sense, not his concern. He would send an article down from his desk with a droll, schizophrenic, pessimistic air, as if to say, "You're on your own now, God help you." And as his own productions passed more and more beyond his control, he relished more and more the control of data, which was the singular achievement of the *Destiny* machine. Jim liked the facts that were served up to him daily by the girl research workers, liked the feeling that there was nothing, absolutely nothing in the world, that he could not find out by pressing a bell, sending a telegram, or taking a plane. He liked the fact-finding trips that he took with a photographer; he had only to mention the name of the magazine and he would be whisked into a farmer's homestead, an actress' dressing room, a Fifth Avenue mansion, a cold-water flat in an old-law tenement, a girls' college, an army camp, a club, a great hotel. And he saw everything *from the inside;* he was free to examine the laundry lists, the budgets, the toilet facilities, the sleeping arrangements, of any American family he chose to visit; he could ransack a desk or peer into an icebox; nobody but a tax assessor had ever had such freedom, and where the tax assessor was detested, Jim's subjects welcomed him into their homes, their hobbies, their businesses. It pleased them that someone should know *all about them* and write it down and publish it with pictures. It pleased Jim too; it gave him a great feeling of responsibility, as if he were a priest or God.

He believed—most of the time—that he was doing an important work. He still considered himself a Marxist, but he saw that the Marxists were never going to get anywhere until they took a real look at the American scene and stopped deluding themselves with theory. Occasionally, after an argument at some literary cocktail party, he felt that he would like to pick up the whole radical movement by the scruff of its neck and rub its nose hard into the good American dirt. He himself, whatever his failings, was at least setting the facts on record; in a time of confusion like the present this was a valuable thing to do. Moreover, he was playing a part, a rather significant one, in the molding of public opinion. It was true that the publisher of *Destiny* was a reactionary in many ways—potentially, he might even be a fascist—but on certain points he was progressive. He believed that the old-style capitalism would have to go, and now and then he would allow Jim to say so in a signed editorial that was termed by everyone in the office "astonishingly outspoken." Jim had come, he told himself frequently, a long way from the *Liberal,* and he was proud of the fact. He looked back on the years he had spent there with a kind of amazed disgust. How could he have wasted his time so? The *Liberal* was no more revolutionary than *Destiny;* it published nothing but muddleheaded opinion; it paid poorly, and it had no influence. No matter what his mood, Jim never doubted for a moment that his resignation had been the most sensible act of his life.

It was not the memory of the *Liberal* that caused Jim, whenever he got drunk, to abuse the publisher of *Destiny,* to contrast his lot unfavorably with that of his radical friends, to protest with tears in his eyes that he was doing it for the wife and kiddies. This lachrymose, self-accusatory stage was usually followed by an aggressive stage in which he told anyone who was still a socialist how he had waked up to himself back in 1937 and what a fine thing it had been for him. These contradictory demonstrations puzzled his interlocutors, who did not see that in the first stage he was comparing his actual work to some imaginary lost vocation, a life of dedication and scholarship which he had

in reality never been attracted to, and in the second stage
he was comparing his present career on *Destiny* to his former job on the *Liberal*. The majority of Jim's friends paid
no attention to the second stage of his drunkenness, ascribing
anything he might say to the effects of alcohol ("liquor hits
some people that way"); it was the first stage that impressed
them. Here, they thought, he spoke from the heart; here
the honest, decent man revealed himslf to be incorruptible;
though obliged to make his living by working on *Destiny*,
he did not deceive himself as to its true character; he re-
belled, if only on Saturday nights. Actually, however, the
utterances of the second stage were "real," and the lamen-
tations were largely histrionic.

The truth was that Jim had changed, though the out-
ward signs of it were still so faint as to pass undetected by
his intimates. He got drunk oftener, there was no denying
it, but, as Nancy said, the strain of being a writer for *Destiny* had made alcohol "an absolute necessity" for him. His
boyish features were now slightly blurred; his awkward,
loose-jointed figure was fatter than it had been, and his
habitual sprawl was not so becoming to it. Imperceptibly,
he had passed from looking pleasantly unkempt to looking
seedy. The puzzled frown had become chronic with him;
he was, in fact, professionally bewildered. And yet there
was something dimly spurious about all this: his gait, his
posture, his easy way of talking, half-belied the wrinkles
on his forehead. In his young days he had been as lively
and nervous as a squirrel; women had been fond of comparing him to some woodland creature. Today that alert-

ness, that wariness, was gone. The sentry slept, relaxed, at his post, knowing that an armistice had been arranged with the enemy. In some subtle way, Jim had turned into a comfortable man, a man incapable of surprising or being surprised. The hairshirt he wore fitted him snugly now; old and well used, it no longer prickled him; it was only from the outside that it appeared to be formidable.

Jim knew that in middle-class intellectual circles his career was regarded as a tragedy of waste. Half-unconsciously, he fostered this illusion, for it permitted him to enjoy what was really a success story, secure from the envy of the less privileged. It was commonly believed that Nancy was the villain, Nancy who had gone and had two more children, Nancy who needed a house in the country, Nancy who kept his nose to *Destiny*'s grindstone. And whenever they had friends in, Jim would grumble good-naturedly about expenses, the children's new shoes, the tricycles, the nursery school. Occasionally, during one of these mock tirades someone would look over at Nancy with a touch of concern or curiosity—perhaps these complaints were a little hard on her? But Nancy would always be smiling with genuine sweetness, for Nancy knew the duties of a wife, and knew too that Jim loved the children, the garden, the new radio, just as much as if not more than she did.

Undoubtedly, Jim was still a good guy. On the magazine, he was always on the side of the underdog. He treated his subordinates with consideration, and he helped organize the Newspaper Guild chapter. He voted for Roosevelt, though *Destiny* was pro-Willkie, and when the Trotskyites

were indicted for sedition in Minneapolis he sent them a
check through the Civil Liberties Union. If he showed a
certain ruthlessness—socially—to people who did not count,
he had the excuse of being extremely busy, preoccupied
with the great issues of the day. And he was always interested in the common man. He could spend hours talking
to taxi drivers, grocers, swing musicians, real-estate agents,
small lawyers or doctors who had married old school friends
of Nancy's. These people and their opinions "counted" for
Jim; it was only the intellectuals, the unsuccessful, opin-
ionated, unknown intellectuals, who had nothing, so far as
he could see, to say to him.

Margaret Sargent belonged to this tiresome class. In
memory of old times, he always talked to her a few minutes when he met her at parties, but her sarcasms bored
him, and, unless he were tight, he would contrive to break
away from her as quickly as possible. It irritated him to
hear one day that she had applied for a job on *Destiny;* he
was perfectly justified, he said to himself, in telling the
publisher that she would not fit in. It would be intolerable
to have her in the office. He owed her no debt; all that had
been canceled long ago. And yet . . . He sat musing at his
desk. Why was it that she, only she, had the power to make
him feel, feel honestly, unsentimentally, that his life was a
failure, not a tragedy exactly, but a comedy with pathos?
That single night and day when he had been almost in
love with her had taught him everything. He had learned
that he must keep down his spiritual expenses—or else go
under. There was no doubt at all of the wisdom of his

choice. He did not envy her; her hands were empty: she was unhappy, she was poor, she had achieved nothing, even by her own standards. Yet she exasperated him, as the spendthrift will always exasperate the miser who feels obliged to live like a pauper, lest his wealth be suspected and a robber plunder him. But there was more than that. What did he regret, he asked himself. If he had it to do over again, he would make the same decision. What he yearned for perhaps was the possibility of decision, the instant of choice, when a man stands at a crossroads and knows he is free. Still, even that had been illusory. He had never been free, but until he had tried to love the girl, he had not known he was bound. It was self-knowledge she had taught him; she had showed him the cage of his own nature. He had accommodated himself to it, but he could never forgive her. Through her he had lost his primeval innocence, and he would hate her forever as Adam hates Eve.

SIX *Ghostly Father, I Confess*

My gostly fader, I me confess,
First to God and then to you,

That at a window—wot ye how?—
I stale a kiss of grete sweteness,
Which don was out of aviseness;
But it is doon not undoon now.
My gostly fader, I me confess,
First to God and then to you.

But I restore it shall doutless
Again, if so be that I mow;
And that to God I make a vow
And ells I axe foryefness.
Gostly fader, I me confess,
First to God and then to you.

T H E eyes gleamed benevolently behind the glasses. If she
turned her head on the cushion, she could see them, and

she kept doing this from time to time, hoping to surprise them in an expression of disapproval, of astonishment or regret—anything but that kindly neutrality. But they did not change, and finally she gave it up, dropped her head back on the cushion, and tried to relax. It was really against the rules (she supposed) to be flopping around there like a fish. He had never scolded her for it; now and then he would say gently, "Don't worry about what *I* think. Just let your own thoughts come."

"I dreamed I was seventeen," she said, "and I was matriculating at a place called Eggshell College." She could not resist a teasing smile and another glance up at him. "I must have dreamed that just to please you. It's custom-made. The womb fantasy."

"Go on with the dream," he said.

"Well," she continued, "there was a sort of an outing cabin. We had one at college. It was supposed to be great fun to spend the week end in it. I never did. I thought it was silly—you know, a vestigial trace of the goofy old days when they had chafing dishes and spreads and college sings and went to the Cider Mill for a binge. My aunt had the idea that college was still like that," she went on. "She tried to give me an electric doughnut-maker to take away with me when I was a freshman. It was the only present she ever offered me."

She knew without looking that she had coaxed a smile out of him. It was all right, then; she could go on. He understood her attitude toward the outing cabin. Often it was not so easy. She would spend half a session trying to show him, say, that a man they both knew was a ridiculous character, that a movie they had both seen was cheap. And it would be hopeless, absolutely hopeless, for he *was* that man, he *was* that movie; he was the outing cabin, the Popular Front, the League of American Writers, the *Nation,* the *Liberal,* the *New Republic,* George S. Kaufman, Helen Hayes, Colonial wallpaper, money in the bank, and two cocktails (or was it one?) before dinner. When she had worn herself out, he would remind her patiently, "It doesn't matter what I think, you know." But it did matter, of course. Sometimes it seemed to her that her analysis could never be finished until he could purge himself of the maple furniture in his waiting room, the etching of the cathedral at Chartres that hung above his desk, the subscription to *Newsweek* that never ran out. Someone had once suggested to her that all this was a matter of policy, that a psychoanalyst in the decoration of his professional quarters aimed deliberately at that colorless objectivity, that rigorous job-lot asceticism that can be seen in its purest form in the residential hotel room. The notion was pleasant but not really plausible. It was impossible to think of Dr. James as a male Cinderella who lived dangerously every night after office hours, and all day Sundays.

"What are you smiling about?" he asked.

"I'm thinking rude thoughts about you."

Damn my stream of consciousness, her mind said. Why must it keep harping on this embarrassing topic?

"Let's have them," he exclaimed, with that ghastly, hand-regulated cheerfulness that seemed to spurt out of him the more eagerly, the more unpleasant were the facts to be faced. To listen to him, you might think that someone had just set a wonderful dinner before him.

"Oh, Dr. James," she sighed. "Let's skip it this time. You know what I think about you. It doesn't give me any pleasure to say it to your face."

"But your picture of me is very important," he said, in his pedagogical manner. "Not for what it says about me, but for what it says about *you*."

This angered her slightly. So he took no stock in her opinion, labeled it "aggression against the analyst," and dismissed it from his mind. Very well, then. . . .

"I was thinking," she said, "how utterly fantastic it is to imagine you on a tear."

"Don't you suppose I have any fun?" There was a certain wistfulness in the question that must have got in by mistake.

"No doubt you do," she said, "but I think you must have to work awfully hard at it."

"What do you suppose I do for relaxation?"

Relaxation, she thought; there is the key word. There the poor pedant betrays himself.

"Well," she said, "you see about six plays a year. Your wife makes a list of the things that are really worth while, and you check them off one by one. You get the tickets well in advance, and you generally take another couple with you. You never go on the spur of the moment; you never take standing room. Sometimes somebody in your party knows the girl who is playing the ingenue, and then you go backstage afterwards. You meet some of the actors and think it's a lot of fun. Once in a while, you go to a benefit concert with your mother or your wife's mother. Myra Hess for the British Relief. You like the movies, and you never miss one that the *New Yorker* recommends. Now and then, if your party is feeling particularly reckless, you go to a swing-music joint. You're not much of a dancer, but you ask the other guy's wife to dance once; after that you sit out because the floor is too crowded. In the summer you commute to your mother-in-law's place at Larchmont or Riverside. There is a nice crowd of young doctors there, and you kid each other about who is going to go into the water first. Probably there is a certain amount of splashing, but nobody loses his temper, and afterwards you play medicine ball on the beach. Your wife likes tennis, but you don't go in for it, on account of your eyes. Your wife has a three-quarter-length silver-fox coat and several very dear girl friends. You take excellent care of your health. You have small feet and are proud of it, and this is your only foible."

"What makes you so sure of all this?"

"Oh, I don't know, I've got a good eye for social types, and I've had a lot of practice. When I was in college, I was a perennial house guest. I never went home for vacations, you know."

She was anxious, now, to change the subject. She had enjoyed doing that malicious portrait, but suddenly toward the end her self-confidence had wavered. Supposing she were wrong? He would not tell her. She would never know. It was like doing an algebra problem and finding that the answers were missing from the back of the book. She felt the ground give way beneath her.

"Nothing I could do would surprise you?" he said.

She began to cry.

"Oh!" she exclaimed. "Why do you lead me on so? It's not fair! You make me say all these awful things to you, and then you won't even tell me whether I'm right or not."

The tears streamed from her eyes. She opened her pocketbook and found, as usual, no handkerchief. He took a box of Kleenex from a drawer and handed it to her silently.

"Thank you," she said, still sobbing. "Do you keep that specially for me or do all your patients weep?"

He did not answer. He never answered questions of this sort.

"What made you cry?" he said at length, in that falsely casual tone he used whenever he asked her an important question.

"You made me feel like a fool," she said. "I extended myself and you sat and watched. It was like one of those exposure dreams. You go into a restaurant and you think how beautiful and chic you are. You even pose a little, toss your head, draw off your gloves very, very slowly, like an actress. And then all of a sudden you look down and you see that you have nothing on but a pair of pink pants. And the worst of it is that nobody shows the slightest surprise; there is no commotion; the headwaiter doesn't come and ask you to leave. Everyone goes on eating and talking, so that you think that maybe your eyes have deceived you, and you look stealthily down again, hoping to find your clothes back on. But no; you are still in the same condition. Then you try to tell yourself that perhaps nobody has noticed anything, that if you behave very, very quietly and do not call attention to yourself, your lapse will pass unobserved. But all the time you know that this is not true. They are all watching you, but out of cruelty they will give no sign. If one of your companions were to say, "Why, Meg, you're undressed," the situation would be saved. You could exclaim, "Why, gee, I am," and people would lend you things and laugh and fuss over you, and the whole thing would turn into one of those jolly Embarrassing Moments that readers send in to the *Daily Mirror.* " *'Imagine my mortification, but there I was without a stitch of clothes!'* "

Dr. James laughed.

"Yes," he said. "But what is there about you that you don't want me to see?" He spoke softly now, in the tone of a conspirator in a Grade B movie. "What is it, Meg, that you are so ashamed of?"

She pressed her hands wearily to her forehead. If he would give up this whispering, she could forgive everything. It made them both ridiculous. She longed to reply in a sepulchral voice, "Dr. James, when I was a little girl, I buried my four-year-old cousin alive." *(Sensation in the courtroom!)* "But don't tell anybody." However, these miserable jokes of hers wasted a great deal of time. She knew exactly what would follow. He would scribble furiously in his notebook for a few seconds, and then the questions would come. Did you ever play with a four-year-old cousin? Did you ever want to bury anybody alive? Where did you get this idea of interment? And so on, through *The Last Days of Pompeii, A Cask of Amontillado,* and the giant, whatever his name was, who slept restlessly under Aetna. Matthew Arnold, Empedocles. And Karl Marx: "weighs like an Alp" on the something-or-other.

"Nothing, Dr. James, nothing. There's nothing I ever did that I haven't told you." (But what about the time she had stolen the ring from the five-and-ten and her aunt had made her take it back and confess to the manager? Could it be that? Oh, surely not, her common sense replied. All children steal, and she had already told him of a half a dozen other childish thefts: the cookies from the pantry, the small change from her aunt's bureau, the dime for the collection plate she had spent on candy. Oh, surely not! And yet . . . What if it *were* important and she failed to tell him? What if her reluctance to delay over a trifle really masked an unconscious fear? In this room, you never knew whether you were putting obstacles in the way or clearing the path. It was a question of relevance, but how could you determine *what* was relevant to the Unknown?)

Fortunately, he was speaking and she did not have to decide.

"Understand me," he said. "I don't think it's anything you *did*. It's a feeling that you have about yourself, a feeling that there is something about you that you have to conceal."

He means sex, she thought with relief. It was not the ring, after all. She could feel her mind wrinkle into a smile. We are heading for the castration complex, she told herself, the horror of the little girl when she discovers that an important part of her is missing.

"I don't believe in it," she said aloud.

"Don't believe in what?"

"All this castration nonsense."

"How do you know I was going to mention that?"

"Weren't you?"

"Well, as a matter of fact, I was." (Ah, she thought, without pleasure, I can read him like a book.) "But," he continued, "I am not trying to foist this idea on you. It was you who brought it up."

"Oh, Dr. James," she murmured reproachfully. "You turn everything to your own advantage. If I can read your mind, you say that I put the idea there."

"No," he said. "Think! What are the pink pants in your dream there for? What are they hiding?"

She looked quickly up at him, struck by his question, proud of him for having asked it. Perhaps he was not so stupid as she feared.

"It's true," she admitted, "when men have exposure dreams, they're always completely naked. Most women, too. The pink pants are a little idiosyncrasy of my own. Maybe you've got it, Dr. James." She felt suddenly excited and gay. Everything was going to be all right. They were on the scent. The fugitive, criminal self lay hiding in a thicket, but the hounds of the intellect were hot in pursuit. Ah, she thought, thank God for the mind, the chart, the compass. Of course, the universe had to be meaningful. There can be no question without an answer; if you throw a ball up, it must come down. Her life was not mere gibberish; rather, it was like one of those sealed mystery stories where the reader is on his honor not to go beyond a certain page until he has guessed the identity of the murderer. She had come to that imperative blank page again and again and stopped and retraversed her ground, looking for the obvious, unobtrusive clue, the thing that everyone overlooked and that was nevertheless as plain as the nose on your face. *"The Clue of the Pink Pants,"* she said to herself. "The publishers take pride in announcing a new kind of detective story by a young author." But, seriously, if that were really it . . .

Then she could go on. She paused to examine this phrase, the vague, dramatic resonance of it, the hollowness of the two *o*'s echoing in a triumph of onomatopoeia the emptiness of the mind that framed it. It was a phrase that came to her lips a dozen times a day. Bumping along on a Madison Avenue bus, she would find herself hammering her fist on her knees and crying out to herself in a sort of whispered shriek, "I can't go on, I CANNOT GO ON." And at home, in the apartment on Sutton Place ("not one of the really smart ones, my dear, just one of Vincent Astor's remodeled tenements"), she would suddenly set her fork down on her plate and say to her husband, "I can't go on. Listen to me, Frederick, I can't go on." She would watch the surprise invade his anxious face, the pain, the irrita-

tion, the Do-we-have-to-go-through-all-this-again, the doubt
(tact or brutality, which was the better method?), the desire to get through the meal in peace, the final decision to
humor her until the maid brought the coffee in. "Finish
your supper, my dear," he would say, calmly, easily, so as
not to put pressure on her. In the end, she would pick up
her fork again and, with an exaggerated listlessness, begin
to eat. This was what she could not forgive herself: the
capitulation. If she had any strength of character, she
would commit suicide. But they would never find *her* body
in the river. Ah, no, not she! She knew which side her
bread was buttered on. Better a live coward than a dead
hero, as her colored maid always said. "Cemetery's full of
heroes," she could hear the soft, wicked Negro voice. *Lace-
daemonians, shed a tear . . . Maestius lacrimis Simonideis.*
The distich of grief was not for her. She remembered how
in boarding school, bemused by sad poetry out of an an-
thology, she had sat half one night with her feet hanging
out her window, knowing that she would never have the
heart to jump, yet telling herself from moment to moment
that *of course* in five minutes, ten minutes, fifteen, she
would. When, at last, she had crept back into her bed, cold
and dispirited, the romantic melancholy had blown away,
leaving her with a mild depression, for she had in truth
secn her own grave, the narrow, schoolgirl's bed with its
regulation blanket which she would always, however late,
return to. It was characteristic, she thought now, that she
had not even caught a cold.

"But why should you have committed suicide?" Dr.

James had said. "You reproach yourself unnecessarily."
"You have got everything upside down," her husband told
her. And from their point of view, they were quite right.
Why shouldn't she finish her dinner, love her husband,
have a baby, stay alive? Where was the crime? There was
the class crime, to be sure, yet it was not for having money
that she hated herself, but (be honest, she murmured) for
having some but not enough. If she could have been very
rich . . . It was the ugly cartoon of middle-class life that
she detested, Mr. and Mrs., Jiggs and Maggie, the Norths
in the *New Yorker*. And the more stylish you tried to
make it, smearing it over with culture and good taste,
Swedish modern and Paul Klee, the more repellent it became: the cuspidors and the silk lampshades in the funny
papers did not stab the heart half so cruelly as her own
glass shelves with the white pots of ivy, her Venetian
blinds, her open copy of a novel by Kafka, all the objects
that were waiting for her at home, each in its own patina
of social anxiety. Ah God, it was too sad and awful, the
endless hide-and-go-seek game one played with the middle
class. If one could only be sure that one did not belong to
it, that one was finer, nobler, more aristocratic. The truth
was she hated it shakily from above, not solidly from below, and her proletarian sympathies constituted a sort of
snub that she administered to the middle class, just as a
really smart woman will outdress her friends by relentlessly
underdressing them. Scratch a socialist and you find a snob.
The semantic test confirmed this. In the Marxist language,
your opponent was always a *parvenu,* an *upstart,* an *ad-*

venturer, a politician was always *cheap,* and an opportunist *vulgar.* But the proletariat did not talk in such terms; this was the tone of the F.F.V. What the socialist movement did for a man was to allow him to give himself the airs of a marquis without having either his title or his sanity questioned.

No, it was not really the humanitarian side of socialism that touched her; though she was moved by human misery when it was brought to her attention, if she went to buy a suit at Bonwit Teller, she was never troubled by irrelevant memories of the slums she had passed through on her way. Her aunt had been one of those pious women who could not look at a garbage pail without being reminded of the fact that there were people in the world who had nothing to eat. "It's a sin to throw that away," she was always saying, and her hyperestheticism on this point allowed her to practice an extreme parsimony with a good conscience. But she herself, thank God, was not like that. In this respect, she took after her father, who in his rather uninspired way had been fond of good cigars, good Bourbon, *eau lilas végétale,* crabmeat, alligator pears, and hotel suites. It was curious, she thought, that all the Puritan penny-pinching should have been on the Catholic side of her family, while her father, that stern Yankee, with his thin skin, his methodical habits, his civic-mindedness, his devout sense of what was proper, should have spent his life buying encyclopedia sets, worthless real estate, patents on fantastic inventions, and have died, to everyone's astonishment, overdrawn at the bank. What a strange childhood she had had! ("No wonder," Dr. James sometimes murmured, in a slightly awestruck voice, "no wonder," meaning no wonder she had turned out so badly. And it was true, she supposed, Freud would have labored in vain if she had not ended up, sobbing, on a psychoanalyst's blue couch. She was a real Freudian classic, and as such faintly monstrous, improbable, like one of those French plays that demonstrate as if on a blackboard the axioms of the Romantic movement. It was not merely a distaste for the obvious that had led both her and the doctor to avoid, insofar as it was possible, lengthy discussions of her childhood. The subject frightened them both, for it suggested to them that the universe is mechanical, utterly predictable, frozen, and this in its own way is quite as terrible as the notion that the universe is chaotic. It is essential for our happiness, she thought, to have both the pattern and the loose ends, to roughen the glassy hexameter with the counter-rhythm of speech.)

Up to the time her mother had died, she had been such an elegant little girl. She remembered her ermine neckpiece and the ermine muff that went with it, her two baby rings with the diamonds in them, the necklace of seed pearls. All a little on the ostentatious side, she admitted, but it had been an era of bad taste. Then, after the flu was over, and mamma did not come home from the hospital, Aunt Clara had moved in, the rings were put in the vault (to keep for you until you're older), the ermine set wore out, the velocipede broke, the white sand darkened in the sandpile, there were prunes and rice pudding on the table, and the pretty little girl who looked (everybody said) so much like her mother was changed into a stringy, bow-legged child with glasses and braces on her teeth, long underwear, high shoes, blue serge jumpers that smelled, and a brown beaver hat two sizes too big for her.

Ah, she said to herself now, I reject this middle-class tragedy, this degenerated Victorian novel where I am Jane Eyre or somebody in Dickens or Kipling or brave little Elsie Dinsmore fainting over the piano. I reject the whole pathos of the changeling, the orphan, the stepchild. I reject this trip down the tunnel of memory which resembles nothing so much as a trip down the Red Mill at Coney Island, with my aunt and her attributive razor strop substituting for Lizzie Borden and her ax. I reject all those tableaux of estrangement: my father in his smoking jacket at the card table with his nightly game of solitaire forever laid out before him, my aunt with her novel by Cardinal Wiseman that she is reading for the fifteenth time, and myself with the cotton handkerchief that I must hem and re-hem because the stitches are never small enough; I deny the afternoon I deliver my prize-winning essay at the Town Auditorium and there is no family there to applaud me because my father is away on a hunting trip, and my aunt, having just beaten me for my error in winning the prize ("You are too stuck-up already"), is at home in her bedroom having hysterics; and also the scene at the summer resort where the lady looks up from the bridge table and utters her immortal tag line, "Surely, Mr. Sargent, this isn't *your* daughter!" It is all too apropos for acceptance.

Yet what were you going to do? You could not treat your life-history as though it were an inferior novel and dismiss it with a snubbing phrase. It had after all been like that. Her peculiar tragedy (if she had one) was that her temperament was unable to assimilate her experience; the raw melodrama of those early years was a kind of daily affront to her skeptical, prosaic intelligence. She remembered the White Russian gentleman she had met once at a party. They were asking him about his escape from the Soviets, and he had reached the point in his story where he saw his brother shot by the Bolsheviks. Here, at the most harrowing moment of his narrative, he faltered, broke off, and finally smiled, an apologetic, self-depreciatory smile which declared, "I know that this is one of the clichés of the Russians in exile. They have all seen their brothers or sisters shot before their eyes. Excuse me, please, for having had such a commonplace and at the same time such an unlikely experience." That terrible smile had filled her with love and pity; she had "recognized" him at once, and afterwards on the street she had kissed him, because she too knew what it was to have a sense of artistic decorum that like a hoity-toity wife was continually showing one's poor biography the door.

If only she could have been disinherited in some subtle, psychological way.... If her alienation from her father could have been expressed in any terms but those crude, shameful ones of food, money, clothes. If that tactless lady's question had not been written quite so large in all the faces she remembered. She had seen it a thousand times, wherever she went with her father, in the eyes of the Pullman porter, the traveling salesman, the waiter in the ladies' annex at the Athletic Club downtown. How she had looked forward to those excursions with him, and how disastrously they had always ended! It was impossible for her to be a credit to him, to be anything but an anomaly, the Catholic child of a Protestant father, the shabby daughter of a prosperous lawyer, the underbred Irish offspring of a genteel New England parent. Her appearance, her conversation, her appetite—everything was wrong. The sight of a menu would be like a poem to her (buckwheat cakes and country sausage with Real Vermont Maple Syrup); inevitably, she would order too much to eat. But when the food came, her shrunken stomach could not accommodate it: a few bites would instantly bring on that stuffed feeling, and she would set down her fork in despair, seeing the feast on her plate as an image of the Unattainable. Her father never reproved her for this, but each time it happened, his lean face with its prominent lantern jaw would set in sharper lines, and she would know that he was grieved, both on her account and his own. He would have liked to "make it up to her" for the loneliness, the harsh, antiquated discipline that his sister-in-law had brought into the house, but it was impossible. Aunt Clara could be bodily left at home but her spirit presided over her niece like a grim familiar demon.

In a way, it had been better at home, for there the social and religious differences had been given a kind of spatial definition and it was easier to move about. Upstairs there were red votive lamps, altars, and holy pictures (the Sacred Heart, Veronica's veil with the eyes that followed you about the room, Saint Cecilia in sepia striking a heavenly chord on an anachronistic piano), a rich, emotional *décor* that made the downstairs with its China shepherdesses, Tiffany glass, bronze smoking sets, and family photographs look matter-of-fact and faded, just as the stories in the *Century* in the magazine rack in the living room seemed unendurably tame after the religious fiction she found in her aunt's favorite periodicals, where people were always being bitten by tarantulas or cobras, struck by lightning, plagued with leprosy or cholera, cursed in the most ingenious and striking ways by an implacable and resourceful God. It was as if the Catholic Church began on the landing, where her father's suite branched off from the stairway that continued on up to her own room, her aunt's room, her mother's empty room with the French perfume slowly evaporating in the silver atomizers on the dressing-table. Her father never entered her bedroom (except once, with the doctor, when she was sick), yet she knew that he was fond of her, thought her clever because she got high marks and talked back to the sisters. It was some peculiar delicacy that kept him from intruding, the same delicacy that made him say, "Aunt Clara knows what's good for you," "You must do what the Mother Superior says."

If he had been truly indifferent to her, she thought, her position would have been more tolerable. She could have set herself to win his love, or fought him as she did her aunt. But she could not win what she had already, and she

could not fight him either. For a long time, she believed
that perhaps he did not notice, and she began to behave
badly in order to attract his attention. She ran away from
home and spent the night in a museum, behind a cast of
the Laocoön, where an attendant found her the next day
and immediately called a policeman. The idea on the surface of her mind was that she wanted to be put in an
orphan asylum, but in the end she confessed her name and
allowed herself to be led home, because the thing she really
desired was to hear her father say, "Why are you suffering
so? Is it so terrible for you here that you honestly cannot
stand it?" When the policeman brought her in, her father's
face flushed, and she knew that she had disgraced him. He
did not scold her, but neither did he ask any questions.
"Get her something to eat," he said to the maid, while the
young policeman shuffled his feet, glancing from father to
daughter with that expression she was so familiar with, not
knowing whether to leave, because the case seemed somehow unsolved. She watched his eyes take in the living
room. She knew precisely what he was saying to himself.
"Good home, nice kid, prominent family, what the hell is
the matter here? Maybe I was wrong about the kid. Maybe
she's the nigger in the woodpile."

And she did not blame the policeman for thinking this.
In fact, she expected him to think it. All the way home on
the streetcar, seeing him begin to like her, seeing the sympathy spring up (her old man probably beats her), she had
known that it was merely a question of time, that as soon
as he met her father, a stupid, suspicious look would come

over his cop's face, and he would feel a little angry and ridiculous, hurt in his professional pride, as if somebody had picked his pocket. Nevertheless, when he had offered to buy her an ice-cream cone at the drugstore at the end of the car line, she had accepted and gobbled it up quickly, just as later on, she would gobble up friendship, love, compliments, with the full prescience of what would come afterwards, the reproachful look, the averted head, the "You are not what you seemed."

Yet what was she to have done? How explain to the policeman a thing she hardly understood herself, that her father's being a good man was precisely what was the matter, that she was the victim of his conscience, as Isaac nearly was of Abraham's? But here there was no God to step in and say, "That's enough, Mr. Sargent. You have convinced me that you are a man of honor, that you practice religious tolerance and pay your debt to the dead. You may now give in to your natural feelings and get that woman out of your house." *Her father had never liked Aunt Clara.* "Your mother," he said once, succinctly, "was cut from a different bolt of cloth." This, she recognized, was for him the sustaining myth, the classic delusion of the frontier, where a pretty woman is a pretty woman, poverty is no crime, and all the nonsense of family and religion and connections has been left behind in the East, and you do not look down on anybody for his race, except of course a Chinaman or a Jap. You do not permit yourself to remember New England and the Irish workers thronging off the boats, the anti-Catholic riots in Boston; you forget your mother, who would draw aside her skirts when a nun passed, and your father with his stack of Know-Nothing pamphlets. If you are to cut down the forests, lay the trolley tracks, send up the skyscrapers, you need partners in business and domesticity, and there is no time to be choosy. You cannot pause to consider that your wife's grandfather is the historical enemy, the jostling, elbowing immigrant whose cheap labor power pushed your own father out into Illinois and sent you as a young man hurrying farther West, where there was still a little space left.

Her mother's youth and beauty had tempered the amalgam. Nobody could have foreseen that she would die and bequeath her husband Aunt Clara, whose complaints, whose tears, whose blue-white mottled complexion, whose medals and dirty scapulars would put his egalitarian principles to the severest kind of test. Aunt Clara was, in truth, more than he had bargained for, and a more realistic man would have felt himself perfectly justified in calling the deal off, repossessing his daughter, bringing her up according to his own ideas, and letting the Pope go hang. Yet the very *injustice* of the legacy, its unwarranted, unforeseeable character, had moved her father to accept it. The fact that Aunt Clara was personally distasteful to him put her beyond the pale of his criticism, rendered her untouchable, sacred, just as the very real aversion he felt toward Catholic doctrine drove him to punish his daughter if her mark in Catechism was low. She understood this now very well, for she had inherited from him the twisted sense of honor that was always overpaying its debts, extorting from herself and

from others the coin of unnecessary suffering to buy indulgence for a secret guilt, an unacknowledged shame.

Not until she was fifteen, however, did she guess the
real nature of her father's sin, and the bitterness of his pro-
tracted penance. She saw then that to have been locked in
closets, beaten, forbidden to read, have a doll, go to the
movies or the pantomime was as nothing compared to the
agony of permitting these things to happen to your child
in the interests of a religious tolerance that you did not
really feel.

He had taken her to a dance at the house of one of her
Catholic cousins. It was her first evening party. She wore a
pink moiré dress with a big, dark-red velvet bow. She was
new to the crowd of Irish boys home for Thanksgiving
from a Catholic prep school and they kept cutting in and
cutting in and bringing her glasses of weak punch from the
buffet. Suddenly, her father had shoved his way past her
admirers and snatched the glass from her hands. "Get your
coat on," he exclaimed in a strange voice, and began to
push her toward the door. She was nearly crying when they
reached the street, but he took her by the shoulders and
shook her. "God damn it," he said, "you ought to have
more sense than to let those little micks get you drunk.
Can't you see they're trying to make a fool of you?" "Why,
father," she said, "that's not true. They liked me. They
thought I was the prettiest girl . . ." "Stop your nonsense,"
he shouted. "Don't you know that they're all laughing at
you?" She had walked sullenly along beside him telling
herself that it was hopeless, that she would never have a

chance to get married if her father was going to act like this. At the same time, she had sensed that he was right; there *had* been something degrading about her success. The boys *were* awfully common, with their red faces and black hair; the whole party was common. Yet it was strange that her father should have noticed this, for he never made social distinctions. She pondered the word "micks," which came so unexpectedly from him, who had taught her that you must never say nigger or sheeny or dago. All at once, she understood; it was as if he had told her the story of his life, and she was both sorry for him and frightened. In that terrible look on his face, in his hoarse voice, she read the living history of the Irish, the Jews, the Negroes. She felt closer to him than ever before; yet there was no doubt in her mind that her allegiance belonged elsewhere. Let her father vote for Hoover! She was for Al Smith, who used such bad grammar and was married to Mrs. Smith, who looked like all her own dreadful Irish relations rolled into one large woman and decorated with a string of beads. It would have been pleasanter, of course, if Al Smith had been a gentleman, if the Negroes were not colored, and the Jews were not Jewish. Nevertheless . . . Her heart quickened with romantic defiance. She shook off her father's arm and stepped proudly into the car.

But by this time she was free. Aunt Clara had been turned into a housekeeper, to whom no one paid any attention, she herself was in her second year at a good boarding school, she had a clothes allowance and charge accounts, took her friends to lunch at the country club, went to the movies and the theater, and read whatever she pleased. *She had lost her faith.* That was what had done it. In her first year of high school, she came home from the convent one day and announced that she was an atheist. Her aunt had had a fit of hysterics and sent for the parish priest. Her father had said nothing, but when she refused to go to Mass the following Sunday, he picked her up and carried her out to the car, while she kicked at his legs and screamed. "You can send me there," she kept repeating, "but you can't make me go in." At the Catholic church she declined to get out of the car. The chauffeur drove her around for an hour and then brought her home. "I didn't go," she said. That night her father called her into the library. "You're old enough now," he said, "to know what you want. I can't make you go to church. I've tried to have you brought up a good Catholic because I thought your mother would want it so. I've let your aunt have her way, though I've told her she was being too strict with you, that there was bound to be an explosion. I can't do any more." He paused. "Are you willing to finish out the year at the convent?" She knew that she must take a strong line. "No," she said firmly. "All right." He smiled for the first time. "You'll have to be tutored then till I can find a good school for you. I don't want you to fall behind." "I won't," she declared intensely, promising herself that she would repay his confidence in her by having a brilliant career. A great writer, an actress, an ambassador's gifted wife. Perhaps he would like it best if she were to study for the bar. But no, that was out of the question; women lawyers wore flat-heeled shoes. A great lady of some sort who spoke six languages fluently, Diane de Poitiers, Ninon, or Margaret of Navarre.

With a conscious sense of drama, she walked over to the bookshelves and took down *The Queen's Necklace*. Dumas had been forbidden her because he was on the Index. "Can I have this now?" she asked. Her father glanced up at the long line of novels in the worn, burgundy-colored bindings. "I ate those up when I was a boy." She smiled and turned to go. "You can read it in here," he said. "No need to rub it in. Your aunt is going to be pretty upset. You must go easy on her." Her face fell. "You must learn to be a good sport, Meg," he said gently. "It's a poor winner that gloats."

Would she have had the courage, she wondered, to have taken up that extreme position if she had not known, unconsciously, that deep down in his soul her father was cheering her on? She was not sure. "You must stop belittling yourself," said Dr. James. "It doesn't make any difference what you would have done under some different circumstances. The fact is that you did the best you could with the circumstances you had. Anybody on the outside would say you acted very bravely." Ah yes, she thought, but again you miss the point. It had not been a real test. That was what she feared and desired, the real test, the ordeal, the burning tenement house with the baby asleep on the fifth floor (would you rush in and save it if there were absolutely no one looking, no God in heaven to welcome your charred but purified spirit, no newspaper account the next day, YOUNG WOMAN DIES SAVING SLUM CHILD; if there were nothing in the world but you and the baby and the fire, would you not say to yourself that it was undoubtedly too late, that the baby must already have suffocated, that the fire was not serious, that the baby was not there at all but in the house across the street?). And of course, as Dr. James said, life is not like that. In life there is always the mitigating circumstance: "Conditions were not right yesterday for the experiment that was to have been performed," "Findings of observers are open to serious question because of the cloudiness of the atmosphere." Yet actually all this is misleading; the details, the environmental factors, the conflicting accounts of witnesses serve merely to obscure the fact that the question has been put, is being put, will be put, but worded so ambiguously, tucked into such an innocent context, that the subject cannot learn whether or not he has taken the test, let alone what his mark is. It therefore becomes important—for the subject who is interested in his status (there are many who simply don't care and doubtless they are the ones who graduate *summa cum laude*)—to examine the data of his life with the utmost severity and cunning, turning the facts every which way, sidewards, upside down, as one turned those old newspaper puzzles to find the face in the cloud.

In her own case, appearances were certainly against her. (Don't look now but isn't she the girl who stirred up all that trouble a few years ago? Treated her husband so badly he drove his car off that cliff. Of course, he was drunk and luckily he wasn't hurt, but still . . . And then that other guy—what was his name—she worked on him till he left his wife and then wouldn't have anything to do with him. And there was another story . . . he was sick and she didn't go to see him . . . The time she made poor so-and-so quit his job on that foundation because it wasn't radical enough to suit her . . . Got them to introduce her to some publishers and then dropped them like a hot-cake . . . Her best friend . . . Now she's married to that architect, you know the one, that does those houses with ramps . . . I guess she's got what she wants, but they fight like cats and dogs . . .) A shady case, unquestionably, a sordid history of betrayal. Yet, in some way, she was not like that. She would look at her face in the mirror and recognize in her features something direct, candid, sincere, some inward innocence engraved there that made strangers trust her on sight, tell her their troubles, ask her to watch their babies, help her carry her parcels. Policemen and taxi drivers smiled at her, truck drivers laughed at her hats. There it was, the unreasonable vote of confidence, which was not quite unearned. She would be, she felt, half entitled to it so long as she refused to become reconciled with herself, so long as the right hand remained on guard, the angry watchdog of the left. Yet in Dr. James' eyes all this was sheer folly.

"Accept yourself as you are," he said. "Stop trying to dig in to your motives. You have set yourself a moral standard that nobody could live up to. Your early religious train-

ing . . ." Ah dear, she thought, how they all deplore my
early religious training. "For God's sake," her husband
said, "give up worrying about your imaginary sins and
try to behave decently. You use your wonderful scruples as
an excuse for acting like a bitch. Instead of telling yourself
that you oughtn't to have married me, you might concen-
trate on being a good wife." "But I do try," she said sadly.
"I really do." "Oh, Jesus," he said, "you overdo it or you
underdo it. One day you're a miracle of a woman and the
next morning you're a hell-cat. Why do we have to live
like that? Why can't you be like anybody else?"

That was what he had sent her to the doctor for—a
perfectly simple little operation. First comes the anesthetic,
the sweet, optimistic laughing-gas of science (you are not
bad, you are merely unhappy, the bathtub murderer is
"sick," the Dead End Kid is a problem child, poor Hitler
is a paranoiac, and that dirty fornication in a hotel room,
why, that, dear Miss Sargent, is a "relationship"). After
consciousness has been put to sleep, it is a very easy matter
(just look the other way, please; it isn't going to hurt, but
the sight of the instruments seems to disturb excitable
people like yourself), it is a very easy matter to cut out the
festering conscience, which was of no use to you at all, and
was only making you suffer. Then the patient takes a short
rest and emerges as a cured neurotic; the personality has
vanished, but otherwise he is perfectly normal; he never
drinks too much or beats his wife or sleeps with the wrong
person. He has returned to the Garden of Eden, the apple
is back on the tree, the snake is a sportive phallus. If there

is something a little bewildered, a little pathetic about this *revenant,* it is only that the ancestral paradise is, like all the homes of our childhood, smaller than he remembered.

Already, in her own case, the effects of treatment were noticeable. "You have lost those unnatural high spirits," her friends told her. "You are not so tense as you used to be. You don't get so excited about causes." It was true, she was more subdued; she did not assert herself in company; she let her husband talk on his own subjects, in his own vein; she told white lies, where before she had only told black ones. She learned to suppress the unpleasant, unnecessary truths: why let an author know that you do not like his book, why spoil a party by getting into an argument, why not tell your friend that her ugly house is pretty? And why mention to your husband that you have spent too much money on an evening dress, gone to the races and lost, had too much to drink, let a man kiss you in the pantry? Pay your debt with the housekeeping money, take your mother's bracelet to the pawnshop, stifle the hangover with benzedrine, say the ice tray stuck and you were a long time getting it out. Do, in other words, what every normal wife does, agree and go your own way (it would only upset him if he knew; it is not important anyway; he would think I was silly to mention it). And if you want the last chop on the plate, the last drink in the bottle, take it, do not force it on him merely because you want it so much—that would simply be making a nuisance of yourself. Stop trying to be fair; only a child insists that everything should be divided equally. Grab whatever you need; he will do the same to you.

What Frederick had not foreseen was that the good would vanish with the bad, that a man may easily over-reach himself in making provisions for his comfort. His situation was like that of a woman who gets a hat altered to suit her features. It is only a small adjustment, the crown is lowered or heightened, the rakish feather is removed; there is no longer any fault to be found, but the customer looks in the mirror and weeps for her folly, because the hat is no longer stylish. Moreover, it is not returnable; it must lie in the closet for a certain number of seasons, till it is old enough to be given to a charity. And she herself was not returnable either. She could no longer go back into circulation, as she had done so often before. The little apartment in the Village, the cocktail parties, the search for a job, the loneliness, the harum-scarum, Bohemian habits, all this was now unthinkable for her. She had lost the life-giving illusion, the sense of the clean slate, the I-will-start-all-over-and-this-time-it-is-going-to-be-different. Up to the day that Frederick had sent her to the doctor, she had believed herself inde-structible. Now she regarded herself as a brittle piece of porcelain. Between the two of them, they had taught her the fine art of self-pity. "Take it easy," "Don't try to do too much," "You are only human, you know," "Have a drink or an aspirin, lie down, you are overstrained." In other words, you are a poor, unfortunate girl who was badly treated in her childhood, and the world owes you something. And there is the corollary: you must not venture outside this comfortable hospital room we have arranged for you, see how homey it is, the striped curtains, the gay bedspread, the easy chair with the reading lamp, why, you would hardly know it was a hospital—BUT (the threat lay in the conjunction), don't try to get up, you are not strong enough; if you managed to evade the floor nurses, you would be sure to collapse in the street.

Certainly, Frederick could not have intended this. He had sent her to Dr. James because he was unimaginative, because he believed in science in the same way that as an architect he believed in model tenement houses, and slum-clearance projects, and the Garden City of the Future, which would have straight streets, and lots of fresh air, and parks of culture and rest. When she had wept and cursed and kicked at him, he had not known how to "cope with" her (the phrase was his), and out of timidity, out of a certain sluggishness, an unwillingness to be disturbed, to take too much spiritual trouble, he had done what the modern, liberal man inevitably does—called in an expert. How characteristic of him, she thought, smiling, this great builder of cities, who cannot fix a leaky faucet! Poor Frederick, she murmured to herself, he did not see it in the cards at all that his spirited termagant of a wife would be converted into a whimpering invalid who no longer raged at him so often, who no longer wept every morning and seldom threatened to kill him, but who complained, stood on her prerogatives, and was chronically, vocally tired. And yet . . . Perhaps he had seen it, and accepted it as a lesser evil to living with her on terms of equality or allowing her to leave him. He was always talking about what he called her "bad record," a divorce, three broken engagements, a whole series of love affairs abandoned *in medias res*. Perhaps what counted for him more than anything else, more than love (did he love her, did he know what love was all about?), more than a stable household with a pretty wife across the dinner table, was that this should not happen to him, that no one should be able to say, "Well, she's done it again." Furthermore, the fact of her illness, a fact she could not talk away, since she went to the doctor daily, this fact was invaluable to him as a weapon in their disputes. He was always in a position to say to her, "You are excited, you don't know what you are saying," "You are not a fit judge of this because you are neurotic," "We won't discuss this further, you are not sane on the subject," and "I don't want you to see your old friends because they play into your morbid tendencies." And under the pressure of this, her own sense of truth was weakening. This and her wonderful scruples were all she had in the world, and both were slipping away from her. Overcome by the pathos of her situation, she began to cry.

Dr. James, who was still talking about castration, stopped in the middle of a sentence.

"What is it?" he said. "What upset you?" He had his notebook ready.

"I wasn't listening," she said, knowing that this was not quite accurate. She *had* heard him, but the mind's time is

quicker than the tongue's. Through the interstices of one
of his measured paragraphs her whole life could flood in.
"Everything you tell me may be true, but it's irrelevant.
Supposing at a certain time in my life, a time I can't remember, I found out that girls were different from boys. No
doubt this was a very poignant moment, but I can't go back
to it. My horrors are in the present."

"But you have never learned to accept that difference."

"Ah," she said, "now you are on Frederick's side. You
think I ought to welcome my womanly role in life, keep
up his position, defer to him, tell him how wonderful he
is, pick up the crumbs from his table and eat them in the
kitchen."

"No," he said, "no. You have a lot to contend with. The
marriage is not ideal. It's unfortunate, for one thing, that
you should have chosen to marry exactly the kind of man
who would make you feel most enslaved and helpless."

"Feel!" she replied indignantly.

"Well," he said in his most reasonable and optimistic
manner, "you could always get away from him. I think
you want to stay with him. I think you are fond of him
and that the two of you have the possibility of a solid
relationship. Mutual interests . . . you could have children . . . you can't keep on the way you were going, flying
from one hectic love affair to another."

"No," she said ruefully, "you can't."

If one only could . . . But it required strength. It took
it out of one so. The romantic life had been too hard for
her. In morals as in politics anarchy is not for the weak.

The small state, racked by internal dissension, invites the foreign conqueror. Proscription, martial law, the billeting of the rude troops, the tax collector, the unjust judge, anything, anything at all, is sweeter than responsibility. The dictator is also the scapegoat; in assuming absolute authority, he assumes absolute guilt; and the oppressed masses, groaning under the yoke, know themselves to be innocent as lambs, while they pray hypocritically for deliverance. Frederick imagined that she had married him for security (this was one of the troubles between them), but what he did not understand was that security from the telephone company or the grocer was as nothing compared to the other security he gave her, the security from being perpetually in the wrong, and that she would have eaten bread and water, if necessary, in order to be kept in jail.

To know God and yet do evil, this was the very essence of the romantic life, a kind of electrolytical process in which the cathode and the anode act and react upon each other to ionize the soul. And, as they said, it could not go on. If you cannot stop doing evil, you must try to forget about God. If your eyes are bigger than your stomach, by all means put one of them out. Learn to measure your capacities, never undertake more than you can do, then no one will know that you are a failure, you will not even know it yourself. If you cannot love, stop attempting it, for in each attempt you will only reveal your poverty, and every bed you have ever slept in will commemorate a battle lost. The betrayer is always the debtor; at best, he can only work out in remorse his deficit of love, until remorse itself becomes love's humble, shamefaced proxy. The two she had cared for most (or was it that they had cared most for her?) had, she believed, understood all this during those last hours when the packed trunks stood about the room and the last pound of butter got soft in the defrosting icebox (it seemed a pity to waste it, but what were you going to do?). They had consoled her and petted her and promised that she would be happy, that she would soon forget them—just as if they had been leaving her, instead of the other way around. The most curious thing about it was that their wounds, whose seriousness perhaps she had exaggerated, had been readily healed by time, while her own, being self-inflicted, continued to pain her. There are other girls in the world, but there is only the single self.

She remembered Frederick's impatience when she had tried to explain this to him. "You couldn't have cared much for him or you wouldn't have wanted to leave him," he had said in a grumpy voice. "Really, Frederick," she had answered, "can't you possibly understand . . . ?" "By their fruits ye shall know them," he replied, sententiously. This was one of his favorite quotations, a quotation which, of course, damned her utterly. Yet, she said to herself now, be fair. This is precisely what you want, to be condemned but condemned unjustly, on circumstantial evidence, so that you can feel that there is still some hope for you, that the very illegality of the proceedings against you will advance your cause in some higher court. The prisoner has been under duress; she has been treated with great harsh-

ness; let me show you, your honor, the marks of the cat-o'-
nine-tails. It was for his incomprehension, his blunt
severity, his egoism, that she had married Frederick in
the first place. She had known from the very beginning
that he would never really love her, and this was what
had counted for her, far more than the security or the
social position. Or rather perhaps she had felt that she was
free to accept these things because the gift of love was
lacking. When that man on the train had offered them to
her she had had to refuse because love had been offered
with them. And yet, she thought, she was being unfair
again, for she would never under any conditions have
married the man on the train, while there had been something about Frederick (the so-called mutual interests, a
certain genuine solidity of character of which the mulish-
ness was only one aspect) that had made her marry him
and even believe for a short while that surely it would
turn out well, that *this time* she would be happy and
good, that a strong, successful architect was exactly what
the recipe called for. An architect, she said to herself
scornfully, the perfect compromise candidate, something
halfway between a businessman and an artist.

"What you don't see, Dr. James, is that I was better then
than I am now. You and Frederick do wrong to be so
deeply shocked by my past. Why, if I forget to send out
his laundry, he can't resist reminding me of my former
sexual crimes. 'You always were a slut,' he says."

"Come now," said Dr. James. "Don't take it so hard.

He doesn't mean everything he says, any more than you do."

"Ah," she exclaimed, sitting up, "but he thinks he does. I still know when I lie, I can recognize a frame-up when I make one. But Frederick is his own stooge, his own innocent front. He has a vested interest in himself. He is the perfect Protestant pragmatist. 'If I say this, it is true,' 'If I do this, it is justified.' There is no possibility of dispute because Frederick has grace, Frederick belongs to the Elect. It's the religion of the Pharisee, the religion of the businessman. It's no accident that Catholicism is the religion of the proletariat and of what is left of the feudal aristocracy. Our principles are democratic; we believe that original sin is given to all and grace is offered with it. The poor man is democratic out of necessity, the nobleman is democratic out of freedom. Have you ever noticed," she went on, forgetting her quarrel with Frederick, warming up to her subject, "that the unconscious hypocrite is a pure middle-class type? Your aristocrat may be a villain, and your beggar may be a criminal; neither is self-deluded, puffed up with philanthropism and vanity, like a Rockefeller or an Andrew Carnegie. And the French, who are the most middle-class people in the world, have produced a satirical literature that is absolutely obsessed with this vice."

Dr. James frowned slightly. It was plain that the subject did not interest him. If only her analysis could be kept on the plane of intellectual discussion! But with Dr. James this was out of the question. Whenever she did manage

it, she was sorry almost at once, for, divested of professional infallibility, Dr. James was a pitiable sight. He was
no match for her in an argument. It was murder, as they
said in the prize ring. And the brief pleasure she got from
showing herself to advantage (now he sees me at my best)
curdled quickly into self-contempt, as she perceived how
abject indeed was her condition, if she could allow this
blundering sophomore to get his hands on her beautiful
psychology.

Would she have done better, she wondered, to have
gone to one of the refugee analysts, or to one of the older
men like Brill? Many of them were intelligent, and they
had another merit, they were peculiar. You could see at a
glance why psychoanalysis had attracted them. They suf-
fered from migraine, divorced their wives, committed
suicide, bullied their patients, quarreled with their colleagues; they were vain or absent-minded or bitter or dis-
honest—there was hardly a one of whom it could not be
said, "Physician, heal thyself." And popular opinion was
wrong when it held that an analyst's personal failings disqualified him as a healer. Psychoanalysis was one of those
specialized walks of life, like the ballet or crime or the
circus, in which a deformity is an asset; a tendency to put
on weight is no handicap to a professional fat lady; moral
idiocy is invaluable to a gangster, and the tragedy of a
midget's life occurs when he begins to grow. What Dr.
James and his young American colleagues lacked was,
precisely, the mark of Cain, that passport to the wilderness
of neurosis that the medical schools do not supply.

Yet for all their insight and cultivation, the others, the marked men, were dangerous. They might give you their own neurosis; they might neglect you or die or go insane or run away with their stenographers, and then where would you be? With Dr. James you were safe. He might never cure you, but he would not kill you. He would try to make up in conscientiousness and sympathy what he lacked in the other departments. Whatever you did or said, he would be unfailingly kind, and now and then in his blue eyes you would see a small, bright flame of pain, which told you that he was suffering with you, that you were not alone. And if, in many ways, he seemed Frederick's ideal apostolic delegate (for Frederick would have been afraid to have you go to one of those showy, gifted analysts), if he seemed a symbol of compromise, of the mediocrity you were rapidly achieving, you must forgive him, pretend not to notice, since he was all you had left. Your father was dead, your first husband, your first lover, and your next-to-the-last, even your Aunt Clara. Your other lovers were married, your friends were scattered or disgusted with you or on bad terms with Frederick. One reason, it occurred to her suddenly, that she continued to go to Dr. James long after she had admitted that he could do nothing for her was simply, if the truth were acknowledged, that she had no one else to talk to. Her conversation had become official conversation—the war, the Administration, the Managerial Revolution, Van Wyck Brooks, Lewis Mumford, the latest novel by a friend. Even on these public subjects, Frederick did not like it if she were too "sharp," and she could never guess ahead of time whether he would laugh uproariously at one of her jokes or rebuke her for a want of taste. Frederick, she thought, must have known that with all the will in the world she could not transform herself overnight into a "public" character like himself, that a certain amount of isolation was desirable but too much might bring on revolt. Dr. James was the Outlet, paid for by the month, the hygienic pipe line that kept the boiler from exploding.

"Let's go back a little," he said now. "It made you angry when I told you that you *felt* enslaved. Understand me, I don't mean that this is a delusion. It's true that you've put yourself in a position that isn't easy to retreat from. You have gone and burnt all the bridges that could take you back to your old life. But you have done this on purpose."

She nodded.

"I asked for it all right," she said bitterly. "I haven't any call to blame Frederick. It's my own cowardice that got me into this, and it's my own cowardice that'll keep me there. Every time I say to myself that I can't go on, it's a lie. Or maybe it's a kind of prayer. 'Let me not go on.'"

"Wait!" He sustained a dramatic pause. In this moment he was very much the magician. Behind him you could see Mesmer and then Cagliostro, the whole train of illusionists, divine, disreputable charlatans, who breathe on the lead coin, and, lo, it is purest gold. In spite of herself, she felt a little excited. Her hands trembled, her breathing quickened. She was ready for the mystery. "I am going to suggest to you a different view of your marriage." He paused again. Now she hung ardently on his words. She would have liked a cigarette, but she was afraid to reach for her pocketbook, lest the movement disturb him. She held her body perfectly still, like a woman who is expecting that any minute now the man by her side will kiss her.

"Yes?" she said in a soft, weak voice.

"You accuse yourself every day of having done something cowardly in marrying your present husband. I want to suggest to you that the exact opposite may be true, that this marriage took more real daring on your part than anything you have done since you left your father's house."

"You're crazy," she said, mildly.

"No!" he declared. "Think! In your childhood you had a terrible experience. Your mother died and you found yourself the prisoner of a cruel and heartless relative."

"She wasn't really cruel," she protested. "She was just misguided."

"I am talking about the way it appeared to you. Your aunt was the wicked stepmother that you read about in the fairy tales. Now where could you turn for help? To your father, obviously. But your father refused to help you. He even refused to notice that anything was wrong."

"He was away a great deal."

"That was what you told yourself. You began by trying to excuse him, but all the time you had the feeling that there was something queer going on, something you couldn't understand. Maybe your father and your aunt had a horrible covenant between them, maybe your own subjection was somehow part of the deal."

He is trying to imitate the way I talk, she thought, but it sounds silly when he does it.

"At the same time, you suspected that you would have been treated differently if you were a boy. You've described the arrangement of your house to me, and you lived in a kind of harem. Your father never went into your bedroom. You began to think that there was something ugly about being a girl and that you were being punished for it."

"Yes. There *was* something odd there. It seems to me now that my father felt that he had committed a sexual crime in marrying outside the clan. Race pollution. That was why he was so strict with me about boys. He wouldn't let me walk down the street—in broad daylight—with a boy I'd known all my life. The temptations of the flesh must have seemed very lively to him."

"We can't go into your father's psychology here. Something like that probably happened. In any case, you were made to feel unclean about your sex. And your religion got into the picture. You compared the upstairs with the downstairs."

Ah, yes, she thought, you are right. The terrible female vulgarity of blood, the Sacred Heart dripping gore, Saint Sebastian with the arrows, the dark red of the votive lamps, and the blue robe of the Madonna, the color of the veins in one's wrists. How schematically it had all been lived out, the war between the flesh and the spirit, between women and men, between the verminous proletariat and the disinfected *bourgeoisie*.

"You thought that you belonged with your Aunt Clara,

that you were a dark, disgusting person, and that your father, though you could not acknowledge this, was the real jailer."

"I see," she said. "And I felt that I deserved my imprisonment, that my father in segregating me from the community was performing a social service, throwing a *cordon sanitaire* around a slum section that was full of typhus."

It was all true. Yet there had been some ambiguity in the situation, arising from the fact that she was, after all, her father's daughter. Yet this element, far from easing her lot, had made it the more intolerable. The ugly duckling might be able to get along in life, adjust, resign itself, if there were not the charming, tantalizing possibility that at any moment it might turn into a swan. And, of course, that was what had happened. The second transformation had been quite as magical as the first. The little girl who looked like her mother had suddenly reappeared, seven years older, but otherwise unchanged. Or so, at any rate, it had seemed. She was pretty, she dressed expensively, she was gay, she made friends, and the only remarkable thing about her was that she had the air of coming from nowhere, of having no past. Her classmates in boarding school could not understand why they had never met her before. When they asked her about this, she would blush and say that her father had kept her in a convent. But this explanation was never quite adequate. "What about vacations?" they would wonder. "Who did you go around with?" "Oh, a lot of Catholic girls," she would answer. "It was very boring." Questions of this sort annoyed her, for she was anxious to think of herself as a completely new person. If anyone would have believed her, she would have pretended that she had spent her former life in some different, distant city, where she had gone to dancing class every Tuesday and been just like everyone else. Unfortunately, her father was too well known; her lie would have been discovered. In a way, she supposed, it was to escape from these questions, from the whole *unfair* business of having to have a verifiable history, that she had gone East to college. There, if you had money and used the right fork, no one could suspect an Aunt Clara in your vague but impeccable background. Later, when she had grown more sophisticated, Aunt Clara had been converted into an asset. It was amusing to have an aunt who said "ain't" and "Jesus, Mary, and Joseph," and ate her peas with a spoon, amusing because it seemed so improbable that *you* could have an aunt like that.

Moreover, the change had not been merely superficial. Her whole character had altered, or, rather, she had believed that it had. She, who had spent seven years in crying fits, spent the next seven without shedding a tear. Where her artistic tastes had been romantic, they quickly became realistic. Everything she had formerly admired became detestable to her. The sight of a nasturtium or a pink cosmos could make her tremble with anger, though these were the very flowers that, at her aunt's suggestion, she had chosen to grow as a child. Most extraordinary of all, she had suddenly developed wit and, even now, she never failed to be surprised when people laughed at her jokes, because for years it had been a household axiom that poor Meg had no sense of humor.

How remarkable it had all been! How very strong she had felt! She used to think back over her childhood and marvel, telling herself that it was really extraordinary that "all that" had not left a single trace. Yet as soon as she had married for the first time, she had begun to change back again. The first time she cried, she had said to herself, "This is very strange. I never cry." The first time she got angry with her husband and heard a torrent of abuse pour from her own lips, she had listened to herself in astonishment, feeling that there was something familiar about the hysterical declamatory tone, something she could not quite place. It happened again and again, and always there was this sense of recognition, this feeling that she was only repeating combinations of words she had memorized long ago. She had been married some time before she knew that she sounded exactly like Aunt Clara. Yet she could not stop, she was powerless to intervene when this alien personality would start on one of its tirades, or when it would weep or lie in bed in the morning, too wretched to get up. And when it began to have love affairs, to go up to strange hotel rooms, and try to avoid the floor clerk, she could only stand by, horrified, like a spectator at a play who, as the plot approaches its tragic crisis, longs to jump on the stage and clear up the misunderstanding, but who composes himself by saying that what is happening is not real, those people are only actors.

"This isn't like you, Meg," her first husband would tell her, in that gentle voice of his, and she would collapse in his arms, sobbing, "I know, I know, I know." She was inconsolable, but he could almost console her, since he shared her own incredulity and terror. It was as if she had lent her house to a family of squatters and returned to find the crockery broken, the paneling full of bullet-holes, the walls defaced with obscenities, her beautiful, young girl's bedroom splashed with the filth of a dog. And it was as if he had taken her hand and said, "Don't look at it. Come away now. Everything will be just the same; we will send for the cleaning woman, the house painter, and the restorer. Don't cry, it has no connection with you." She was glad to believe him, naturally. Never-theless, before long, she began to think him a fool. At the outset, it had seemed to her that he was right, that she was being impersonated by some false Florimel; however, as time went on, she herself became confused. She was losing the thread of the story, which was getting fearfully in-volved, like one of those Elizabethan dramas in which the characters change their disguises so often (Enter the Friar disguised as a Friar) that the final unmasking leaves every-one more perplexed than before. She came at last to the place where she wondered whether the false self was not the true one. What if she were an impostor? The point could only be settled by producing the false self in all its malignancy, and asserting its claim to belief. To say, "You were wrong about me, look how dreadfully I can treat you, and do it not impulsively but calmly, in the full possession of my faculties." Her first husband, however, had not been convinced. (And how could he be, she thought now; it was far easier for him to believe in her innate, untarnishable virtue than to believe that for three years he had been the dupe of what her present husband called a natural-born bitch.) He had grieved over her and let her go, remarking only that her fiancé would never understand her as he did, that she must be out of her senses.

At once she was restored to herself. She knew that she did not cry or make disgusting scenes or have cheap tastes or commit adultery (unless she were *very* much in love). Yet whenever a new love affair grew serious the usurper would crowd in again. Each time she would persuade herself that with this particular man her defenses would be impregnable, and each time the weak point, the crumbling masonry, would be discovered too late, when the enemy was in occupation. And she would reflect sadly that of course she ought to have realized that this one was too selfish, that one too lazy, the other too pliant to permit her being herself, though actually it was these very qualities that she had relied upon for protection. And unfortunately she had used very little realism in her selections. She was not in a position to ask herself any of the conventional questions (are our tastes congenial, will he be able to support me, will I still want to sleep with him after the first few weeks?) because precisely what she dared not look into was the Medusa-face of the future. "I will have to take a chance," she would always say, and her friends, marveling at her recklessness, did not see that she was exactly as gallant as a soldier who moves forward flourishing the standard, because he knows that if he does not do so, his officers will shoot him in the back.

"Now," said Dr. James, "you were helpless, you had no one to turn to, not even the Juvenile Court. And yet . . ." He paused again, even more impressively. This is the moment, she said to herself. This time surely he will get that rabbit out of the hat. "You won your freedom. And the thing to remember, Margaret," he pronounced her full name with all its syllables, "is that you did it yourself!" His voice was full of triumph.

"Perhaps," she said sadly. "But I can't do it again."

"I think you can," he answered. She felt belief stir, faintly, fondly, within her. It would be nice if he were right. However, the whole tone of his address was so deplorably YMCA. "I think you can," he repeated. "The very fact of your marriage indicates that you can."

She looked up at him. At last he had surprised her.

"Let me suggest to you, Margaret, that this ordeal of your childhood has been the controlling factor of your life. You forgot it, blotted it out of your consciousness, just as you blotted your aunt out of your family history, yet you have never ceased to think about it for a single moment. You did not understand how you had escaped, you could never really believe that you had. Everything that happened afterwards seemed unreal to you, like a story, but you disguised this from yourself by turning everything upside down, by pretending that your child-hood was the fantasy, the thing that never took place. Nevertheless, as you grew older, as you found yourself able to get along, to graduate with honors, have friends and a husband and a job, as you began to feel more secure in your role, the past reasserted itself. This could not have taken place earlier because you were still too frightened. When it did come out, however, it expressed itself in various ways, not all of them bad. It expressed itself in neurotic symptoms, but also in your political beliefs, in a taste for colorful language that has been useful to you as a writer. It expressed itself in what you call emotional greediness, which has done you good as well as harm.

"As soon as the past showed itself, you tried to run away. At the same time you set yourself various tests to find out what you were like. None of the results appeared to be conclusive, though, because the tests did not seem to you real. What you were being drawn toward all the time was a re-enactment of the old situation, but your first marriage and your other relationships fulfilled practically none of the conditions that had prevailed in your father's house. And the essential thing was lacking: you felt free; you were an equal; you could always get away. You say that you were happier in these relationships. In the end, though, they proved unsatisfactory. You dropped them abruptly. However, as you got older and—you must not forget this—stronger, you began to choose men who more nearly resembled your father. A middle-aged man, married men, even, once, a New Englander who came from your father's home state."

"That was nothing," she said. "A flash in the pan. One afternoon."

"Yes. All these affairs are mere signposts of a direction. Finally, however, your father dies, and you are free to make a real marriage. You at once marry Frederick and imitate, as much as it's possible for a grown woman, your own predicament as a child. You lock yourself up again, you break with your former friends, you quit your job; in other words, you cut yourself off completely. You even put your money in his bank account. You are alone: if you cry out, no one will listen; if you explain, no one will believe you. Frederick's own weaknesses contribute to this picture; they affirm its reality. His own insecurity makes him tyrannical and over-possessive; his fear of emotional expenditure makes him apparently indifferent. On the one hand, he is unjust to you, like your aunt; on the other, like your father, he pretends not to notice your sufferings and to deny his own culpability in them. Religion appears again, but now (this is very significant) it is the Protestant religion. A doctor enters the scene. If I remember rightly, you say that the only time your father came into your bedroom, he was bringing a doctor with him."

She nodded, unable to speak.

"You reproach yourself with cowardice for having contracted this marriage. But look at the facts. Isn't this the most dangerous action you have ever performed as an adult? You have run a terrible risk, the risk of severe

neurosis, in putting yourself to this test. For that's the
thing you are asking: will I be able to get out? And once
again you have the answer in yourself."

"No, I haven't," she said. "I'm turned to water. I'm
finished. I'm overrun by barbarian tribes. Two or three
years ago, perhaps . . . Not now."

"Two or three years ago, Margaret," he said gently,
"you wouldn't have had the courage to put yourself in this
situation, let alone to save yourself."

"It's not true. I was wonderful then."

He smiled.

"In those days, you were avoiding the things you feared.
Now you are eating breakfast with them."

"Not eating breakfast," she said. "Frederick prefers to
breakfast alone. I disturb his train of thought."

"The weakness you feel is a result of living with these
fears. You must find your way out, and you'll discover
that you are just as strong as Frederick."

"But what can I do? He won't allow me to leave him.
I have nobody left to borrow money from. I could run
away and sleep on a park bench, I suppose."

But she did not want that. Ah, no! The days of romantic
destitution were gone for her. It was no longer possible
for her to conceive of herself as a ribbon clerk at Macy's.
Now there was not so much time left in the world that
you could spend two years or three in the unrewarding
occupation of keeping yourself alive. Her apprenticeship
was finished. If she took a job, it would have to be a good
one, one that would keep the talents limber. No more

secretarial work, no more office routine, that wonderful, narcotic routine that anesthetizes the spirit, lulls the mind to sleep with the cruel paranoiac delusion of the importance, the value to humanity, of the humble-task-well-done.

"You tried running away as a little girl, and it didn't work," he said. "No. You misunderstand me. I'm not advising you to leave Frederick. You must win your freedom from him, your right to your opinions, your tastes, your friends, your money. And, of course, your right to leave him. Once you have it, I believe, you will cease to want to exercise it. You can become truly reconciled with Frederick, and you may even be happy with him."

"It sounds impractical," she said. "How am I going to get these rights?"

"You did it before," he answered. "You did it with your mind. That and your beauty are the two weapons you have."

He closed his black notebook.

"All right!" he announced in a totally different voice, high and unnaturally sprightly, as if he were giving a bird imitation. The hour was over. She looked at the electric clock. He had given her five minutes extra. This pleased her, and she was ashamed of being pleased over such a small, such a niggardly present. What a pass indeed she had come to when the favors of this commonplace little doctor could be treasured, like autumn leaves in a memory book! The knife of terror struck at her, and she saw herself as a transient, and this office with its white walls as the last and bleakest hotel room she would ever lie in.

Guests who stay after one P.M. will be expected to pay for the extra day. When she was gone, he would empty the ash tray, smooth out the white cloth on the pillow, open the window for an instant, and the room and he would be blank again, ready for the next derelict. She put her hat on carefully, trying not to hurry, lest he see how humble and rejected she felt, how willing to be dislodged; and trying, on the other hand, not to take too much time, lest he think her inconsiderate. He picked up her coat from the end of the couch and held it out for her, an attention he rarely paid her. She glanced at him and quickly lowered her eyes. Does he think I am unusually upset today, she wondered. Or was it something else? "My beauty," she murmured to herself. "Well, well!" She slid her arms into the coat. She turned, and he offered her his hand. In slight confusion, she shook it. "Good-bye," she said softly. He patted her arm. "Good-bye. See you tomorrow," he said in a rather solicitous voice. He held the door open for her and she slid out awkwardly, half-running, not wanting him to see her blush.

On the street, she felt very happy. "He likes me," she thought, "he likes me the best." She walked dreamily down Madison Avenue, smiling, and the passers-by smiled back at her. I look like a girl in love, she thought; it is absurd. And yet what a fine rehabilitation of character that had been! *The most dangerous action . . run a terrible risk.* She repeated these phrases to herself, as if they had been words of endearment. *I think you can . . .* Suddenly, her heart turned over. She shuddered. It had all been a therapeutic lie. There was no use talking. *She knew.* The mind was powerless to save her. Only a man . . . She was under a terrible enchantment, like the beleaguered princesses in the fairy tales. The thorny hedge had grown up about her castle so that the turrets could hardly be seen, the road was thick with brambles; was it still conceivable that the lucky third son of a king could ever find his way to her? Dr. James? She asked herself the question and shook her head violently. But supposing he *should* fall in love with her, would she have the strength to remind herself that he was a fussy, methodical young man whom she would never ordinarily have looked at? All at once, she remembered that she had not told him the end of her dream.

She was matriculating at a place called Eggshell College. There was an outing cabin, and there were three tall young men, all of them a sort of dun color, awkward, heavy-featured, without charm, a little like the pictures of Nazi prisoners that the Soviet censor passes. They stumbled about the cabin, bumping their heads on the rafters. She was sorry she had gone there, and she sat down at a table, resolved to take no part in the proceedings. Two other girls materialized, low-class girls, the kind you said, "Hello, there" to on the campus. A sort of rude party commenced. Finally one of the men came toward her, and she got up at once, her manner becoming more animated. In a moment she was flirting with him and telling one of the other girls, "Really he is not so bad as the others. He is quite interesting when you begin to talk to

him." His face changed, his hair grew dark and wavy.
There was something Byronic about him. He bent down
to kiss her; it was a coarse, loutish kiss. "There must be
some mistake," she thought. "Perhaps I kissed the wrong
one," and she looked up to find that the Byronic air was
gone; he was exactly like the others. But in a few minutes
it happened again; his skin whitened, his thick, flat nose
refined itself, developed a handsome bridge. When he
kissed her this time, she kept her eyes shut, knowing very
well what she would see if she opened them, knowing
that it was now too late, for now she wanted him anyway.

The memory of the dream struck her, like a heavy
breaker. She stopped in the street, gasping. "Oh my God,"
she demanded incredulously, "how could I, how could I?"
In a moment, she told herself that it was only a dream,
that she had not really done that, that this time at least
she need feel no remorse. Her thirsty spirit gulped the
consoling draft. But it was insufficient. She could not dis-
own the dream. It belonged to her. If she had not yet
embraced a captive Nazi, it was only an accident of time
and geography, a lucky break. Now for the first time she
saw her own extremity, saw that it was some failure in
self-love that obliged her to snatch blindly at the love of
others, hoping to love herself through them, borrowing
their feelings, as the moon borrowed light. She herself
was a dead planet. It was she who was the Nazi prisoner,
the pseudo-Byron, the equivocal personality who was not
truly protean but only appeared so. And yet, she thought,
walking on, she could still detect her own frauds. At the

end of the dream, her eyes were closed, but the inner eye had remained alert. She could still distinguish the Nazi prisoner from the English milord, even in the darkness of need.

"Oh my God," she said, pausing to stare in at a drug-store window that was full of hot-water bottles, "do not let them take this away from me. If the flesh must be blind, let the spirit see. Preserve me in disunity. *O di*," she said aloud, *"reddite me hoc pro pietate mea."*

It was certainly a very small favor she was asking, but, like Catullus, she could not be too demanding, for, unfortunately, she did not believe in God.